THE
GATEKEEPER

THE
GATEKEEPER
AWAKENING SLEEPING MINDS

JOY PETERSON

Second Edition

ISBN: 978-0-9920654-0-9

Edited by Elegant Editing and MAKN Productions.

I thank God, who gifted me with this remarkable journey, Rubin Carter for being my first teacher about consciousness, Darrell for providing what I needed to get here.

Dedicated to those who encouraged, supported, and motivated, and most importantly believed that "I Can". You know who you are.
I love you!

Joy Peterson.

CONTENTS

AUTHOR'S BLESSING

If you:
Have come to these pages to be uplifted,
May you be uplifted by within them.
Need a reminder to always treasure the gift of love,
May you be reminded within these pages.
Believe there's danger in having thoughts,
May you find the gift of wisdom to fear not using them.
Seek your purpose of life,
May this story lead you to the path of your fulfillment.
If you seek courage,
May this story be the uplifting wind beneath your wings.
May you find the true meaning of peace,
And know it in your reflective soul.

- Joy Peterson

CHAPTER ONE

WHO'S DEMISE?

"You better open this door, Patience! Don't make me break it down!" The door bulged with each strike. Trevor Jefferson-Johnson, their uncle, was trapped on the other side of the basement door. He continued to yell furiously, turning and shaking the wooden doorknob.

Patience, Theo, and Marcus stood four feet away from the door. They all jumped when the next blow loudly struck the door.

"Pat, he's going to kill us if we don't open that door," Theo said loudly.

"Oh yeah, Theo, it's not like he would change his mind about that if we did open it. So we open it now and he'll be grateful and laugh like it's one big joke? Are you for real?" Patience said.

"Open it!" Theo said.

"I think we should listen to Theo." Marcus said. He stood behind his twin, Theo, who looked back at him nodding his head in approval.

"I should have known you two brats would chicken out. All talk but no backbone!" Patience said. She faced her twelve-year-old fraternal twin brothers directly. Marcus, the taller of the two was chubby and dark skinned with long corn rowed hair, closely resembling their father.

Theo was the exact opposite, despite being his twin. Theo was tiny, caramel-skinned and wore a big Afro, closely resembling their Uncle Trevor.

Patience was fifteen and had delicate features. She was the mirror-image of her mother with high cheekbones, full lips and caramel toned skin; a tall lanky girl with long braids down to the center of her back.

She walked towards the duo standing side by side stopping in front of Theo to stare down at him, with large beautiful almond-shaped hazel eyes, brimming with fury. He was a foot shorter than both his siblings.

Her eyes narrowed, lips pressed together as she shook her head in disbelief and disgust, fighting the impulse to slap him.

"Look, we all decided this was the only way to keep our home. Did you forget about his plans to send us to an orphanage? Now you're going to let his ranting and crazy words scare you into letting him out. You can't deal with what will happen if you do."

"Let him out!" Twins said. "No. You losers do it!"

They just stood there silently trying to stare each other down. The only thing that moved was Patience nervous foot that tapped anxiously on the wooden floor. *Oh Lord what am I going to do now? Patience you can't stop them if they try to open the door. I better not look at them because*

I may lose my nerve and want to open that door too.

When the next blow did not fall, they all turned to look at the basement door, bewildered by the eerie silence. The blows that had rained like clockwork thumping against the door had unexpectedly seized. To their surprise Patience sprung towards the basement door.

Her brothers' eyes widened when they saw her brace her back against it. She never took her eyes off them while she wedged herself tightly against the door, legs wide apart as if bracing herself to stop a bull from breaking through.

Surprisingly, their plan to trap Trevor worked. It didn't backfire despite their mistakes. She wondered if maybe locking the boys up with their uncle would have protected them from Trevor's rage and put the blame solely on her.

Did I do the right thing? Keep hiding your hands. Patience, don't let them see them shaking. She held her hands behind her back against the door. Even though Theo and Marcus gave her plenty of reasons to hate them, the promise she had made to their Grandmother outweighed any animosity she had. She had promised to take care of her brothers and protect them in spite of how they felt towards each other. She kept her word honoring her promise to a grandmother she missed dearly.

"Trevor's fixed good. Now I can relax my mind for a minute and rethink our get away from all this drama. You two fools must realize we're too deep into this, and surely he will kill us if we open that door. We have got to focus on what to do next!"

"Pat, move or we'll make you move. Marcus, she's forcing us to open it. I'll help you but we've got to let him out!"

"Forget it Theo! I'm not fighting her. It's better if she opens the door. Maybe Trevor will forgive her too when we explain why we did it."

"You good for nothing spineless brats make me sick! All those nights we put into this plan to make it successful. You now want to change your minds? I would have been better off having nothing to do with this mess and just leave you two to deal with his wrath. You all aren't worth it. You hear me? This plan was a total waste of time!"

"You're selfish and you ruined a good home and family situation for us! So leave! We don't need you so get out now so we can open the door. None of us want you here. Isn't that right Marcus?"

Patience looked at them and her expression was pure anger. Marcus suddenly looked down at his feet while Theo glared, hands on his hips. Theo had pushed her rage button and she did not care about what he thought and decided to make him pay. She was never one to be malicious but dire circumstances make strange bedfellows.

"Hey, rat food in the basement! Guess who is laughing at you now? Thank Theo for your new name. The joke is on you thinking I started all this when it was Theo! He talked us into helping him. Your favorite nephew is your worst hater!"

Theo was taken aback and rushed at the basement door. Patience however sidestepped him, fed up and marched boldly towards the front door. Theo raced back grabbed Marcus's hand and tried to drag him towards the basement but he could not move him. He stood rooted to the spot and as Theo turned following his gaze the basement door exploded. It was as if rage had made Trevor stronger because he burst through the door like a loose wild cannon. The wooden door splintered with the impact sending Trevor and the wooden doors' remnants crashing to the floor. He sat up slowly and faced the children smiling maliciously while he started to rise like a villainous movie bad guy.

"Run!" Patience yelled. Patience, Theo and Marcus sprinted off before Trevor could take his first step from his basement cage.

The Robinson children, Patience, Theo, and Marcus ran so fast not even their shadows could keep up with them. There was no going back, Patience realized. Her choice to run on her own was gone now. She had to escape with her brothers to save them from Trevor's revenge.

They kept running until the house was no longer in sight and reached the cornfields. The golden cornfields stretched for miles and miles. The husks were tall enough to hide. So high that it would make it hard for their uncle to see or follow them. Though the cornfield offered them protection, it however did not offer any comfort as the trio found it very difficult and tiring to move through the thick corn field, as if trying to fight their way around endless lines of football defensemen. Furthermore it was so hot. Hot enough to make the corn pop right out of their husks.

The massive field was too thick and impossible to run through entirely. They had to break the husks with their bare hands to avoid getting hurt. The siblings continued slowly walking while dodging and zigzagging in the massive cornfield to escape their uncle. The fear of what would happen if he caught them was a powerful force within

Patience and nothing was going to stop her from escaping her nightmare. Patience was far ahead of Theo and Marcus. She heard her brothers calling out when they began to get lost in the field.

Should I ignore them?

Her energy was about to give out. Frightened and out of breath, she stopped and glanced up at the sky. What she saw captivated her gaze.

"Look at the sky!" They all yelled in unison. In the sky, just low enough for the children to see, hundreds of butterflies in an array of beautiful shades were led by unusually large neon colored butterfly so vibrant you would think it was glowing.

They were flying in an arrow formation with the large neon one being at the tip. It was as if it was showing them where to run.

"Are you seeing what I'm seeing?" Patience yelled.

"Yeah they're trying to help us! We gotta follow them!" Marcus yelled. Within moments, the kids found themselves in a field of tall golden wheatgrass. The spiritual buoyancy of their surroundings caused their fear to dissipate. Their fears were momentarily forgotten as they ran after the butterflies, especially Patience, who in that moment could have raced Usain Bolt and won. All three children were infused with adrenaline from their excitement and exhilaration of receiving help from the butterflies. All three raced through the wheatgrass. Patience gave her brothers time to catch up then motioned for them to keep moving while she rested and looked behind her but saw no sign of Marcus or Theo.

Not wanting to lose sight of her twin brothers, she took off running fast and elegantly like a gazelle, not stopping until she had edged past Theo. She prayed the butterflies would lead them to safety and her prayers were being answered. She stopped again and yelled out to her brothers but only Theo responded. Theo began to run towards his sister but stopped when he saw her. As she approached him, they heard Marcus' voice carried faintly over the wind. He could be heard but not seen. Together they ran towards the sound of Marcus's voice.

"Help get me out this hole!" Marcus yelled.

They were nearing the sound of Marcus's voice, when suddenly Patience reached out and grabbed Theo's arm just in time before he fell in too. They looked down and saw Marcus trying to jump out of the hole that was three feet over his head. Patience quickly pulled her belt off then laid down on her stomach she crawled to the edge. Theo got in behind her and grabbed onto her ankles as she extended herself over the ledge. They quickly lowered the belt down the hole. Marcus reached up and grabbed it tightly and they together pulled him out within seconds. Patience quickly put her belt on as her brothers stood by watching out for their uncle. She stood up, scanning the sky then pointed upward. The boys looked up and Patience, Theo and Marcus began running again in the direction she had pointed too. She passed them once more but stopped and ran back when Marcus called out.

She returned to her brothers, looking at Marcus who was sitting on the grass. Theo was holding his brother's hand, trying to pull him up onto his feet.

"I'm tired. Leave me alone Theo!"

"Stop being a punk and man up. Pat, we can't leave him here!"

If Marcus didn't want to move, moving him physically would have been a difficult feat. In desperate times ideas dawn and Patience knew what had to be done. "Theo grab some wheatgrass to cover up the opening of the hole. Hurry!" she yelled.

"Marcus go hide behind that big tree while we cover this hole. Call out if you see Trevor!!"

Patience and Theo sprang into action covering up the hole quickly. The wheat grass placed evenly over the willow branches left no evidence of the hole beneath. The duo then ran to hide behind a tree and waited with their brother. Anxiety caused Patience to abandon the trait she was named for and the ever impetuous leader made another split second decision.

"You guys stay quiet. I'm going to make sure Trevor falls into it."

Before they could respond, Patience further surprised Theo and Marcus when she took off and ran back towards the hole and Trevor.

Her brothers watched frozen from behind the tree. Marcus feared the outcome. He covered his eyes, peeping out through his fingers when he saw Trevor appear. His fear caused him to jump, startled when Theo squeezed his shoulder. Marcus looked at Theo about to shout but Theo put one hand over Marcus's mouth to stop him. His eyes were as wide as saucers too. Trevor was visible and with his appearance their fear rematerialized. They saw him huffing and puffing, trying to catch his breath hunched over, hands on his knees.

Mocking laughter pierced the air and he suddenly looked up to see Patience in front of him. Driven by his anger he immediately leaped forward, running directly at her. Theo and Marcus shook their heads while they watched what happened. Patience made fun of Trevor, mimicking a big fat man who could hardly walk. She edged him on and called him names. Just as Trevor was about six feet from the hole, she turned and ran. Patience stopped when she heard her brothers' cheers.

Theo and Marcus were on their feet jumping up and down, excited. Looking behind her there was no sign of Trevor. Patience fell to the grass and lay on her back and breathing hard. She slowly got up when her brothers stood beside her. All three of them were about fifteen feet away from the hole. They walked over to look at the hole.

"We did it. I bet that big butt of his would make it impossible for him to get out of that hole. He's going to be down there for a very long time." Patience laughed.

"Get me out of here!" Trevor yelled.

"You get yourself out! You're bug food. A dirty rat like you belongs in a hole!" She yelled back.

Theo was mad and happy because everything was going to be different now that Trevor was gone, and wanted to reassert his authority. "I'm going home to eat. Come on Marcus." Theo said. *I hope she doesn't want to come back home. Marcus better not say anything.*

Patience tip-toed quietly over to the opening and looked down quickly. She jumped back when she saw Trevor looking up at her vengefully, causing her to run back to her brothers. Marcus was amazed by how his sister always found a way to save them. Suddenly all three of them went closer and stood a few feet away, pointing and laughing towards the hole. Theo and Marcus were laughing while Patience stood there watching them quietly.

"Alright get to step-in. I'm sick and fed up with the both of you. That evil rat Trevor can't get out so I don't have to be stuck taking care of you two. Go. Thank God I'm free so go back home. I'm not coming. You got everything you need. The helpers are thrilled we got rid of him. Thank God he was hated by them too. Now everyone is better off, and we hooked up our money situation. There's enough to keep everyone happy. No one will report he's missing. I set that up too. The helpers do the shopping, driving, and live in the house, so you guys are safe. Finally I can focus on my life. How I hated that place and all of you too!"

"Pat you got to come back with us. Trevor can't hurt you anymore. We promise you'll have a better life. Theo, tell her things will be different. Isn't that right Theo?"

The danger passed and the catastrophe momentarily averted, Theo returned to his cocky self. "She wants to leave. I think that's the best idea she ever had!"

Marcus frowned as he watched Patience walk over to Theo. She slapped him hard across his face. His eyes widened in anger, his hand suddenly shooting out but Patience grabbed it before it touched her.

She held his hand tightly then suddenly shoved him so hard that he almost fell. Theo stood there yelling while Patience did the same.

Marcus kept his distance as they argued. Marcus did not move. He was scared and confused. His eyes were misty then he quickly rubbed away a huge tear- drop with the back of his hand.

Why doesn't she want to come back? Theo wants her to leave. Has everyone lost their minds? Oh Gram, I wish you were here! Marcus never spoke up for himself, the second fiddle stuck between the orchestras that were Patience and Theo's constant bickering. Characteristically he disassociated himself from the quarrel and looked away. As he looked towards the hole, his eyes became round as saucers.

Suddenly, he pointed towards it with a trembling hand then started to back away.

"Guys, look! He's going to get out!" Marcus shrieked.

Marcus stumbled having backed away too fast. He lost his footing, fell then got up quickly. Theo and Patience did the same from trying to run backwards too. As they all stared wide-eyed at the big, creepy fingers that clawed wildly at the earth, Trevor's massive hands then his thick muscular arms slowly became terrifyingly visible.

"Run. Now, before he gets out!" Patience yelled.

Patience took off with her brothers not very far behind. Patience, Theo, and Marcus desperately scanned the darkened sky for the flock of butterflies. When they saw them in the distance they followed. They did not know where they were going, but it had to be better than where they had been. Theo ran by Marcus's side, following their sister as the beautiful butterflies led them to foreign parts of their Grandmother's massive farmland. Suddenly, the butterflies scattered, leaving the children standing side by side in surprise. They were surprised by their surroundings, afraid to move or make a sound. "This place is creepy. I can't believe it's on our land." Patience said quietly.

"Yeah, but we never went near this area cause Gram said the land was dangerous and unstable. Remember?"

"We were all so focused on following those butterflies. I didn't even think or worry about where we were going. I can't believe I trusted those bugs!" Patience said. "Did you guys realize that the danger zone signs are gone?"

"No." The twins said.

"I know they were a few miles back. I wonder who took then down cause I never would have passed them if I saw them."

"I did too. What is this weird place?" The twins said, again unison, awed by the landscape.

"This is the strangest looking forest I have ever seen," Patience whispered. "How come a creepy place like this is on our land?"

"Check out those clouds. It looks like they're alive," Theo whispered. "They're making faces. That one just stuck out its tongue," Marcus whispered.

At their remarks, Patience wondered if it was their fear or uncertainty about this place that was making them see things. "Wow live clouds with red faces, black eyes and long pointy teeth. I don't see the sun, just the light green clouds but everything else, like all the plants, look so big, overgrown, and it's weird how they're all grey too. How could anything grow with no sunlight? But it's not a dark we can see. It looks like we're in a scary movie." Patience said quietly.

"Yes it does." The twins responded, following closely behind their big sister. Marcus grabbed his brother's arm but Theo slapped it away. Theo did not want his brother to feel him shaking. Their sister nearly fell when Theo bumped into her because he was focusing on keeping distance from Marcus who followed too closely. She spun around to rebuke them. The fury on her face frightened Marcus more than the forest. "I don't care if this place is scary. I don't want you brats following me. No more help. I need to get as far away as possible from you two. So don't follow me, you hear?"

Theo equally abrasive, scoffed back. "Following you? Following you Pat, leads to nothing but trouble. You agree, right Marcus?"

Before he could answer, Theo and Patience ran off in different directions, leaving Marcus looking frantically from left to right, scratching his head, afraid and indecisive trying to figure out who he should follow. In this state and unable to move, Marcus did not notice the vines, leisurely and quietly slithering towards him from behind.

They quickly wrapped around each of his ankles and violently yanked Marcus down on his back. Like a car driving fast in reverse, they dragged him backwards despite his wailing. He screamed until he passed through to the other side of the massive grey bush with black curly thorns. It closed back up quickly enveloping all trace of Marcus ever having been there, leaving behind only an eerie silence.

Patience and Theo, not too far off, having heard Marcus's cry for help turned back to help. They raced to where they had left him to find only an empty space. They both looked from left to right expecting to see him in the clutches of Trevor.

"Theo, why was Marcus screaming? What happened to him?" "Pat you should have watched out for him too!"

Patience looked around her anxiously, concerned more for Marcus' safety than Theo's ignorance. They screamed when they felt something touch their ankles. The Vines at a lightning speed had wound themselves around their ankles tightly and in similar fashion to Marcus, yanked them down onto their bellies. They clawed at the earth as they frantically tried to stop what was happening. The thorny grey bush quickly closed back up after they passed through to the other side. The Vines quickly released them and slithered away; leaving all three of them, face down on the grass, their hearts beating heavily in fear. They were less than three feet away from Marcus and covering their faces too frightened to look or still their trembling bodies.

"Marcus, Theo, where are you? Are you okay?" Patience whispered. "He got you too. Oh no," Marcus shouted, responding to their voices.

"Whatever did this, I don't think Trevor made those vines attack us," Theo said. "What happened was done by magic, but a magic beyond anything Trevor just wishes he knew!"

Marcus removed his hands from his head slowly turning to look at his sister and felt relieved when he saw Theo too. "Theo if it wasn't Trevor, then who or what made those things grab on to us?" Theo uncovered his face to respond to Marcus but saw Patience and was surprised at how much she was shaking. She too looked at Theo's head then turned towards Marcus while peeping through her fingers.

"Theo, go look around and see what you can find."

"Pat it's your fault why we're in this mess. You go look," Theo said. Patience, though furious with Theo, slowly rolled over onto her back. With her eyes still covered, she sat up. She peeped through her fingers quickly. Her eyes opened wide and her mouth stood agape, amazed by what she saw.

"You guys won't believe this. Look up at the sky!"

The boys, still trembling, rolled onto their backs also before sitting up. What they saw surprised them all and all three looked at each other wide eyed and mouths opened.

"Wow Pat! That's amazing!" Both twins said in unison. This caused Pat to smirk. Even though they were not identical twins, they sure did mirror each other verbally a lot. Patience, Theo, and Marcus stood up slowly and looked around nervously, keeping close to each other. She had her hands on top of her head, shaking it in disbelief, her eyes as round as saucers. She looked down and up repeatedly, completely fascinated. They wandered of separately as if in a trance, to explore.

"Check out this grass. It's like a thick shaggy blue carpet. The sun, I mean everything here is mad, crazy, sick bro!" Theo said.

"Yes it's like we are in another world. Like we were dragged through a Gateway and ended up on another planet," Marcus said.

"First, that scary forest and now this place? It's like two different worlds exist in the same place on and through our land. Are we even on our land? What's happening is crazy. I thought Grammy had the most beautiful garden, but this place, whatever it is, it's amazing. It's like her stories came to life!"

The children knelt on their hands and knees gently touched the grass and plants to see if they were real. Patience was smiling as she caressed the uniquely shaped large petals with snow flake like patterns.

The flowers were a beautiful mélange of colors. She rubbed her face against the delicate petals. She smiled from smelling the sweet fragrance while her brothers were rolling in the grass, loving the way it felt.

"Can you believe how different the sun looks? How it's like glittery orange, kind of yellow. It looks like a big candy, and those clouds are like floating weird shaped rainbows. The sky is a very light blue making those clouds look extra pretty. It's like we really are in another world?" Patience said.

"Yeah thank God it's not creepy like the other one," Marcus said. "It wasn't that bad. It was kind of cool," Theo said.

"Those vines should have left you in the forest Mr. Big and Brave Theo! Right, Marcus?"

"Pat you're always talking junk. You needed my protection. Consider yourself lucky that I ended up in the forest too. God only knows how you would deal with things without me!"

"You're always running your mouth when you're nothing but a little punk! Always lying through your teeth when we both know who was going to have to do the protecting, Theo!"

"Ah man!" Marcus interjected. "Can't you guys ever stop the warring? Look at this place. It's amazing! Gram woulda loved it here.

Can you imagine if she was here with us and all she saw was you arguing?"

"I believe that she is." Patience whispered. "Gram, we miss you." Theo said.

"I miss you too, my babies!" The all too familiar voice of their Grandmother echoed around them, sharp and clear but disembodied as if carried on the wind. The wind swirled around them rising and showering them with leaves causing them to look up and as they looked up a further surprise greeted them. The children looking upwards in unison, pointing at the most remarkable Kaleidoscope colored cloud, with their grandmother's Image smiling down at them. It zoomed downwards towards them and just as it seemed it was almost close enough to touch them, they fainted in fear.

*   *   *

Mistick Krewe of Jefferson in New Orleans was the largest parish plantation in the state of Mississippi, going as far back as the 1700s. It was known for its unique manifestations of life's energy. Other plantation owners were never as fortunate to foster the same habitat and bountiful harvests, and as a result jealously was rampant in the location.

However the southern code of conduct between white plantation owners prevented any destructive acts of sabotage against the Jefferson family, by their surrounding peers. That might not have been the case if they knew what made the Jeffersons so blessed. Any foreign seedling planted on the land grew and thrived because of the descendants of Mable Jefferson-Johnson.

The Jeffersons had two generations of family living on the plantation. They were unique in that their slaves primarily originated from the South

African region. The Jeffersons on their travels to the south of Africa had befriended many free blacks and developed a close kinship. When they became aware of the misfortunate that had befallen their beloved friends of Zulu heritage who had been relocated to areas of West

Africa, they their lives to helping them.

They used their resources and connections to locate and purchase as many South African slaves as they could. In a short time, their plantation became a home for slaves of South African descent. The Jeffersons' home was a beautiful white mansion with a wraparound veranda that was admired by all. Bertram Jefferson was the only son of James and Samantha Jefferson and as such was deeply loved by his parents.

Bertram and his father James shared a powerful bond and through him he learned to respect the concept of equality, seeing how his father chose to treat the "slaves" that worked and lived on his plantation.

Within this environment, his son Bertram befriended a boy child slave birthed under the name of 'Thulani'. Thulani meant "quiet" but he was anything but. The Jeffersons came to know Thulani who they had renamed Theodore Jefferson as an extremely rambunctious youth.

Theodore's father, a Zulu named Gabangaye was renamed with the English word "Noble" because he was trustworthy and stoically dignified.

Theodore's mother Thandeka became affectionately known as 'Thandee.' She embodied everything that the English equivalent of her name 'Beloved' meant. The family of slaves shared a close relationship with Bertram's father James and even more so with his mother Samantha. She was very close to Bertram and Theodore; they were unusual pair, inseparable in how they played and saw the world. Their parents taught and encouraged unity between the two families. This created a rare but powerful social connection between both families who lived on the plantation. The boys' parents shared a deep spiritual bond too. They all believed that they were united because of their beliefs in one creator, God.

Isineko's Johnson slave name was 'Isi'. Her birth name Isineko came from a Zulu clan known as the Xolani tribe. She was proud of being born free unlike many children in her age group on the plantation. She was proud, strong, and refused to marry until slavery was abolished as she wanted her future children to be born free too.

Isi had received many proposals and broke many hearts, sticking steadfast to her promise. That was until she met Theodore Jefferson.

Isi knew immediately that he was special. Theodore's special nature showed in how he loved nature and animals with a deeply spiritual passion. While he may have not matched her in physical stature, Theodore had surprising athletic skills. She found his dark skin and long corn rowed hair appealing. However it was primarily his eyes that captivated her. His eyes and smile made the pain from missing her family in her heart ease. She was his from the moment she looked in to his eyes and she decided to marry him after only one month of courtship. Together they made a pact that if their children were not born free, they would work until they were!

The union between the young couple was beautiful and special. There was a spectacular ceremony officiated by Bertram's father who was accompanied by a chieftain from the South African Zulu nation named Yengwayo. Publicly he was also known as Clement. Both men were Elders in their own respective communities and shared a strong friendship and respect for each other. Yengwayo in his community was very strong, wise and kind, often providing wisdom and encouragement.

Despite being separated by the oceans, Clement had maintained his connections with his people through prayer and meditation.

As such, he had been very successful in reconnecting broken families stolen into slavery. When Clement saw Isi suddenly he dropped to his knees in shock then slowly rose. He knew of her great gifts and the sad tale of her family's fate too. He stood before her, tears of joy flowing from his eyes. Speaking in their tongue he shared with her the fact that he knew who she was and that her parents were alive. At this revelation which spread quickly through the crowd in attendance, the ceremony was stopped. The Jeffersons knew of Clements's gift and accepted his help. Within days they found Isi's parents and they reunited the family.

Her parents Kwanele and Ntokozo had been living on a plantation less than fifty miles from her. Isi was excited but she feared seeing them too, given the circumstances under which they had parted. This haunted her. When her parents came face to face with her the love and miracle of being re-united made all the pain they had carried a thing of the past. Theodore and Isi were married the following day, in a blessed ceremony witnessed by both sets of parents. Their ceremony was spectacular and included rituals from their South African heritage.

In honor of her husband she took his last name and became Isi Jefferson. Isi eventually shared with her husband her secret story and her pain and guilt about what she believed was the cause of the villagers' curse of becoming enslaved. Theodore and her parents eventually convinced her she had nothing to do with their misfortune. He learned of his wife's unique gifts and encouragement from her parents and husband helped her to embrace and practice her mystical powers again. Together Isi and her mother Ntokozo committed to the creation of a new world on Mistick Krewe of Jefferson. They talked and dreamed of creating a new world free of slavery, racism and hate.

They, Isi and her mother were thrilled to discover that Theodore had unique powerful gifts too. Their gifts combined empowered each of their abilities, taking them to supernatural levels and making it possible for them to foster the enhancement of plant and animal life, creating hybrid life forms. Life in shapes and forms that represented what they believed to be the utopia of beauty. They were secretive and protective of each other, Isi especially as she never wanted history to repeat itself. The young but wise couple often disappeared and returned as silently as they left. Their parents were delighted by their children's' powerful love and bond. They prayed and visualized their incredible new world that would not be contaminated by the evils of greed, jealousy, haste or sadness. Isi and Theodore's parents instilled the vision and virtue in their children that they should live a life of pure minds and hearts free of malice, beliefs which they transferred into the vision of a new landscape. They encouraged them to pursue their destiny. Isi shared with her husband about her dreams about other worlds where the Stars lived and how her dreams would guide her to find seedlings from these worlds on the plantation.

She had a secret box which housed her precious seeds. One day she had a vision as to the purpose of the seeds. Together Isi and Theodore went to their beloved friends asking them to help and provide a home to give birth to this dream. Bertram and Mable were gifted the plantation once they married. The young couples were very close and loved each other dearly since childhood. With the blessing from Bertram and Mable, a small plot of land became a gift for Isi and Theodore enabling them to make their dream a reality. Together Isi and Theodore through the gifts bestowed to them, created a secret, special place that was the birthplace of a remarkable world called, "Mbaba Mwana Waresa." The land was named the Zulu of Natal after the Goddess who rules over rainbows, rain, crops, and cultivation.

They were blessed with a remarkable girl child whom they named Mable Jefferson. Her mother adored her because Mable was the chosen one too. Her gifts were much more powerful than her mother's.

She looked identical to her mother too. Her parents raised her to be proud of her Zulu heritage and most of all about her sacred gifts. "As living beings we must be proud of the difference we can make and what we can do." Mable Jefferson grew up and learned of her unique gifts and together shared in the caretaking of this world. Mable was young and considered by some not yet ready. Despite these reservations she dedicated her life to learning all she could.

Mable Jefferson met and married Frederick Johnson from the Johnson plantation. She hyphenated her last name to Jefferson-Johnson to honor both families of the plantation's former owners. Frederick adored his wife and committed to nurturing her gifts and protecting the secret too he choose to live with his new wife on her family's plantation. She felt comfortable with him and normal in spite of her mystical gifts and he helped his wife and in-laws with the building and creation of their Mbaba.

Mable Jefferson-Johnson and husband Frederick collaborated on all things concerning their mystical world but he ran the plantation too.

He respected his wife's family tradition that only a female could be the caretaker of the remarkable world.

Mable received help and guidance from her mother Isi who empowered her daughter in collaborating in the cultivation of their sacred plants. They harmonized and bred together mother seeds from foreign worlds with father seeds from exotic and faraway lands on earth, creating unique original flowers and plants. The combining process was best described as a marriage ritual. These special seeds were known, by the most apt translation possible as 'Star Seeds' each having its own unique name. A stunning star seed named Zelfari was married to a male Lotus seed from Egypt. They married a male Folaxi star to a female Iris from France. The star seed Samasi was partnered with a male Chrysanthemum from Japan. A beautiful mother star seed Lomarro was joined with a male carnation from the Soviet Union. Through these and many other unions an entire race of unique plants and flowers were created to support the other life forms of Mbaba.

The new seedlings grew into plants and trees of varied colors, adopting the combined shapes of its parents making for many peculiar designs in tree trunks and petals. So many tones and hues created a visual sensation of a mystical wondrous world. Ms. Mable believed that God bestowed this mission upon her and her Ancestors. A special mission that was not only meant for growing plants but also discovering how to grow the mind and soul. Mable was a beautiful replica of her beloved mother Isi Johnson but gentler in spirit with an over active imagination and gifts more powerful than her ancestors. She learned from her mother Isi as she grew older about her mother's tribe the Xolani and her grandparents. Her grandmother Ntokozo and grandfather Kwanele Silongo as well as tragic tale Ntokozo parents' Isineko Kuleni wife of Jubulani Mebena. The shocking betrayal she experienced from Chief Mandla Silongo. She watched her mother's Isi sad eyes as she shared about her terrifying journey to Mistick Krewe of Jefferson.

*   *   *

Isineko Kuleni was from the Xoloni Tribe and the rarest of all children from her village in great beauty and earthly gifts. Her ability to heal plants, animals and people was remarkable. At the age of seven, she could mate seedlings' together from different species of plants – seedlings that she later shared in confidence with her only child that came from other great worlds. Ntokozo spoke of her fascination when she watched her mother Isineko Mebena wife of the great warrior Jubulani Mebena do and create many remarkable things. Speaking to plants and communicating with animals, was one of her most prominent unique gifts.

These were gifts that she used to help her fellow villagers have a better life. Isineko adored her daughter who also possessed great wisdom beyond her tender years. Ntokozo Mebena studied her mother and wrote and documented her mother's gifts.

Her mother was delighted by her daughter's devotion to learning and understanding her rare gifts. Ntokozo was destined to marry Kwanele Silongo only male child of Chief Mandla Silongo. It was foretold by the village midwife that his only son would grow into a great and proud warrior. Kwanele was chosen for Ntokozo by her parents. A union was easily arranged, as from the time of their birth the children's parents' had shared a very close friendship. From early on, it was clear that Ntokozo gifts were not as powerful as her mother's. It was foretold by Isineko that her daughter Ntokozo would bear a girl child who would have sacred powerful gifts more powerful than her own. This grandchild would be the re-birth of her must bear her name Isineko.

Ntokozo from the age of six kept a journal and documented everything – sacred prayers, chants, herbal remedies, and powerful medicines – to pass on. She wanted to be well prepared to raise her gifted child. The chief and all the villagers' were excited upon learning of the preordained birth of the future Gatekeeper.

However fate acted contrary to their favor and Ntokozo was orphaned from the age of thirteen. Her parents' death was tragic. Her father Jubulani committed suicide in the wake of defending his wife and Ntokozo's mother Isineko from Ntokozo's Uncle Lizwi. Upon returning from hunting, her father Jubulani had caught his brother Lizwi trying to force Isineko to submit to him. Jubulani's rage and blind fury at his brother's transgression caused him to unthinkingly plunge his knife into his brother heart killing him instantly. Isineko distraught by her husband's actions and knowing that his life would be forfeit under Southern customs and local law plunged the same knife into her own heart, taking his place. When Jubulani learned of her sacrifice, the truth was too much to bear and he killed himself. He couldn't live with the pain of knowing he killed his brother Lizwi and Isineko had sacrificed herself to save him, in the wake of them sharing forbidden intercourse whether involuntarily or naught. The tragic deaths cast a dark shadow over the once peace loving village. Ntokozo screams of terror as she ran from her home to the arms of Kwanele could be heard from miles around. Kwanele's parents' also vowed to protect and help nurture Ntokozo who struggled for years to recover from the shock of seeing her mother, father and uncle's lifeless blood soaked bodies. She was so loved, cherished and protected living with her future husband and family until the chief and council felt she was ready for marriage. All believed that she would give birth to the next Gatekeeper. Kwanele was tall, handsome, powerful, strong and wise for a boy his age. He knew of his wife's destiny and vowed to protect and guide his gifted soul mate their love was as powerful as her parents.

Ntokozo and Kwanele Silongo married at the age of sixteen. One year later they were blessed to give birth to a daughter Isineko Silongo. She was extraordinary in beauty and wisdom. Their baby was the rebirth of Ntokozo's mother Isineko Mebena but with caramel skin and eyes which held the brilliance of her parents own, changed colors with her moods. Isineko daughter of Ntokozo shared with her mother about her incredible dreams about other worlds. Seeds sent to her from other planets destined to know life on earth. Her dreams would lead Isineko to the location of these remarkable seeds that came to their village. With her mother's help she put the seeds in a secret box that was handed down to her from her grandmother Isineko Mebena. Together the granddaughter and daughter of Isineko Mebena performed the ceremony that would give them life. . .

Isineko would lovingly enchant the sacred vows and rites, knowing instinctively what to say and do. At the age of seven, her wisdom and gifts were so shockingly advanced that her parents believed that she would become more powerful than her namesake, her grandmother Isineko Mebena. As such they feared for their daughter's safety. Her boldness caused them to be concerned that it could put her in danger. Isineko Silongo wasn't secretive or subtle, but bold wanting to flaunt her extraordinary gifts. This was in stark contrast to Ntokozo who like her mother was extremely private and protective doing all things with discretion. Their daughter believed she was privileged and partly because they spoiled her. She fought with her parents, refusing to hide what she believed should be public. From the five generations past, one single female had been blessed with her sacred gifts. The Gatekeepers' gifts were not supposed to be exposed or used for self-elevation. The bearer of the 'gift' was to be modest, humble and help in secrecy. Her parents' Ntokozo and Kwanele became fearful of their daughter's need for attention. They threatened to take Isineko away from a home, the village she loved but refused to leave.

Her gifts grew from creating plants to healing people and many had seen the healing take place including the chief, Silongo. Her parents' worried if she did not curtail the exhibitionism of her gifts. She insulted her parents, in the spirit of teenage, youthful rebelliousness laughing in their faces calling them old and simple minded. A thing she had seen her age mate counterparts do, ignorant to the redress that occurred in private beyond the public eye. Isineko had never been subject to this private homestead disciplining as her parents believed she would not require physical curtailing. In this moment however they realized they were wrong and the truth of this hurt them even more. No good deed goes unpunished. She screamed at them to leave her behind as she would not forsake what she believed was hers. She stormed out leaving them to their own silence.

Hurt and saddened her parents could not fathom abandoning Isineko and they refused to leave without her. They prayed that she would change her mind. If she didn't they would do what they had never done before and physical control their daughter. In planning their escape they forgot to be mindful of the Idiom "Eyes have Ears" and these eyes soon found their way to the Chief's ears. When the chief discovered their plans he had her parents captured, imprisoning them as captive in another village. He told Isineko her parents abandoned her because they no longer loved her.

She was heartbroken but her pride wouldn't let her show her pain. She decided she didn't love them anymore. Their daughter's powers' continued to stun and awe the villagers'. There were animals near death and many witnessed her powerful ability to bless and heal instantly to make plants grow regardless of draught, or famine. Rival tribes attempted to kidnap Isineko creating war and more corruption, in the wake of which peace vanished. Isineko was willful, stubborn, and disrespectful of their ways too at the tender age of thirteen. Many villagers' admired but feared Isineko especially now that their chief would possess and control her powers. There was no escaping the power hungry village chief Silongo. Silongo saved Isineko for himself, warding off other suitors, publicly protecting her but secretly wanting to make her his bride as soon as she was sixteen. When she learned of the fate in store for her terror filled her being and she regretted her feisty impertinence that had brought to this eventuality. But now it was too late. She was confined within a house and room that was heavily guarded and from which there was no escape this prison became her home for two years.

She now realized what her parents had tried to warn her about.

Under the weight of being separated from her parents and imprisoned, her love and joy turned to resentment and spite. Hatred filled her young heart and she cursed the land and village. She was constantly in a state of rage, sometimes so disturbing it caused the chief to have the healers' force her to drink a sedative, which sent her into a deep sleep. Things continued in this manner until the eve of their wedding she now was sixteen. The next day was to be the biggest celebration ever known to the villagers' and to all surrounding villages. The day in which her "marriage" to chief Silongo would be celebrated, a day she deeply dreaded.

That day however had a very different beginning than expected. Isineko was awakened not by her bridal party but by a man whose skin color terrified her. The strong hands that held and grasped her tightly were white and very pale to her eyes. The eyes that peered deeply into hers were steely blue and almost lifeless, devoid of any emotion. Before she could fight back or resist the large white demon suddenly looped ropes around her hands and ankles, before throwing her over his shoulder as he carried her out of the house. The sedative had weakened her and she found difficult to fight or walk as once outside he pulled her roughly along. The burning Village struck fear and awe in her being and she screamed loudly but to no avail. Her screams were lost in the cries of help from other women and children. She lost her footing, got up stumbled and fell repeatedly while being dragged towards the others also held captive. She suddenly released a piercing scream as the blood of chief Silongo stained her feet. He laid there lifeless, sliced wide open with his guts hanging out, mouth agape, silent with his eyes sightless.

Death surrounded her and as she looked at the destruction about her, she was horrified. She believed that she had invoked this calamity and the demons were her to claim her. Sorrow filled her soul but rage filled her being. Rage against her own self for having brought such a horrible, evil curse upon her village. Isineko remarkably survived the long agonizing voyage on a ship from hell that was returning with her on it. She was taken from her home to a faraway land called, 'Mississippi'. Isineko believed she was cursed, being punished for what she had done to her village. Her gift had become evil and tainted and now she would die living amongst the white demons.

This evil land was far worse she realized because animals were treated better than her people. This ugly world was filled with horrors.

However as every cloud has a silver lining, she survived due to small graces. Her captors recognized her beauty and it was her beauty that saved her. Her captors protected her from rape and sexual abuse. She was to be preserved for breeding and sold to the highest bidder, either for personal use or profiteering through the numerous pleasure houses prevalent through the land. Blessings can sometimes come from curses and she was fortunate to be sold at the very auction that Donald and Anne – Marie infrequently attended. She was also fortunate that Donald and Anne-Marie Johnson purchased her despite the very high price.

This saved Isineko from a life of being used like an animal for breeding and sexual hire. Isineko hated her fate and resented these white demons too. She was only sixteen and yet her eyes were those of a hardened, tortured old soul.

Anne-Marie and Donald Johnson knew Isineko was different from others they had encountered and she similarly recognized they were not like the other white demons. When they looked into her eyes they saw and felt a life force that exceeded anyone they had previously met.

This white female demon was strangely kind to her. Isineko didn't fear her or the slave Rebecca that had accompanied her. Rebecca spoke her tongue and the white female's words too. Rebecca became the bridge between them. Rebecca had been living on the plantation for three years and adapted to her new world and life. She was friendly, warm and nurturing. Very much like an older sister to Isineko. They deeply cared for each other and trusted each other too. Isineko had a new home, a cabin with a bed, food and water. In these circumstances Rebecca soon bonded with the frightened young woman.

Within two months Isineko learned much about her new life and how to survive in it. Within six months her intelligence had enabled her to learn the white man's language at a speed that shocked Rebecca. The slave owners' Anne-Marie and Donald had one child, a daughter named Mable and it was easily foreseeable that a relationship of sorts would develop between the two. At the age of sixteen Mable developed a deadly fever and word spread throughout the plantation about her illness. A fever had been spreading throughout the locality for over a year which had coincided with Isineko's arrival. As there are two sides to every coin, Rebecca having shared her home with Isineko knew of her gifts to heal and convinced Isineko to help the sick white girl. Together they went to the big white house, where Rebecca explained to Mable's parents that Isineko could heal their daughter, through the use of natural medicine.

Anne-Marie and Donald loved and trusted Rebecca and were deeply grateful desperate to save their only child. They however at first refused but with Rebecca bringing to light the number of people she had helped cure they agreed. They all left Isineko alone in the room with their dying daughter for one hour. When they re-entered the room Mable was sitting up in her bed talking with Isineko and there was no sign of the deadly virus. Her parents' were stunned and profoundly grateful that she saved their beloved Mable's life. Mable insisted that her new friend

Isineko should live in the house with them. Her parents agreed and after much kindness trust developed and something more, Love. They were inseparable and the best of friends, more like family. Mable and Isi had a very unique bond both girls sixteen they shared a powerful love for each other and were like sisters. Their Friendship grew over the next three years, transcending the racial restrictions that permeated the South.

Mable's father Donald was a sensitive man who always respected his wife's and daughter's wishes and as such. Isineko eventually bonded with the Mable's parents too. They accepted and loved her dearly and let her keep her first name but shortened it to 'Isi. In the following year, Mable while at a charity ball meet Bertram Jefferson and it was mutually love at first sight. They were married after a short courtship and soon after Mable moved along with Isi to the Jefferson plantation.

The marriage didn't break their bond and it became a local joke that Bertram married two wives that day.

Mistick Krewe of Jefferson had a new generation now running things.

Bertram's parents retired early and went away leaving Martha and Bertram as the youngest plantation owners in recollected history.

Through the couple's marriage, the two remarkable young Johnson and Jefferson families maintained a strong bond, enjoying a rare and powerful friendship. The two couples, Mable and Bertram Jefferson and Isi and Theodore Jefferson-Johnson lived an independent existence, happy because they lived more of a free life. Mable and Bertram believed that all men were equal but trapped by the laws in the south.

They never wanted slaves a fact that was known to all "slaves" on the plantation which fostered an endearing relationship with blacks living on the plantation.

Between the two families, Bertram and Mable enjoyed learning about African history and tales their tales. They often expressed fascination when they saw and learned about seedlings from Africa too.

This mystical world thrilled and fascinated Mable and Bertram. Although they were forbidden from visiting it but despite this they still forged a deeper bond between the two families through their mutual love for nature. Isi and Theodore did make a significant contribution to plantations' success in harvesting the most beautiful crops of corn, wheat, fruits, and rare one-of-a-kind plants and flowers as well as vegetables exported to different countries. Eventually Theodore and Bertram shared many adventures together that expanded their knowledge, trust, and respect for each other thus providing unique and rare seedlings from far away countries too. The Jefferson's' wealth provided a lifestyle that was extremely private, creating remarkable opportunities for all, with everyone on the plantation being educated to read and write in English.

After the emancipation from slavery, Mable and Bertram bestowed the deed of the Mystic Krewe plantation to Isi and Theodore Jefferson.

They were the first and only slaves' to receive such an incredible gift. They were given title to the land, the homes, and a small fortune. It was no longer safe for Mable and Bertram to stay now that they had many reasons to fear for their lives. There was a bitter begrudging suspicion among their southern neighbors that they Bertram and Mable Jefferson and their in-laws had supported the North and helped them to win the civil war. A suspicion based on truth. The former slave owners were grateful to have the chance to help any runaways they could escape to the North. However it seemed that wanted had befallen Isi a long time ago was set to happen to Mable and Bertram, especially given the fact that all freed slaves chose to remain and sharecrop, while slaves on all the other plantations had departed for new properties of their own.

They had indeed secretly supported the war and were happy that the North had won. Their friends the Johnsons' decided to stay behind knowing they were safe due to Mable and Bertram actions to protect them. After the war there was a lovely, quiet celebration in their home.

They were all excited about the new beginning for the families' of Bertram and Mable Jefferson and Isi and Theodore Jefferson.

Mable's parents the Johnsons' kept a powerful image that protected them from repercussions' from the North and South. Mable and Bertram quietly left to begin their new lives too. The Plantation owners' the Jefferson's and Johnsons' wanted their extended family of freed slaves to live in a land that supported their beliefs. All believed their land became all the more blessed because of the beautiful hearts, minds, and souls of those who came before them and those that continued to live at Mystic Krewe of Jefferson.

When their friends left to honor them, their names were incorporated into naming the descendants and future generations that were born on both plantations and first and last names carried forward in future generations. Theodore Jefferson and Isi Johnson were Mable Jefferson parents.

Mable Jefferson married Frederick Johnson she decided to hyphenate her name to Mable Jefferson-Johnson were the parents of Trevor and Thandee Jefferson-Johnson. Patience Robinson's first name was the

English translation of Isineko named after her great grandmother Isineko Mebena and great great grandmother Isineko Kuleni. Theo and Marcus Robinson were also the children of Thandee Jefferson-Johnson and Anthony Robinson. Ms. Mable was their grandmother and the matriarch of their family.

Thandee and Trevor loved their family's history and had tremendous respect for their ancestors' remarkable gifts and their sacred mission.

Her son Trevor especially was proud and wanted more than anything to carry on the family tradition. Trevor expected now it was his time, given that fate had worked in his favor due to the unexpected passing of his sister Thandee and husband Anthony whose lives were tragically taken by a drunk driver.

He remembered repeatedly having sat with his father Fredrick, waiting for his mother and Thandee to return from Mbaba. It was during these times that his dad spoke of having the same capabilities and that he could fulfill the role of the Gatekeeper if needed. Believing he knew his father wanted him to continue his legacy. Trevor adored his father and remembered the promise he had made on that fateful day to his grandparents also. He never knew that would be the last time he would see his father and grandparents. Isi and Theodore were blessed with remarkable health in their senior years and had one last wish to return to their place of birth. Ms. Mable encouraged her husband to accompany them on their journey and there was a big celebration on the day of their departure. Two months later Trevor was awakened by a piercing scream from his mother's room. He raced in to her bedroom and found his mother collapsed on the floor distraught from a vision of her beloved husband and parents having died in a horrific plane crash.

Within hours they received a phone call that confirmed her nightmare that they her husband and parents were killed in a plane crash on a flight from Africa returning to the United States. Trevor withdrew from public life and consumed himself with making the plantation the most extraordinary vegetative land in New Orleans and used his gifts like his father as well as protects the health and welling being of his beloved mother too.

He committed himself to safeguard the mystical world his grandparents and mother had created regardless of having been forbidden from visiting it. Ms. Mable shared her vast knowledge and family secrets during private moments with her daughter and Patience. She cherished her granddaughter Patience the most as she was the incarnation of her mother, 'Isi'. No one could create the beautiful plants they were capable of growing. Mistick Krewe of Jefferson was the most spectacular plantation in the South of New Orleans.

Ms. Mable honored and kept the original name her mother Isi bestowed, "Mbaba Mwana Waresa" from the Zulu language of Natal, named after the Goddess who rules over rainbows, rain, crops, and cultivation. Ms. Mable Jefferson-Johnson affectionately referred to the mystical world as Mbaba, pronounced as "ba-ba".

* * *

"Oh man every plant is glowing neon. I'm surprised that my eyes can take it," Patience said.

"Yeah it's like living in a cartoon animation!" "How can this be possible?" Patience asked.

The surroundings were a remarkable cornucopia of trees and bushes of varied shapes. The soft, glittering grass was parented from unique harmonized seeds. Other fauna included Pink Pampas, Korean Feather Wood, Rye Brome Grass, and Sweet Vernal Grass textured like a thick shaggy carpet so silky and soft, surpassing any grass in their world. The trees were also unique. Some were tall, gigantic with milky white trunks, others colored in aqua, red, green, orange and blue in color. They had several shapes some formed like coke bottles, thick spirals, triangles and other unique shapes with leaves of similar fashion.

There were fruits on trees that were smaller in size with vegetables yellow for apples, red for bananas and green for oranges. Every shade represented a different flavor of fruit and the vegetables looked like over grown fruits from the plantation. This garden was a botanical paradise because of how the plants looked and smelled. Trees from the Methuselah and Prometheus plants, the oldest trees known to man in the world were all the more unique with the seeds from these ancient trees having been merged with ancient seeds from other galaxies. All of the plants were wild and crazy-looking because of the weird designs and sizes.

No matter what their shape or size, color or appearance, everything was strikingly beautiful. Now as the children wandered, they started to recall more of their Grandmother's stories. She shared more with Patience because she was the only female left to continue her legacy. Patience looked cautiously around herself, fear and fascination making her heart race.

"Pat and Theo, so Gram wasn't making up stuff. Look at this place. It's so like the stories she use to tell us, especially you Pat."

"Yeah and how many times did I pretend to be listening? I would be daydreaming, just waiting patiently for Grammy to finish. You'll know I have no interest in plants." Patience said.

"Well, if you had listened when Gram talked then maybe we would know what to do next!" Theo yelled.

Marcus interjected before she could retort back at Theo.

"You know, Pat I think she wanted you to know more than us for some reason. Like it was important to her that you were into plants and nature like she was. Mom said that you were the only girl and she wanted you to be like her and Grammy into plants and stuff like that." Marcus said.

"Oh yeah? Well, it wasn't like you brats paid attention either. You're just as bad as me. So none of us knows what's going on here or how to deal with it? How was I supposed to know it was for real? It's not like we would believe her if she said it was." Patience said.

"Pathetic excuse, Pat. She talked to you mostly about this stuff and you should've paid attention, but you're too selfish to care about what's Important to Gram." Patience walked up to Theo and stared him down.

She raised her hand then suddenly dropped it to her side while she clenched her fists tightly. She suddenly marched off on her own. Theo looked at his brother and shook his head then grabbed him by the arm went off in another direction. Unknowingly, the children were wandering towards a place that bore the rarest fruit in the entire garden.

*   *   *

"What are you brats doing here? Did you follow me?" Patience asked. "Pat, how many times have you screwed up every situation? Like we would want to follow you? Would we Marcus?"

"Oh man, I can't take any more of this constant warring. We got away from Trevor right? Let's not forget that we'd be worse off if he caught us. Can you move beyond your petty animosity?"

Both were taken aback by his bold outburst and in the wake of his stern words, they both conceded to his demand.

"Yeah," They said together, shame hanging over them.

"So chill man. Relax and let's get along. Okay?" Marcus said. Patience was tired and, suddenly feeling the weight of her burdens, decided to lie down on the downy, soft grass to pull together a plan. She put her hands behind her head. Marcus and Theo did the same then all of them stared up at the remarkable sky.

"Wow, did we ever get lost!" Patience said.

"We definitely did! Imagine getting lost and found right into another world," Theo whispered.

"Did Grammy ever tell us the name of this place?" Marcus asked. "No, how could she? It's just a coincidence. This place is kind of like her stories. I don't remember her mentioning any name though." Patience said.

"Yeah, Marcus, this isn't the same place that had the weird name. I don't remember."

Not wanting to talk to them, Patience retreated into her internal solitude and enjoyed a peaceful feeling of tranquility. She spoke quietly, not wanting to being awakened back to the harsh world and wrath of

Trevor. She feared that this all was just a dream and she would inevitably return to the nightmare she tried to escape.

"Oh yeah, that's right. I bet he can't find this place," Marcus whispered.

"Those vines aren't strong enough to drag Trevor's big butt here." Theo said.

They all laughed became silent while they looked again at the incredible sky. One minute it was blue, purple, pink or turquoise but the clouds made an impact because they were a spectacular glittery rainbow. Patience pointed upward and smiled as she watched the sky show off bright tones in unique shades. The sun was bright glittery light orange. Patience was curious about what the stars looked like. She thought of how much more beautiful her Grandmother, Mother, and Father would shine here too. Oh God why did you take them away from me and leave me here with these brats?"

Her tears slowly dropped down her cheeks as she listened to her brothers snoring while she remembered the funeral.

*   *   *

It was a beautiful sunny day when seven-year-old Patience stood tearfully holding her Grandmother's hand tightly. She watched them as they lowered the caskets of her Mother and Father into the ground.

Patience buried her face into Ms. Mable's tummy because she could not stand to see what was happening. Her uncle Trevor was between her brothers and held their hands as they cried too. Everyone cried except

Trevor. He just stayed there silently and watched. Patience suddenly looked at him and what she saw in his eyes made her blood run cold.

Now he had confirmed what she always believed; that he hated her parents.

Seven years later, she would see that look again but it was worse because his hate focused on her alone. Since the day her Grandmother died, he always looked at her as if she had caused his mother's death.

Patience knew he blamed her and her brothers' too. He often spoke about how Patience had argued with his mother and believed the stress on his mother's heart was why she died in her sleep. He also resented that she never helped his mother enough especially when it came to the garden he and his mother loved so much. Although it was a massive farm with many helpers, he felt like Patience had taken advantage of her. She had brothers but they never experienced the burden of continuing to do all the chores their grandmother had for them. All of that stopped after her death. He kicked all but one of the helpers out of the house and sent the rest home. Patience struggled to survive their constant tirade of words, neglect, and being used as a personal servant, taking care of them and that very large house too.

Worst of all, was when he drank. He would send her brothers out so that there was no escaping him. She learned not to scream, fearing the consequences. She believed it was best that she alone was beaten.

Finally the day came for her to escape but it did not happen the way she had planned.

*   *   *

On her knees, Patience was hiding behind the couch crouched down low with her hand over her mouth to silence the rage that rumbled in the core of her being. She couldn't believe what she'd heard as she listened to Trevor and Loretta talking as they sat on the couch watching TV.

"Trevor it's just not right, you having to raise them. Maybe you should send them to an orphanage," Loretta said.

"Loretta, you're brilliant. Why didn't I think of that? They shouldn't be my burden."

"I bet that car accident was Thandee's fault. Probably being reckless and not paying attention. Her husband was weak and wasn't much of a real man to me, I never liked him. They're dead and that lazy daughter of theirs doesn't do enough around here. How I hate that brat."

Patience forced herself not to scream and crawled around the corner on her hands and knees into the kitchen. The well-oiled hinges of the door helped her to be escape. Once in the kitchen, she jumped up, marched over to the stove, and leaned her back against it. Her arms folded tightly across her chest to prevent her hands from smashing everything in the kitchen. She stared up at the ceiling then quickly wiped away a tear.

His burden in life? Oh man, has he really lost touch with reality?

Since when did taking care of that worthless, lazy, ungrateful man and those brats make me his burden in life? Patience slammed the cupboard doors so hard she almost broke them off its hinges.

Fool! How I hate Trevor.

It was almost dinner time and she thought how to distract herself. The kitchen door swung open and her brothers were standing behind her as she faced the cupboard. She grabbed the plates from the dish rack and with them in hand moved to set the table. She however froze with plates in her hands motionless, as Theo spoke out.

"Pat, can't you do anything on time? We're hungry. Where's dinner?" Theo asked.

She spun around and holding the plates high above her head let them go. The plastic Plates landed and spun on the floor like tops twirling. Her hands shot to her ears to block out Theo's nagging voice and she ran out the back door leaving her brothers staring after her.

Marcus attempted to follow her but Theo stepped in his way. Marcus frowned but backed away, looking down not wanting to meet his gaze.

He wasn't sure what to do and didn't challenge Theo's directive. "Marcus, leave her alone and get our dinner. Trevor will deal with her later."

Stepping outside into the beautiful, dark, clear starry night, she sat on the double-seated rocker on the massive veranda that wrapped around the beautiful white mansion. The night air seemed to free her and she covered herself with the soft wool blanket her grandmother knitted for her. She rocked on the lawn chair while staring up at the sky.

She looked up at her angels; now beautiful bright stars. Her Grandmother, Mother and Father always waited and shined no matter how dark it was in her life.

The nightmare of her living situation since their passing was a daily struggle. There was no one to run to because Trevor controlled the entire plantation, a vital part of the town's economy. No one wanted to risk making an enemy of him so she was entirely alone in her pain.

Patience searched the sky for her three very special stars.

"Thank God, I can still feel some love when I look up at you guys.

Dear Grammy! Dear Mama and Papa! When are you guys going to get me out of this mess?" She whispered. Suddenly three very large stars, side by side sparkled brightly and made every other star appear dim.

This caused her to smile as it seemed as if they were waving hello. She began to sing. Her voice resonated throughout the whole house carried by the winds of the night breeze. Despite their vicious animosity towards Patience all within the household were taken back by this.

Despite her maliciousness, Loretta could not help but voice her surprise.

"That child has the most amazing voice! Trevor, baby we could make all kinds of money off of her singing. I could be her agent and make things happen."

"No. She won't and can't sing for the public." His hatred blinded him from seeing the benefit of the development of any of Patience's talents.

Angry he shushed Loretta with his hand. "Don't ever talk about this again, Loretta! Now quiet I want to listen".

At the same time in the dining room, the boys stopped setting the table mesmerized by her singing. Theo stood there silently in awe while Marcus quietly sneaked outside and sat unobtrusively in a corner to hear Patience better. Even the animals quieted and listened. Her voice was so beautiful it could make angels come down from heaven to enjoy her gift.

Starlights in my Soul . . .

You will always shine in me and I will always look above to the light of your love . . .

Starlights in my Soul . . .

You are angels in the sky and although God called you home, I know I will never be alone . . .

Starlights in my Soul . . .

You are stars to light our way for all to learn and know how to light each other's days . . .

Starlights in my life . . .

I am grateful for your love and how your love fills my lonely heart . . . Starlights in my soul . . .

You are everlasting Stars and will always be the Starlights in my life . . .

Just as Patience stopped, she heard her brothers on the other side of the porch. She got up and approached them. Theo frowning, chastised Marcus for getting them caught listening. "Marcus you gotta stop chasing after Pat when she messes up. You know how pissed off Trevor will get when you try to help her, so leave her alone." He was about to continue until Patience cut him off. Theo stared up at her tight-lipped and Marcus had his head bowed.

"Theo and Marcus, do you have any idea what your Mr. Wonderful uncle is planning on doing?"

"What?" Twins asked.

"He's going to send us all to an orphanage," She whispered.

Theo and Marcus looked at her with eyes and mouths wide open in surprise. She stared at her brothers faces and then up at the sky before looking back at them smiling.

"I've got a plan."

*   *   *

What was I thinking? Anytime I help those two, I always end up paying the price for it. They're so ungrateful. Now I'm stuck here in this weird place with them. How are we going to survive here? Patience bit her lip and tried hard to fight away the painful memories and tears that came with them. She rubbed her eyes and continued to look up at the sky, praying that another miracle would happen, not caring that Theo wasn't back yet.

"Pat, Marcus, come check this out. Look at what I found hiding behind these Vines!"

Patience and Marcus got up and Marcus followed his sister towards Theo. Theo jumped up and down while waving frantically, on top of a massive pile of multi-colored vines. Not very far away stood a spectacular looking tree half hidden by the vines and unlike anything they had ever seen. Puzzled, Patience and Marcus went towards it. Theo had discovered the most beautiful and delicious looking fruit tree.

"Wow. Have you ever seen berries that big and beautiful?" Theo asked.

"Forget the Berries. Check out that tree it kind of looks like a horseshoe on a stand. It's so weird, but kind of cool too." Marcus said.

The tree unknown to them was called "Inhlakanipha." A Zulu name meaning wisdom. It grew the rarest giant fruit like berries called, 'Uhlamvu'. The tree trunk was straight, thick, and silver, about ten feet high. The lower branches formed silver horseshoe and stood about seven feet high and was very wide. Two rows of smaller branches on each side that framed the horseshoe, each about a foot apart, totaling about thirty wands on each side. The wands had different solid colors on them no two the same beside each other. Hanging off each wand was one Uhlamvu the fruit heart-shaped, all with a different colored striped pattern that glittered in the sun.

"Remember Grammy's lesson on color, ROYGBIV. R for Red, O for Orange, Y for Yellow, G for green, B for blue, I for Indigo, and V for violet. I have never seen a berry with so many tones on it. Now for sure that's some kind of fruit tree. A funky -looking one too! Just like Grammy would say." Patience said.

"Yeah I remember," Theo and Marcus said.

The Uhlamvu were the size of a dime, larger than the berries grown in their world. Mouth-watering, plump, and magical, they glistened temptingly on the tree.

"Man I wonder why this place exists. I just don't get," Marcus said. "Pat we haven't eaten in hours or what feels like days. We have got to eat them. I can feel and hear my stomach growling. I'm starving." Theo said.

"No stupid! We don't. How do you know if they're not poisonous?" she said.

"Yeah, what if they're poisonous Theo?"

Marcus uncharacteristically spoke out against Theo and this time Theo put him back down.

"Marcus, stop being such a punk and always letting her boss you around. What does she know?"

Patience did not hear their exchange being focused on the berries. Patience walked away from the berries then suddenly returned, cautiously. She slowly approached the tree and got a closer look. Theo is right. They're some kind of berry, and we're so hungry, but should we eat them? If we don't, we'll die of starvation.

Theo and Marcus picked one berry each and held it in their hands, fascinated by them. Patience looked over at them, frowning, and quickly walked over to Marcus, slapping it out of his hand. Marcus jumped back, surprised. He hated this about Patience and Theo. They were two battling control freaks. Theo was smarter, faster and considered better looking. Although Marcus was bigger and stronger, Theo always won every fight through sheer will and determination Theo could kick his tail any day of the week. Marcus's bossy twin never let him forget who the 'better' twin was. Marcus was cautious and disliked confrontation too. They were almost thirteen, but sometimes Marcus felt like he was a little kid when it came to Patience and Theo.

He loved his brother and was fiercely loyal, no matter how he treated him. Marcus defended him, no matter how wrong he was. He also wanted to protect Patience too. He hated how Trevor and Theo treated his sister, but he could not do anything about it. Their big sister always favored Marcus because to her, he was the good twin. She knew if Trevor and Theo became abusive and abused her or Marcus. Her more if Marcus tried to help. Still she resented Marcus for his weakness. Marcus did always find the good in the bad and tried to make the best out of an ugly situation. She struggled with constant emotional confusion. One minute she hated Marcus, the next she loved him but she never felt any love for Theo.

"Marcus! Don't pick another one," she said.

Marcus stopped and backed away. He avoided his brother's eyes and looked down at the ground.

"Man, are you still going to listen to her? Don't be a punk. We know I run things here. Now get another berry!"

Theo never feared his sister and always challenged Patience authority. Patience marched over and stopped just in front of him, hands on her hips as she glared menacingly at Theo. It was like looking at a little

Trevor because he did resemble his uncle. He walked over to his sister and stood face to face staring up at her. How he hated that she was more than a foot taller. He drew himself up, always trying to be taller than her in every way. He was the man after all and Patience was just a stupid bossy girl.

"I'm the King of this world and I say we eat them. Girls have no authority here, right Marcus?" Marcus looked at them both and stayed silent. He walked over to the tree and picked another Berry.

"Theo, you little fool. Now you think that you're all that because Trevor's not around. Okay, king of this world! You eat the berries first. Pray that they don't kill you."

"Alright, you'll be lucky if I leave any for you to eat. So you'd better eat them too!"

Oh man what if she's right? But I can't punk out now. I have got to show Marcus that she's wrong again.

Theo approached the tree and boldly looked at Patience. He took his time picking a berry before he popped one in his mouth. His eyes opened wide as he grabbed his throat and dropped to the ground under the branch. Suddenly Marcus ran to his side. Patience however knowing better didn't move and watched. Theo quickly sat up, laughing as he got to his feet and started picking more berries to eat. He began to eat them faster and made a lot of noise as if he was eating the best food he had ever tasted.

"Man, they're so good I don't care if they kill me. They're worth dying for. I don't care if you guys don't eat them, because they're too good to share."

He maliciously smiled at his brother and sister with multicolored berry-stained teeth. Marcus had one berry in his hand and Patience picked one and stood there staring at it. She held it up high to examine it hoping she could tell if they were dangerous. Suddenly she held her belly with one hand because it growled so loudly the berries could have fallen off the tree.

"He isn't dead yet. So maybe they're okay." Still Marcus waited. He feared what might have happened if he ate the berries and he was tired of listening to his bossy brother too. Marcus looked upwards as if seeking guidance. Patience did the same.

No food, no water or place to get prepared food. Marcus is hungry.

We all are, but if we ate the berries they might kill us. If we don't, we would die from starvation. Those berries do look good. Lord, you always make my life so hard. Why did I get this stupid name? I'm just a kid, but I always have to make big decisions for my brothers. It's taking all the patience out of me.

Suddenly the most incredible looking butterfly landed on the berry Marcus held.

"Pat, Theo, look at this!"

Curious, Patience and Theo quietly walked over and stood beside Marcus then looked at it, both fascinated. Surprised by how calmly it sat on a berry, fearless of humans.

"Hey that's the same butterfly that helped us to get out of the cornfield. Amazing," Patience whispered.

"Yeah Pat, you are right. Maybe it's trying to tell us something like it's okay to eat the berries," Marcus whispered.

"What if it's trying to stop us?" Theo whispered.

"Oh my God guys, look at its face. It kind of looks human and it's smiling. I think I'm losing my mind. Butterfly should we eat the berries?" Marcus asked.

Do not fear me children or this world! You belong here.

Patience was taken aback. *I can hear you. But you're a bug! I must be dreaming.*

No one can hear me but you. It seems the others are not yet in tune with this world.

The butterfly smiled and nodded its head in approval and then suddenly flew away. The trio was stunned and stood there, looked at each other, then at the berry tree.

"You guys heard her right. I can't believe what just happened. I can't believe any or all of it!" Patience said.

"Heard what Pat?" Both asked.

This weird place is making me lose my mind now I'm imaging talking bugs.

"I trust her. She has helped us before, Pat. The berries are okay to eat. Have some. Berries that taste this good couldn't kill us!" Marcus said. "Well at least I got to eat more than you guys. I don't need some bug to tell me what to do." Theo said.

"First we hear Gram's voice and she's a cloud, and now this weird butterfly. Maybe this place has something to do with her. I believe Gram is trying to help us," Marcus said.

"Okay let's do it together. Ready on the count of three we eat them. One, two, and three," Patience said.

"Oh my lord, thank God! They're so good," she said. "You ought to listen to me from now on," Theo said.

They were at the tree picking, eating and loving the delicious berries. Patience closed her eyes as she slowly sucked on one to enjoy the unique tingling sensation making it linger. As hungry as she was, still she did not want to rush, it was so delicious. They ate and ate until there were no berries left on the tree.

Patience, now we are one. Suddenly Patience looked around her then up and down she looked frightened upon hearing the voice of the butterfly again.

Wow this place is playing with my mind.

"I can't believe we ate all those berries. We shoulda saved some. What are we going to do when we get hungry again?" Patience asked. "Pat, you always take the fun out of every situation. We're in a weird garden. There's gotta be other things to eat too." Theo said.

Don't worry about it," Marcus said.

"Yeah, for once you're right," Patience said.

For the first time in months they were all together laughing and smiling. Each of them made funny faces because of their weird glittery colored teeth. Suddenly, Patience, Theo, and Marcus held out their arms then started to twirl and spin wildly as if they became out of control propellers. Somehow, they were spinning and jumping at the same time no longer looking or moving as human. They were spinning out of control, unable to stop trying to soar into the sky. They just kept twirling and spinning until the children collapsed on the grass, now laid flat on the backs. You could see their chests heaving up and down as they tried to catch their breath.

"Wow! What just happened?" Patience asked.

"That was totally sick. I was out of control," Theo said.

"I was almost flying. That's crazy!" Marcus said.

"Me too. I can't move but I feel like I'm spinning," Patience said. "That was scary. Unbelievable, but feels so incredible I feel happy. I never felt that good before," Patience said. "Yeah," Theo and Marcus said.

"But know I feel sleepy. I don't know about you guys but I'm going to fall asleep in a minute." Patience said.

Drowsiness seems to have crept up on all of them and Patience tried to fight it as long as she could. Patience heard her brothers snoring loudly before she closed her eyes, smiling. Her hands stroked the big beautiful cushiony purple and black striped dandelions scattered on the silky plush colorful blue grass. As she stroked them she imagined they were laughing happily. Then they stopped laughing and were crying begging her to save them. Not long after, she was snoring too.

CHAPTER TWO

ACCEPTANCE?

"What's that noise? Oh man shut up, Theo! Stop the noise!" Patience said.

A loud buzzing sound filled her head. Her body felt heavy – her eyelids too. She'd never felt that sleepy before. The noise was too much. She finally got her lids to move but everything was foggy. She blinked then rubbed and blinked her eyes repeatedly. Patience continued to rub them to focus on what she thought she imagined.

"No way! I can't be seeing what I'm seeing. Oh my God. They're for real," she whispered.

The shock made her eyes as round as saucers. She jackknifed into a sitting position and screamed. The trespassers moved back, frightened by the sound. Theo and Marcus woke up and screamed too when they saw what she was looking at.

"Now, now what's going on here? Why did you kids come here?" The unknown entity demanded.

The kids stared at the largest and most bizarre looking creature they had ever seen. It looked like a human and bee combined together.

Before them stood a spectacular looking humanoid bee with a beautiful human face, crowned with long antennae that seemed more like metallic prongs. From her torso extended two slender but strong arms with large hands, covered in black glittering gloves. Her lower half extended downwards into two strong muscular legs wrapped in bee-like fur legs leading down to stylish golden heeled boots. Her skin was covered very short soft fuzzy hair all over. The colors were the most stunning neon shiny black, purple, and gold stripes from head to toe. She was dressed in a fabulous gown made of three quarter length light gauzy gold fabric that had sequence all over. On her head was a gold tiara decorated with stunning jewels. A gorgeous cape spun in the finest gossamer gold shimmers under which rested on her remarkable wings. They had incredible patterns, with the same colors on her body outlined in gold. They would come to know her as Queen Star.

Queen Star was an evolved, advanced species of insect divergent from the ancient bloodlines of the Africanized Killer Bees. They were known as 'Nyuki' in Mbaba. The most powerful of all Queens that ruled in the world of Mbaba.

"Child, I asked you what's going on here. I can see what you foolish children have done. You all are in some serious trouble!"

The children sat there and stared up at her and the hundreds of these strange looking humanoid bees. They were too shocked and frightened to respond. All they could do was just look at the swarm of massive bee-like creatures. They were all dressed and some were smaller and different in color from the Queen's, but brown and gold.

Another humanoid besides the first spoke out. "Oh lord; I can't believe what you greedy little children have done. You have eaten all of the 'Uhlamvu' berries from the sacred 'Inhlakanipha' tree!"

"The inhla-what tree?" they asked.

"The Inhlakanipha tree. The Inhlakanipha tree is our sacred wisdom tree."

The first bee-like creature turned to the second. "Violet, these kids are acting like they don't know what I'm talking about!"

"Yes. How Strange! Maybe its shock affecting their minds, Star." Hundreds of glowing eyes stared at them. It was eerie and the children felt as if the multitude eyes were laser beams that could burn a hole right through them. The Queen's eyes were more intense – large and round turquoise, with gold colored pupils. They glowed on and off like a flashlight.

"Who are you?" Patience whispered.

"I am Queen Star from the land of Harmony, ruler of Hope's Mountain. I am a Nyuki and ruler of the Uju-inyasi colony. Now you know that, I will be the one asking the questions. I can't believe that you brats would dare to violate the most precious tree in Mbaba!"

"What?" Theo and Marcus asked.

Queen Star, offended tossed her cape back and flew closer to the children. Within moments she was suspended directly in front of Patience who was amazed by how enormous she was. When Star glared down at her she fought the urge to run.

"I said what you have done here is criminal in Mbaba. Where are you children from?" Star asked.

Taking charge, Patience spoke to alleviate any punishment that might befall them in this unknown place, surrounded by this unknown army. "I am sorry Queen Star but we don't know what you're talking about!" Star looked from Patience to the other children who had scared and dumbfounded expressions on their faces, eyes as round as saucers in awe. "Can't you say anything more than sorry and you don't know? Is that all you brats are capable of?" she asked.

"I have never heard of this place or of bugs that talk," Theo said. Violet who seemed to be second to Star responded to his snide remark.

"You're ignorant, and rude, for an inyasis. Your colors are different but that doesn't give you the right to disrespect your elders, child!"

Patience was terrified, surrounded by so many large humanoid insect creatures. They scared her more than anything did. Patience eyes opened wider then narrowed into angry slits from the insult as she glared back at her.

"Have you been flying in the sun too much, Queen Bug or bee, whatever you are? You must have got sunstroke or something and are seeing things? Are you kidding me? Don't you know what a human looks like? Humans and Bugs don't look alike and thank God for that!" Patience said.

To the children's surprise, Stars entourage started to laugh at her, including the Queen. Patience sucked in her lips then gave Star a nasty and most fierce look. "Do you find that funny?"

Star replied chuckling, even though her eyes blazed fire at Patience. She felt annoyed by the attitude from this rude child. "The only thing I find funny is that you are confused as to what you look like.

Just look at yourselves you little fools. Tell me if I'm looking at humans now?"

But how could these kids not realize what would happen if How dare this brat talk to me that way? Doesn't she know better? What if they don't? They ate from the Inhlakanipha. Surely their Grandma, Ms. Mable, must have warned them.

Her lady in waiting, Violet, fluttering close by voiced her thoughts. "My goodness! Ms. Mable didn't tell them about us or that our world is real, Star."

Star and Violet kept a comfortable distance, and her entourage, all of them, where silent and in awe of what happened in front of them.

"Theo and Marcus, oh my God, look at me!" "Pat, you're not human!" Twins yelled.

Patience, Theo and Marcus looked like humanoid bees similar to the ones before them, with gorgeous colored stripes of red, orange, yellow, green, blue, indigo and violet. Their wings were adorned with amazing patterns outlined in silver. Their facial features were similar, but their eyes stood out the most. Each eye was neon in color, but always two different colors. They had tiny ears, earlobes and antennas. The boys were blue, Patience's were dark purple. From their torsos extended one set of arms that were thin but well-muscled.

Their lower half extended downwards into two lengthy legs wrapped in bee-like fur. The boys wore blue metallic boots while Patience wore purple. Their clothing was fashioned in simple uniform shear vests and shorts, also matching the different color schemes. Light blue for the boys while Patience had on a sheer purple sleeveless top with matching purple shorts. Their entire bodies were covered in multicolored fur with striped patterns.

"We're like human bees and we have wings too! Look at what's on my skin – short, fuzzy fur. The stripes, weird colors are crazy too. I got weird looking bug like arms and hands and mad bug like crazy legs too. Check out the sick shiny boots. This is totally nuts. Theo, Patience do my eyes look like yours are they two different colors."

Marcus asked excitedly. He was the only one who seemed to relish the change.

The other children looked down then slowly up suddenly realized they stood side by side but alone on top of the strange plant that looked like a dandelion. They looked at their weird-shaped bodies, frantically touching their faces as they watched each other. Suddenly they screamed from shock of how high up they were from the grass.

There was a very loud gasp of shock then a burst of frantic whispers from amongst the Queen and her subjects. Not even the Queen herself had witnessed anything as wild or crazy as this but it was self-evident.

Star suspected the sacred fruit had powers but never knew that it could be capable of this. She wondered if they could do that to a human what would they do to them. She looked at the transformed humans with curiosity. They were humanoid insects like her but their colors were extraordinary. The human inyasis' she was seeing were quite remarkable looking too.

"You inyasis' have the most remarkable colors I have seen in this world. I can't believe your gorgeous stripes! What amazing patterns on your wings too, with the same colors framed in silver.

And your eyes when they're lit. Amazing, too alternating colors like two different color flashlights. Fascinating," Star said.

"Theo and Marcus, your eyes are different colors," Patience said. "Yeah this is crazy. So are your eyes too, Pat," Twins said.

"Check out the wild crazy gorgeous patterns on their wings," Star said to Violet.

The children only stared at each other and continued to touch their bodies while silently being observed by the creatures. Suddenly they looked up at Queen Star and at all the strange insect like creatures that had flown a little closer, frightening the children. They fainted overwhelmed by the circumstances and the effects of the fruit and fell lying flat on their backs on top of the large purple and gold striped plants known as Dandelilys.

"Should we wake them, my Queen?" Violet asked.

"No let them rest. I need time to think," Star said. "We will take them with us. Aren't they the most stunning looking Inyasis you have ever seen?" Star asked.

"Who would have ever thought that our berries could actually make humans look beautiful?" Violet said.

"How in the world am I going to deal with this? You know, before I met Ms. Mable, I couldn't believe that humans were real," Star whispered.

*   *   *

Queen Star had observed Ms. Mable Jefferson-Johnson on several occasions. She knew of her as the Gatekeeper for years and that she cared for her beloved plants and inhabitants of Mbaba. She knew of the human Gatekeepers remarkable powers from stories told to her by Queen Tulip and Violet. When her mother, Queen Tulip, passed away, Violet continued her education. Then one day while on a private outing alone as a teenager, she came face to face with Ms. Mable. Only Queens and princesses in this world had the ability to see her. Star was shocked and suddenly went down on her hands and knees bowing and trembling in fear. Ms. Mable patted her on the shoulder and Star looked up at her at the smiling Gatekeeper who beckoned her to stand up stood face to face. "Blessings, Queen Star, there is no need for formalities. I'm so happy to finally meet you. Don't be shy. You know my presence here is about love for you and all that is here in Mbaba. I've been waiting for this opportunity to meet you. I've got so much to tell and learn from you. Isn't this exciting?" Ms. Mable asked.

"Yes I've heard so many wonderful things about you, but what can I teach you? Didn't your ancestors create our world?" Star said. " No. We worked with God, our creator. He gifted us with the ability to help Mbaba to become a beautiful world and thrive too. All the plants and flowers are a unique blend of two seeds from many worlds married to create a beautiful new species for Mbaba. Everyone here is to learn how to develop their minds by studying the plants."

"I don't understand what you said about how our minds can be influenced by plants. Can I visit with you in your world and learn more about it?"

"Plants have a wisdom that requires a mind that can stay still and quiet to learn. Yes, Star, please do. You can visit anytime."

One day while Ms. Mable visited her she showed Star how to find the fruit that would be the gateway to the human world. She explained that this fruit could change her appearance too. Star ate of the magical fruit she put in her hand. After swallowing the berry, Star placed her hand in hers. Within moments she was on the other side of the garden, eyes widened in surprised that she was no longer neon but looked exactly like her ancestors. She appeared as an Africanized Killer Queen bee. She looked about her amazed and made sure to stay close to the Gatekeeper. Ms. Mable informed her that she looked different in the human world but would appear to be the same to others who were from Mbaba.

It was scary to behold. This world lacked animation and colors. The sounds were so different and frightening that nothing about this world resembled Mbaba. Ms. Mable's garden had a very powerful and overwhelming loving energy that filled Star with a completely new excited feeling. Star discovered it was beautiful and like her home was very special too. She loved its unique smells and only liked visiting the garden, terrified of what possibly lay beyond. Star watched discreetly, hidden from view and learned as Ms. Mable tried to teach her grandchildren about God's beautiful earth why they must love and respect it. What the Queen loved most was the story time this old human woman shared with them in her garden.

Star frowned while watching Patience who clearly had no interest in nature, always reading a book or magazines. The twin boys were interested but often asked a lot or silly questions because they got bored. All they seemed to enjoy was eating her delicious apples and the break they got from their chores. While their grandmother talked, Star would be sickened when the boys would run off tried to catch insects and pull the wings off them, or seeing Patience try to slap away the flies.

Ms. Mable looked frustrated at times. She knew they were not really enjoying her stories but were just respectfully there because they had to be.

As Star watched, she felt very discouraged about any of those kids becoming a future Gatekeeper, one born with special gifts that would enable him or her to heal and help all living things in the mystical world of Mbaba. The only human respected by all was the rare and special Gatekeeper who was not visible but always known for their acts in the preservation of Mbaba.

The gifts of the gatekeeper if passed on to them would be wasted. Star enjoyed many visits from the time she was a teenager into adulthood before becoming a Queen. She loved Ms. Mable so much her generosity, kindness, playfulness, and ability with her enlightened mind, heart and soul.

*　　*　　*

Star gave her drones the approval and they woke the children up. Patience, Theo, and Marcus slowly got up and stood on their Dandelilys to look at the Queen who was a few feet away from them. The children looked at each other. Patience and Theo were touching themselves slowly and looked upset while Marcus was smiling as he examined himself.

"Oh no. I'm a still a nasty bug," Patience said. "I want Trevor. I wish he was here," Theo said.

"I'm a weird creature. This is so sick," Marcus said.

Marcus was the only one who has happy and this set Theo off. Theo suddenly started to bawl like a baby, shocking his sister and brother.

This silenced everyone as they watched Patience who looked at her arms and legs. She started rubbing her body as if she could remove what was on her. "Ah, Ms. Bee Queen, please help me to change back. I hate bees and I can't live like this." Patience said. "Child, I am not a Queen of bees. I rule a tribe of 'Inyasis'. I don't know how to fix this but I can help you to deal with how to accept your transformation. It'll be all right and I will help you to learn how to love your new self. Becoming a beautiful Inyasi, I believe was meant to be blessing."

"I'm flying, I'm flying." Marcus said. That transformation enabled him to not be restricted by his siblings. He loved being in the beautiful sky and the funky clouds and what happened to him. He was waving as he flew over his sister's head. Patience stood there looking up and frowning. Theo did not wave feeling left out as he watched his brother.

"Marcus, come down from there. You'll get hurt!"

"Never! Wow I'm flying so high. This is so sick, bro! Pat, Theo, come on – it's fun!"

Patience was even more taken aback when she saw Theo get up and, after several determined tries, suddenly soar into the air, flying alongside his brother. She watched her brothers, struggling to believe what her eyes were seeing. Theo and Marcus were now bees, the worst of all the bugs that terrified her the most. *Could it get any worse? She thought.*

They flew in circles and loops while surrounded by a large number of inyasis whooping and hollering in excitement as they watched her brothers trying to out-fly each other. Theo and Marcus were laughing and whizzing around doing loops had all kinds of fun as if they didn't have a care in the world. Patience now looked at Star and Violet as they quietly stared at her about a foot away, fluttering so close. Violet flew back leaving Star alone to deal with the female child. Patience was crying as she touched herself with shaky hands then put them on her face to cover her eyes.

"I can't believe I have wings and a stinger. It's so awful and disgusting. I hate bees more than anything on earth. Does or will this, horrible spell ever wear off? Dear lord, please wake me up if this is some bad dream!" she yelled.

"Patience come on, man. You gotta try this flying thing – it's crazy! Come on!" Theo yelled.

"Patience, it's so much fun, there's nothing like it. It's totally amazing. Come on!" Marcus yelled.

Patience just stood there watched and Queen Star landed on the same Dandelily instinctively Patience backed away while Star kept her distance smiling. She trembled before the Queen but stood tall and faced her directly. "What is it, child that you fear?" Star could see the terror in her remarkable eyes as Patience tearfully shared their tale of what they had suffered from since their Grandmothers death. Their names, becoming orphans, and why they had to run away, her Grandmother, Ms. Mable, stories and she thought it was just fantasy. No way would she believe in another world.

"I would never want to be a bug-like thing especially a bee!" Patience said.

"I don't know why you hate Bees so much. How ironic you transformed into an Inyasi, the most advanced species of bee-like life in your eyes. However you're here and need help. You won't make it on your own. I don't know why this happened but I can relate to unexpected change."

*   *   *

"Oh my goodness, what is happening here and what unusual looking Nyukis they are. That poor Mother and her child," Violet said.

As she hid behind a bush in the human garden, Violet watched in horror. She saw a brave Queen, who alone tried to rescue her child from being harmed by a human. The Queen was of a species of Inyasi she had never seen before, adorned with magnificent gold, purple, and black stripes and patterns on their wings. Her crown and gown were afro centric in design and spectacular. Her child wore the same royal Afro centric designs and stunning little crown on her head. Violet could still see the Queen's true identity in spite of appearing like her ancestors from being in the human world. To others who were not from Mbaba she appeared to be a very large bee and her child much smaller.

This remarkable Queen was now forced to sting the human child to save hers but suffered a lethal blow doing so. The human child ran away in tears, leaving behind the helpless little Nyuki buzzing around her mother tried to get her to move shaking her gently.

"I must help that poor Queen and Child!"

The Nyuki Queen laid there motionless as the child cried, still shaking her mother in vain. Violet flew away and quickly returned with her Queen Tulip, a stunning Uju-inyasi who ruled the colony she came from.

The Queen beautifully striped with colors of a mahogany and gold patterns. She too wore a jeweled crown, stunning ivory beaded gown and gossamer cape under her wings. Violet and her Queen resembled large honey bees. Upon hearing of the matter, Queen Tulip quickly followed and then watched the orphaned child before making a decision. She knew of this species – the deadly Nyuki – that the young child came from.

The colony of Nyukis from the south and were the largest and most lethal species of all inyasis. These colonies never mixed. If Queen Tulip left the child, she wouldn't survive but Queen Tulip knew their entourage had gone in search of their Queen and princess. They were too far and it was dangerous to stay here where other humans wandered. She had her guards take them back to their homeland.

First she needed to deal with the child in shock and immediately make her feel safe.

"Sweet baby, what is your name?" Queen Tulip asked. "Star! My Mama won't wake up. Can you help her?"

"Your Mama needs our help. We will take you and your Mama to my house until she gets better. Okay, sweet Star?"

"Okay. I'm tired, thank you."

"Violet, I believe this Queen too was on a royal visit. Ms. Mable receives visitors' from Mbaba with the exception of Enchantress and her drones. This poor Queen was most likely here to introduce her child to our Gatekeeper."

Queen Tulip had her entourage help. They made a carrier and placed Star's mother on it. The strong Drones flew away with the Queen after princess Star was fed and comforted. Princess Star was led away by Queen Tulip and they soon arrived at Harmony Castle where she began her new life. After a week of bonding, she explained to Star that her mother was gone to sleep and she wouldn't wake up anymore. Queen Tulip had a special quiet ceremony in honor of the deceased Queen.

She lovingly raised Princess Star as her own and adopted her so that everyone would respect and protect the new princess with the exception of her half-sisters. Princess Star's acceptance wasn't an easy task he was the only Nyuki in the colony. Eventually, her new colony of Uju-inyasis' loved her and when Queen Tulip passed, Star became their Queen. As Star remembered, she now smiled at Violet who was thinking of Star's past too. Thankful for Queen Tulip's decision to raise her, she too loved the princess now Queen, and shared a powerful bond that survived many years.

*   *   *

Star suddenly flew towards Violet, sensing that her Queen was scared too.

"Your Highness, these children as strange and frightening as this is maybe they were sent her by divine guidance. Perhaps they were sent into your life for you to mother them. Maybe for the same reasons our Queen Tulip loved and adopted you long ago as a child into our colony. I couldn't think of anyone more capable of performing this challenging task. To help these children remember they are just children – ignorant, innocent, helpless, and incapable of surviving in our world. Your wisdom, courage and love will guide you through this," Violet said.

Patience watched the exchange and realized in that moment that they did need them. Now that there were many of these strange, humanoid bugs like creatures around, she feared what they could to her. "Please change me back and send me home. This place and you bee-like creatures are freaking me out so much. Please do something.

Please!"

Star watched and seeing her upset compelled Star to return the siblings. She obeyed and landed on the same large Dandy lily and stood beside them. *I must help remove the fear from her. Fear is unhealthy and can't manifest in Mbaba.*

"I don't know what to do. No one has ever eaten from the tree. Maybe the spell will wear off. We just have to wait." They talked it over between themselves leaving the children to wait.

While they waited for Queen Star's decision, Marcus and Theo tried to comfort Patience. "Patience, don't be afraid of what's happened to you. Being an inyasi is a whole lot of fun. You can do something so amazing that humans can't. Fly! You can be one with the clouds, touch the most awesome clouds, fly up high, and sit on the incredible trees.

Flying is a remarkable gift that allows you to view the world on so many different levels, but the best part is the freedom." Marcus advised her.

Theo seconded his belief. "There's nothing to wait on. No traffic lights, buses, cars or trains. You don't have to depend on the same things that humans need to travel. Just spread those beautiful wings and I promise you will fall in love with your new self. Look at my wings."

Theo spread out his magnificent wings and up close, they were even more spectacular. Shimmering delicate patterns with radiant colors and the edging of his wings were shiny silver. Patience slowly approached him, fascinated, and gently touched them. She asked earnestly, "Will it hurt doing this flying thing?"

"No. You won't feel a thing but joy." Star said.

Patience looked at them doubtful. Then hesitantly and then ever so slowly spreads out her wings. Patience eyes widened and she smiled then gently touched her wings mesmerized by their beauty. "Wow they're gorgeous. They're even finer than yours and I can make them move too. It's so easy, like they do what I think. That's so awesome!"

Watching from a distance and having listened to the conversation, Star and Violet gave her more encouragement. "You're right, Patience, they are the most beautiful wings I have ever seen," Star said.

CHAPTER THREE

WHO'S DEMISE?

A large entourage of female worker inyasis' and large male drones encircled Queen Star, Violet, Patience, Theo, and Marcus. Star and Violet were in the second row while the children flew behind a row of male drones. The children separated from Star and Violet, but the siblings didn't realize they could hear them talking.

"Violet, we're bringing home a whole new species of inyasis'. I can't keep it a secret that they are human kids. Everyone will be able to tell by their colors that they're Inhlakanipha Inyasis'. I must get the colony to accept criminals and humans. I need a miracle."

"Amen on that one. These kids still are Jefferson-Johnson. We all know their family created our world, so maybe that might help."

"Thanks, Violet, for reminding me of that." "Have faith, My Queen."

Lord help me to provide wisdom and assistance to Star to deal with these children.

From above the children were astonished by how everything looked. Patience was frustrated because she couldn't hear the conversation ahead and she believed she would hate everything in sight. She did not intend to fall in love, but stopped herself from being impressed with this world. She flew close enough to her brothers to talk.

"You know this so-called kingdom belongs to a bug-like weird creature. I'm not looking forward to living in a bug's house. You brats act like this situation is cool!"

"Her crib will be like a crazy old golf ball in clear plastic from hardened honey. It will be so sick living in a bee crib. I hope we get servants because Pat, you sucked at taking care of us!" Theo said.

"Theo, I wish I could stick this stinger in your junk-talking mouth!" Patience yelled.

"Look at how beautiful this Queen looks – and her jewels, too! Come they are the most beautiful wings I have ever seen," Star said.

"Yes Star, they truly are the most remarkable wings we have ever seen. Your wings look like they're spun from magic material. Don't they?

Doesn't it just make you want to fly?" Violet said.

"Yeah!" Patience took a tentative step and set her wings in motion. To her surprise and delight she suddenly soared into the sky.

"Oh my goodness, I'm flying too!"

Patience was whooping, hollering, and laughing aloud as she flew just below the clouds but close enough to be in awe of what she was doing. Her brothers flew close by, following her. All three of them laughed and played tag. Queen Star watched Patience, Theo, and Marcus in wonder and fascination from the ground but was fearful for them too. She looked at Violet.

"I have never, never had to deal with humans before on this level. I'm not sure if I should try to take this on. Responsibility for these children could turn out to be a big mistake. They might be too much for me to handle. How can I, a Nyuki, be a mother to these humans? Is it too crazy to try?"

Star turned to Violet whom she loved and was like a big sister and best friend for as long as the Queen could remember. She glanced at Violet with a faraway look in her eyes as she remembered long ago how she became a part of an Uju-inyasi colony.

"Violet I really don't have a choice do I? They are kids, human Inyasis', and my beloved dear Ms. Mable's' grandchildren. They are a part of us. We just have to find a way to get them and everyone else to accept that."

Violet responded with a cryptic comfort – "The way will be revealed in time!"

Patience, Theo, and Marcus returned to the Queen and Star announced that they would be happy to live in her kingdom as they learnt about Mbaba.

"Oh. You know her crib is happening." Marcus said.

"It's going be primitive and lord, I won't have a phone. I can't call my friends," Patience said.

"Patience, take a chill pill. Like you have any friends to call? Get real," Theo said.

Theo shot her a pissed off look then buzzed off to get closer to the strong male drones he thought were wicked.

"Patience I really like what's happening to us. If you relax you'll learn to like it too," Marcus said.

"The best part of all of this is that you brats have finally stopped calling me Pat."

Star was an Empathic, a telepath who was able to read the emotional energy of those around her. As such, she knew about the kids' issues long before they arrived at Mbaba. Star decided that it was time to take a break, and instructed her drones who led them to a large Sungold Flower.

Star decided they needed to sit and talk. She didn't want a war zone coming into her kingdom. Star landed on a beautiful pink and yellow striped flower with a long yellow stem and sat in the center of it. Her drones escorted Violet, Patience, Theo, Marcus, and a few of the loyal subjects to sit on their own petals. Now sitting, they faced her while she smiled with all of them but Patience who rolled her eyes and looked serious, arms folded across her chest.

"Do you kids know what the word harmony means?" Star asked. "Yeah, it means peace. Having everyone flow in the same direction, smooth." Marcus said.

"Yeah, you can't have haters if you want harmony, so you better get rid of Patience," Theo said.

"Theo! You nasty back-stabbing little brat. You're going to pay for that," Patience yelled.

"Silence. Ms. Mable would be ashamed of you all for coming into our world and having no respect for each other!"

"You knew our Grandmother?" Patience asked.

"Oh course I did and she loved this world just as much as the one she lived in," Star said.

"I knew it." Marcus exclaimed! "I knew our Grammy had something to do with this place!"

"So how do you think she would feel knowing her grandchildren bring hate, anger, and disrespect into our precious world?" Star asked.

"Disappointed," Patience said. "Sad," Marcus said.

"Ashamed of us," Theo said.

"How did my Grandmother learn about this place? Did she get kidnapped here too?" Patience asked.

"No, child. She came here of her own free will but I will explain that to you'll one day. I don't get how you got here or why clearly you're not prepared. Now I need you three to recognize I'm taking a big risk bringing human inyasis' into our colony because you violated the most sacred law of Mbaba. Trying to integrate a new species into Mbaba is the most difficult thing I have ever tried to do. I realize for your protection, I will have to tell everyone their Queen adopted children.

From now on Patience, Theo, and Marcus, you all are my children – and royalty because you all are adopted by me. But I really can't make any promises that it will work out if you continue to war with each other. I won't help three miserable, argumentative, brats who don't try to get along and respect each other and their seniors. So what's it going to be? If it's 'No' then your new home will be Prison!"

Patience glanced around and saw that everyone stared at them.

Theo and Marcus had their heads hung low. Marcus looked up and stared at his sister and spoke while Theo refused to acknowledge her.

"Patience, It's all on you and Theo. You know we can't survive here without Queen Star's help. She is a very nice Nyuki to help us like that." Patience responded speaking earnestly. "We have to do this to be safe. It's totally crazy that it's something like you; a totally different species from another world came to our rescue. I'll try if Theo can stop talking junk, but we might get lucky and find a way back to our world too," Patience said.

"Yeah, I'll learn to ignore Patience and not let her get on my nerves," Theo said.

Star smiled briefly focusing on all of them in turn. "Great. All right then, I expect you three not to create stress and drama in my home.

You hear? Now let's get going. You kids are draining me."

While the Queens entourage clapped about the outcome, Star looked at Patience and caught her wiping a tear from her eye. When Patience looked up and saw Star watching her, she tried to fake a smile.

However, it didn't reach her eyes.

Violet knows that Patience is going to be the ultimate challenge. She doesn't want to be here. Lord, help me to find a way to connect with her.

* * *

Queen Star and Violet flew side by side with Patience, Theo, and Marcus following closely. The powerful swarm encircled them to protect the Queen and her guests.

Suddenly, they saw different colors in the sky's horizon, highlighted by a shimmering massive rainbow of gold, black, and purple high. The Rainbow extended above a massive structure whose exterior consisted of shiny glass and gold. It was shaped like a large cylinder, extremely wide and tall with a massive dome shaped roof. The roof had a transparent retractable glass dome that opened remotely for entry or exit to the building.

As they flew inside the structure, the children glanced around in earnest. The interior consisted of one hundred floors that rose so high and had a unique circular stairwell you could climb up to the clouds. It was magnificent. One step was gold, the next black and each stair an alternating color, making it easy to climb up to the remarkable large glass dome and stand on a circular platform to watch the stars. The castle was encircled by a moat with a gold brick bridge filled with golden honey like substance that flowed like water beneath it. The garden grew flowers with colors to compliment the tones in the rainbow. The sky's unique colors complimented the structure.

There were numerous miniature uju-inyasi guest homes behind the massive structure. All were surrounded and protected by a tall gate that was almost sky high of gold and black colored metal poles. The structure made the Trump Tower look like a third rate hotel. Impressive was not enough to describe this work of art. The fortress had three-dimensional lettering in purple outlined in gold. Star titled her castle, Hope's Mountain.

"Wow!" the children said.

"Not bad for a bug, eh," Star said.

"Yeah, how could someone like you hook this up?" Patience asked. Star and Violet chuckled. "I'm a Queen who rules in a magical world. Everything is possible."

Violet motioned the children forward. "Come in. Let's get you kids settled and remember my number one rule is to behave don't touch anything useless you have permission. Got it?"

"Yes!" All three kids said.

Once inside, the children looked at each other, eyes and mouths wide open. Each of them wondered how that Queen bug had created such an amazing place. They stood in the large foyer and noticed about ten feet away was a formally dressed male behind a large Marble desk.

"There is a royal elevator operating by a manual lift system. There is no electricity in Mbaba. "Where do you live?" Patience asked.

"My private quarters are on the top ten floors and the ladies in waiting and servants live below me. There are more than one hundred floors in my castle."

"Oh man, it's amazing how the rooms are shaped like hexagons. All of them lined up evenly beneath each other, from top to bottom. It's amazing, the interior shape of your castle," Patience said.

"Where am I going to live?" Patience asked. *Please make it as far away as possible from the brats!*

"Since you all are family and now a part of mine, I want to keep you kids close to me. Now your rooms are on the ninetieth floor. It is best for now – drones never lived so close to a Queen, only a king can. You children don't know our ways, but you will learn. You all are a part of my royal family now and will learn just how amazing life is because of it."

"I just can't believe a Queen bug can live this way. It's so sick," Patience said.

"This place is beyond sick," Marcus said.

Queen Star suddenly turned around and walked up to Patience, Theo, and Marcus. Her eyes suddenly a fiery shade. The kids slowly backed away.

"Watch it juveniles! I will not tolerate your disrespect of me, by calling me a bug and insulting me in my own home. If my home is sick to you brats, then would you all prefer the prison that's worse than your former residence? For the last time we are not Bees but Uju-Inyasis."

Violet admonished them in equal fashion. "Mind your manners and show respect towards your Queen. A Queen is a Queen no matter what species she is. I demand that you show respect!"

My poor Star! These kids are a nightmare to deal with.

A semi-circle of large drones, drawn by the noise surrounded Star, Violet, and the children. Patience looked at Theo and Marcus. She could tell by their expressions they were mad at her too. Their expressions were cold and she sucked in her lips as if trying to prevent herself from talking.

Theo silently cursed Patience. Patience ruins everything for Marcus and me. I hope that Queen gets rid of her.

"Oh no, Queen Star, neither Patience, Theo or myself meant to be rude to you. In our world the word, sick means beyond awesome. We're sorry for making you feel disrespected. I promise you no one will ever call you a bug again," Marcus said.

"Patience, why do you always mess up and take us down with you? Don't listen to Patience. We never do. You run things here and show her whose boss. She doesn't represent what we feel right Marcus?"

Not always. Marcus and Patience thought to themselves.

"We know you're a Queen Nyuki not a bug, Patience ought to know better than us!" Theo insisted.

I hate the way they're all looking at me because they know I hate what happened. Why me, lord how could you turn me into a disgusting bee. Making me look like an ugly human bug is beyond disgusting.

Suddenly Patience felt terrified by the expressions the Uju-inyasis had looking at her with blazing eyes. They were frightening when they stared and she didn't like what she saw in their eyes. She felt the impulse to escape and instinctively looked behind her but there was no way out.

Could I survive by myself? No there are too many bugs and strange things beyond these walls.

"I apologize, Queen Star. I'll show you how respectful I can be. I apologize for what I said, okay, and I will never call you a bug, Queen Star – you're a Nyuki."

Patience looked at Marcus. He smiled broadly while Theo shook his head at her. Star and Violet watched Patience, their eyes narrow and still tight lipped. They nodded at her acknowledging her promise. Violet looked at Star, her expression changed and smiled broadly.

"Patience, you will really have to learn how to conduct yourself respectfully as a part of my royal family. You're not just a female but a rare new species of Inyasi, now you're a Princess and one day you might become a Queen!" Star said.

"What?" The children exclaimed.

Star looked at Patience with a kind expression and her eyes were not so frightening.

"A Queen?" Patience whispered. Patience looked around at everyone with eyes as wide as saucers. Patience stood up and glowered at Theo. Everyone laughed except Star and Violet. Star now observed how remarkably beautiful Patience was and wondered if that would make dealing with her more of a challenge. Suddenly, Patience standing at her full height approached and stood before Star.

"Before I was just plain old, ugly, invisible, Pat, emotionally abused and feeling used up by my uncle and brothers. I was a slave to my heartless uncle Trevor and his gold-digger girlfriend, Loretta. I had no life after my Grammy died. It was my fault she died. We had argued prior to her death and I'm so sorry about that. I still had to keep my promise to her and take care of my brothers. I wanted my grandmother to be proud of me while trying not to lose my mind. Stressing all the time about acting like a mother was awful and nothing but hard work. What's worse is because of my hateful uncle, who treated me like a servant; no one cared, tried to help or even respected me. I felt like God put me on this earth to suffer." She took a deep breath wiping tears which had formed on her cheeks.

"I guess I deserved it because of what happened to Grammy. No matter how much Trevor beat me I would never let them break me or give those brats' a reason to laugh at me. Maybe becoming a bee, an inyasi isn't such a bad thing now that I'm a princess. No more slavery or abuse. I don't have to deal with being a parent to my brothers anymore. You can have them. I never have to see Trevor again. My life doesn't have to be like a nightmare anymore."

I hope this creature gets why I hate them and finds a way to keep them out of my life.

Violet was also an Empathic and was taken aback by her admission.

There is so much hate; pain and rage here in Mbaba because of these kids. Lord help my poor Star.

At this point Star felt it was best to address the matter right away. "Boys, your sister will always be your family, even though she might become your future Queen. Patience, you must always love and respect your brothers. Everyone here can learn to forgive, Right? You must make a good start in your new life!"

Patience emotions got the better of her with the idea of forgiveness having triggered memories of past wrongs.

"No! I disown them. They are not my brothers, just stupid drones. I don't have to deal with them like before." Patience looked defiantly at Star as if she was trying to challenge her.

Her words had a stinging effect. "Patience, you don't want to be my sister anymore? I am sorry about everything. We didn't know that Trevor was beating you. Honestly, we're sorry!" Marcus said quietly.

Marcus had spoken before Star could address Patience's outburst. Star looked at Marcus and his head was down. She saw him wiping at his tears. Theo moved closer and sat beside him, patting his back and when he looked at his sister. His eyes were narrowed and blazing, one orange the other red.

"Marcus we don't need her. She's nothing but trouble. We're better off without her. It is her fault why Gram died!"

"Why, Patience? You're my sister. You can't change that just because we live here now. Trevor is gone. We're sorry. Well treat you better, I promise. You can't blame her, Theo! It's not right!" Marcus yelled.

"Brats like you never change, but you're a drone! Forget we're related. I plan to spend the rest of my life forgetting how much you brats ruined my life! You're a drone and I'm a princess inyasi. Everything is different. I don't want to have brothers anymore!" She yelled.

Now Marcus was bawling, his shoulders shaking. It was heart-breaking, watching him fall apart. Patience suddenly went to him. Theo tried to block her from going near him but she knocked him out of the way. Theo, furious, looked like he was about to attack his sister but the guards quickly stopped him. Suddenly, Star flew over and grabbed

Patience's hand, and led her to the center of the Sungold flower. The female guards were fluttering close by looking ominous and ready to intervene.

Star wasn't sure whether to voice her opinion. *That Patience makes me sick and uncomfortable. What a nightmare to deal with. Maybe we all would be better off without her here. I wonder if Violet feels the same way too.*

Violet thought to herself as well. *These children are dangerous, especially Patience. They are causing an eruption of so many unpleasant, hostile emotions in everyone. I am seeing and feeling reactions we are not use too. Maybe I was mistaken in encouraging Star to raise them.*

"Patience, girl, you got a long way to go before you can become a Queen. If you can't forgive or care about your family, how you could be capable of being a princess?" Star asked loudly.

"Queen Star, I think you should get rid of Patience. She's no good and doesn't deserve to be here."

"No, Theo, Patience is our sister no matter what she says."

Marcus opposed Theo's suggestion "We are a family and we stick together, just like our Gram wanted us to do. We got to stick together were blood!"

Suddenly, Marcus broke away from Theo and tried to get closer to Patience. She quickly went to him and put her arms around him.

Surprised, Star and Violet, who looked at each other, were so close that they could read each other's thoughts. Star smiled then whispered to Violet, who nodded in agreement but her expression was grim.

Marcus and Patience share some kind of bond but it will be Theo and Patience that will be the real challenge!

"Okay then, let's get you guys settled into your new home to learn and enjoy how to be a family."

CHAPTER FOUR

LIFE RENEWED?

"Where did you get the inspiration to create this place?" Patience asked. "Once I visited your world and I was given a vision of how to build a castle worthy of its title by Ms. Mabel. I fell in love with the possibility, so when I returned home I used my magical powers to create Hope Mountain, working alongside my fellow drones. Gifted with divine abilities as females, we can design just as good, if not better than anyone. No Drone can be considered to be above me. I am a Queen and I represent us. If you know what I mean."

She winked at Patience smiling. The boys were fascinated by what they saw too. The floors were polished black marble with a massive woven rug of the finest neon threads in a spiral design of gold, purple, and black. Patience suddenly remembered where she had seen that design before. It was in the basement the day after her Grandmother had passed away. She went down there looking for her things.

Any memento she could use to remember to keep her grandmother's memory close to her. Suddenly, she found herself standing in the center of a glowing spiral. It was eerie in how when it glowed she saw things, strange things that frightened her. It vanished within seconds and she never told anyone. The large sparkling eight-layered tiered golden chandelier lit by singing fireflies created a warm magical feeling. Large portraits of former Queens including Star hung on the walls.

Expensive ornate gold furniture with chairs shaped like oversized stuffed Daismar looked to Patience funny, but nice in a weird kind of way. To the extreme, right along a winding gold circular banister, marble stairs were visible. In the massive foyer on the far left hand side stood a long gold inyasi symbol, behind what resembled a King Protea flower shaped table that was the reception desk. It was supervised by a very stylish and formally dressed drone, Manfred who wore a special suit. He looked up from his desk with a smile, standing to greet them as they entered. "Welcome home, your Highness Queen Star and Ms. Violet. I see here we have guests!"

"Manfred, it's good to see you. I'll hook up with you later and explain the situation. Please have the children escorted to their rooms, Theo and Marcus you must not enter your sister's room." Star told the children to go with Manfred who escorted them to the royal elevator.

He was quiet but smiled in spite of feeling terrified of them. He knew by their colors where they came from. He first took Patience to her room, before ushering Theo and Marcus to their rooms. The children's reactions were equally priceless.

"Oh my God, I can't believe this is so glamorous. I'm going to feel like a Diva living here."

"Wow!" Theo and Marcus said.

Patience's antennae clicked repeatedly as she wandered about. Her room was shockingly big and bright. The color scheme was gold, pink, and black. The walls were light pink and gold striped. There was a large crystal chandelier that was magically lit from the beautiful fireflies that sang softly from within the lamps. A carpet with spiral designed patterns in gold and black on top of a pink marble floor. She had a large Daismar shaped bed in gold, the mattress made the bed appear high covered with a pale pink satin blanket with thick puffy matching pillows.

There was a dresser, desk and chair and on it was a gorgeous bouquet of flowers in an antique gold honeycomb shaped vase. The mirror on the wall was Daismar shaped and large too. Her bathroom had the same color scheme. She hadn't realized that Manfred left and Star had returned. She too smiled because of Patience reaction, seeing her dancing around her room like a happy child.

"Oh my goodness, I can't believe this is for real and it's mine too, this is crazy. I love this. It's so beautiful. I feel like a princess. Thank you Queen Star!" Star smiled and then went to the door to talk to the boys. "You two little drones are on the other side of Patience comb. You boys can't ever go into your sister's room. The conduct is different here because with male drones there are rules. Patience might shock us all and become your future Queen. In spite of her ways, you must act like the other drones and show her respect always." "Are you serious?" Theo asked. "Absolutely!" Star said.

Theo turned his back on them while Marcus stood there and stared puzzled and frowning. At that exact moment Violet appeared advising them to go to the dining room before going to get Patience. Her lady in waiting, Violet, waited outside Patience bedroom door too. The children followed the royal chef, who had prepared their feast, into the octagon-shaped royal dining room. The room's interior was spectacular with gold colored mirrored glass, also on the ceiling. There was a six-tier crystal chandelier illuminated by stunning fireflies, creating a uniquely beautiful ambience while they sang a soothing melody softly.

"See how special you boys are? Never before has a drone dined in this room." Star said.

They were seated, the Queen at the head of an oval shaped gold table with eight ornate high back chairs hand carved in multi-toned metal finish. Violet on her left side while Patience, Theo, and Marcus, were seated on the far right. The table had settings and was formal like a human dining room with plates, bowls, cups, utensils, and fine linen too.

"I'm surprised that everything tastes so good with everything being liquid. It's not like I'm not missing human food. I wonder why?" Patience asked.

"It's because everything changed when you transformed into an Inyasi, but you still have the thoughts and feelings of your human self. Now that you are inyasi, you'll discover new things that you will love too."

They ate, laughed, and told stories of the first pleasant experience Star and Violet shared with the children. All of them were enjoying themselves.

"What do you all know about bees? Your grandmother taught you about why they're special?" Star asked.

She looked at Marcus and winked at him, and his checks glowed pink.

"They have tempers and will attack if you piss them off. I ought to know. I couldn't sit for days," Marcus said.

"They're smart. You can't outrun them. I enjoy the honey they make but when there's a swarm, look out. They're small but scary. Don't mess with one because then you got to deal with all of them," Theo said.

"You don't want to know what I think about bees. I just can't deal with that right now. Let's talk about something else please," Patience said.

"Oh, she hates them more than anything in this world," Theo said. Everyone looked at her as Patience rubbed her hand and looked very sad. She suddenly tried to smile but they knew she was faking it. "Did you know that there are three types of bees and inyasis?" The kids looked at her and shook their heads no.

"Females are our warriors – well, not so much with uju-inyasi because we believe in harmony and peace. They have stingers and protect us if necessary. The males are the workers who build and maintain the colony. They care for the babies too. The Queen and princesses have the most important job in the world. She is the only one who can have the babies. That is the highest honor of all."

Star smiled but her eyes looked sad. She couldn't have children because she was from a different species. None of the drone uju-inyasi would dare court her fearing for their lives if they tried to mate. Star as a Nyuki believed she was domed to live a lonely life. Her sisters filled the castle with babies, but no other child could rule if Star became a mother. Now her sisters would possibly resent her once they found out about her newly adopted children.

"What? The Queen or princesses are the only ones that give birth? Having hundreds of babies with different baby daddies too? How come the royal female ends up in the worst situation? That's disgusting,"

Patience looked at the Queen with revulsion in her eyes. Tight lipped, Patience arms crossed her chest as shook her head. She looked at Star as if she should be ashamed of herself. "I am a princess now. I plan to change things when I become a Queen. I will never let myself become a baby-making machine!" she said loudly.

The Queen and Violet laughed so loud it almost shook the kingdom. Star continued laughing while Violet and her brothers looked at Patience and laughed too.

"Young lady, when you become a Queen, I bet you will want to have hundreds of babies. It's the most important job in the world and, oh yes, you only need one special husband to have babies. No multiple baby daddies required, Patience!" Star and Violet laughed as Patience, Theo, and Marcus' cheeks glowed a bright red. Then suddenly they burst out laughing too.

Overcoming her embarrassment Patience asked, "What makes having babies so important?"

"In your world there are Bees. In Mbaba we are Inyasi or Nyuki from the same family and there are other pollinators too. We identify ourselves as an advanced species of insects but respect our pre-historic relations and the function they play. Our ancestors are insects from your world and we are similar in the fact that we pollinate to help plants to grow. The plants in Mbaba need Inyasi to survive and we help plants to grow by performing a ritual called Krulisa with our thoughts and loving words too. As either Inyasi or Nyuki, we make one of the most important contributions to all of the plants in the world. Personally, I believe they are more significant than any other animal on this earth."

"For real?" the boys asked.

"Wow. To think I use to try and kill them." Theo said.

"Yeah, Gram told us to respect bees and that we needed them too," Marcus said.

"Are you kidding me? You think bees are important, but they're dangerous to humans. Everybody knows that. I think you're biased and trying to play us for fools. You will never change my mind about that."

Patience said loudly. Patience rolled her eyes and shook her head once again, her arms crossed against her chest. Suddenly, Star looked upset.

She stood up walked towards Patience than stopped right in front of her.

"Child, it's going to be fun waking you up out of your ignorance. Didn't listen to anything your grandmother tried to teach you. I was there listening or watching while you were reading a magazine or daydreaming. Now here you are, in the most amazing garden on earth, experiencing what most kids your age would think is incredible. Even here, Patience you still have an attitude! You're ignorant, unconscious it's like you're not allowing your mind to understand wake up about what's important. The way you kids are so ignorant and disrespectful about nature, life it's like your mind is asleep when it should be awakened because of how your grandmother raised you. It's extra frustrating because of your ancestors. You are so mindless, it's pathetic!" Star said loudly.

Star and Violet were taken aback. How could these kids be related to Star's beloved Ms. Mable?

The children were taken aback by Star's reprimand.

Patience rebuked her silently. *That Queen thinks my brothers and me are stupid? I'll show her that humans are smarter. She'll see.*

Marcus broke the silence with his scientific curiosity. "How can creatures like you come to our world? And you came to our home and watched us too? Why?"

"There is so much to explain – in time, hopefully, you will understand and try to be patient. Eventually, we all will understand.

" Patience interjected before he could get an answer. "You act like we should know more, like we got something to do with this place, but that doesn't make sense." Patience said.

"No, it wouldn't – but it's too complicated to explain. Right now I don't understand enough about what's happening. When I know more, you will too." Star said. Star looked at Violet who then nodded her head at Star approvingly.

"Do we have any special powers? Can we destroy things?" Theo asked.

"No. We are not inclined to destroy or harm anyone or thing. It is not our nature Theo."

Marcus continued his scientific queries. "We inyasis' are kind of like insects from our world. In our world insects help out humans a lot when it comes to having food to eat. Do other bugs, sorry, I mean uju-inyasis' pollinate here, Queen Star?"

"Yes. Others like cousin Adui whose ancestors are Wasps, as well as our other cousins who have ancestors that are butterflies, ants, and birds too. But inyasis' and bees from the human world are the best pollinators."

"Wow!" Marcus said.

Patience's curiosity was piqued by this unknown person. "Who is this cousin Adui?"

Violet answered on Star's behalf. "You will meet him soon enough. It's time to escort you kids to your rooms. We have a very busy day tomorrow."

Star broke up the meeting. "I'm very tired, so Manfred will see to your needs. Remember to behave. Good night, my Funky little Inyasis', you'll probably don't know that word but it means, 'sick' to us old folks and sweet dreams."

"That's funny. My Grammy always used that word too." Patience said.

Manfred escorted Patience to her room and said good night as she closed the door. Patience, refreshed from her mist like shower loved how clean she felt. It was all stone the room with no faucet. There was a small bench to sit on with vanity mirror. She was surprised to learn that there was no rain only mist in Mbaba. When she finally lay down on her bed, Patience sighed loudly. She felt as if she was on top of the lightest cloud. She covered herself and looked up at the ceiling, smiling while watching the fireflies in her crystal chandelier now they sang a different song that sounded like a lullaby in a different language. She had a final thought before falling into slumber. *I can't believe the way I'm living now even though I turned into the creepiest thing on earth.*

Star, restless, got up and went to check on the children. She smiled as she watched them sleeping. She stood there, so amazed by their beauty then returned to her suites. Star was in her bed but the thoughts that filled her mind kept her up. No matter how many obstacles she encountered, she vowed to protect Ms. Mable's babies, but worried about Patience. *Dear lord, where or how do I begin to teach these new species of inyasis' how to merge their human nature with their inyasi one? How do I teach them how to appreciate and value their new inyasi nature as much as their human one?*

Violet knocked and entered Star's room. She felt the need for a sincere chat. Violet sat beside her bed and took her hand while she faced her. She moved when Star got up and together they paced the room.

"Violet, I haven't seen that crease in your forehead since Adui came into our lives. Relax, everything will be cool."

"Oh, my lord, what have I done? Maybe it was a mistake encouraging you to bring those children into our home. They are so complicated with their human ways and attitude towards us. Star we are changing I don't believe it's for the better. All of us now have very complicated thoughts and feelings. We never worried or had doubts.

Our lives had balance and we never had fear. These children bring new challenges to our world in how they will affect our mental state. This frightens me I am very concerned not use to worrying too. It's not too late to change your mind. I think it would be best if we make the Humans' leave and send far away from here, banish them. Star, have you noticed that our world is starting to look different too? All this negativity is weighing heavily on us and Mbaba."

So I am not alone in realizing that our world is looking different, as if the beauty in our world is slightly, ever so slowly fading. I cannot let Violet focus on these thoughts. "Yes, we are changing they do affect us emotionally because they came into our world with serious issues. The way they came here too, so shockingly transformed. Evoking feelings of anger because they violated our sacred Inhlakanipha and we fear each other's species. They have no respect or understanding towards nature in both worlds. We fear each other because we are different. Does that mean we should turn our backs on Ms. Mable's grandchildren, relations to the ancestors' that helped our creator to make our world? Violet, they are not just some ordinary human kids here, and what if there are consequences for doing that?"

"Well, what if having them here destroys our kingdom – or even worse, what we are and our understanding of life as a species?"

"Violet, where is your faith? You had it when I came into your life, why not for the grandchildren of our Ms. Mable? I learned a lot from you and my mother about faith. Please don't lose it now. I'm counting on you to help me through this."

Violet reached out and held Star close to her. She placed both hands on the side of her face and kissed her then hugged her. "I will, but what will it cost us if you are wrong? You came to us from a different kingdom and species of our world. That was different. They are human; humans have so many thoughts and emotions that can be contaminating to our world. Okay, baby girl, I've got your back. Lord knows you need all the help you can get," Violet said.

"Violet, this situation with these kids is scary and confusing. Stay with me as I think this over. I don't want to be alone."

Violet held Star's hand as she climbed into bed together and they held hands Star fell asleep.

*   *   *

"Wake up my little Funky inyasi. We've got work to do and plenty of it!" Star said.

Patience jackknifed up into a sitting position and looked at Star defiantly.

"What work? First you tell me I'm a Princess, and now you want me to work. So you were trying to play me for a fool? All that talk about three different kinds of inyasis' and the drones do jobs and you expect me, a human kid, to do labor. Now you flip the story and are treating me like a drone too. How dare you mess with my mind like that?"

Suddenly Patience lay down and then pulled the blanket over her head. Star walked over, reached down grabbed Patience by her antennae and lifted her suspended in the air before dropping Patience down on to the floor. Patience stood up quickly, rage blazing in her eyes, but she was no match for Star and stood there breathing hard.

"Child, if you want to be treated or respected as a Princess you need to learn about what it takes to become one. You had better stop with the attitude or your days are numbered. Now I'll give you five minutes to get ready and meet me at your brothers' room. Rosa will be waiting outside your room to escort you. Don't make me have to come and get you!"

Patience looked at Star as if she was some nasty smell she couldn't stand. She turned around and stormed towards her bathroom. Star took a few steps and stopped, looking at Patience shaking her head as she left her room. Star paused stood outside her door before leaving.

Will I ever learn how to deal with that child? Lord help me.

Star then headed to the boys' room. The Guards bowed, stepping aside as she entered. Star stood there smiling as she watched them sleeping. She then walked towards them, standing close to Marcus.

"It's time to rise and shine! We have got work to do, you Funky Inyasis, and don't give me any attitude. I had enough from your sister."

The boys sat up and looked at each other. They were rubbing their eyes and just sat there and stared at the Queen.

"Work? We're too young to work." Marcus stretched and yawned then looked at Theo who had the expression he got when he's about to have a fit.

"Theo! Cool it! Don't make it worse for us."

"It's against the law to make kids work in our world, don't forget. We don't come from here. We're not really inyasis' and we might change back one day so it's a waste of time to make us work like one," Theo said. "You won't be working for me. You'll be working on how to awaken your minds and become caring and conscious inyasis'. You will feel better about yourselves when you not only learn but enjoy doing something special that helps to make your world a better place for all. Have you kids ever tried something that was fun while working on helping our planet?" Patience had entered the twin's room and walked begrudgingly past Star, Violet, and the guards, then stood in front of her brothers' bed, arms crossed and defensive. "No. Work and fun never go together." Patience said.

She ignored the spectacular décor that was surprisingly masculine. They had a massive elaborate bunk bed that was curved in dark mahogany like plastic. There was a matching desk and chair, dresser, chairs for sitting, large black and gold spiral rug. A huge mirror framed in mahogany faced the large dressing table. They too had a large chandelier with fireflies that lit the room but were now silent. Theo and Marcus still sat on their beds arms crossed. Star, Violet, Rosa, and three large female drones stood facing them but no one was smiling.

"You all are getting off easy. Don't forget the crime you committed here and what punishment I prevented. I could have you three arrested and in prison for the rest of your lives. Now, you choose to abide by my laws or face judgment. Don't waste any more of my time. You'll have been here for what? Two days now and I am almost about to give up. Do you want that?"

"No!" they said.

"Okay, now, you'll have a lot to learn. So come! Let's get out there and teach you kids all about it."

Theo and Marcus got dressed and when they were ready, everyone went with the female guards with Star, Violet and Rosa following behind them.

*   *   *

"I'm so glad we came out today. It's a glorious day and a blessing to live amongst so much beauty. I don't always get to go on outings. A Queen has her duties and there are responsibilities that only I can deal with. Maintaining my loyal subjects and keeping up with the production of, 'Insingani' is my job. My male drones work hard as providers, seeing that everyone is happy here. The worker uju-inyasis gather pollen and which my sisters guard within our home. Patience, honey child, check out your stinger. We girls got the power to defend ourselves – not that would ever be necessary, since we are a peaceful species."

Twenty guards were flying in front of Star, Violet, and the children. There were more behind them. Star landed on a massive flower. A Wasazi flower which was pink and blue in the center with massive purple petals.

Violet and the children joined her and went to sit on their own petals while the guards remained suspended above.

"How can you take care of a castle and have so many babies too?" Patience asked.

"That's none of your business, child," Violet said.

"I'm a different species of Inyasis', so I can't have babies. My step sisters do. I have three of them who keep the colony very busy."

"Oh!" They said.

Star's stepsisters Cornita, Kandrella, and Dosetta never expressed negative emotions. It was not allowed in their colony. Jealously, hurt, or resentment of the fact that their mother favored Star the most or how a outsider could be the chosen one to become Queen was forbidden. Star always sensed their thoughts no matter how hard they tried to suppress them. Star knew that they never forgot that she was different. They would talk to her and be nice, too nice. Star would felt something or thought she would but then would fight against her negative thoughts because they were not of pure love. Their mother and Violet were aware of how they treated Star and protected her, raising her with so much love. Uju-inyasis' were about pure love thoughts only. Star grew up feeling proud of whom she was instead of ashamed. Star, so strong willed, would not allow their nasty thoughts break her. Her determination to honor her mother's wishes and rule her kingdom as a pure in loving thoughtful Queen was a promise she planned on keeping no matter what it took to do it.

"In this world females rule and run things. The male drones must be worthy, humble and willing to support the females of the population."

At these words, Star saw Patience face transform from one of fury to total bliss. Her eyes had a warm, tranquil sea-blue in one and a warm purple in the other. The color that further illuminated a radiant, beautiful smile. Theo and Marcus stared at her.

Theo was angry his eyes blazing red and green at this revelation. "Why are you giving Patience all kinds of reasons to disrespect us? Don't you realize she will be extra nasty? Queen Star, why are you messing with my family? Can't you see that it's a mistake to make Patience a princess? She's human! We don't come from here." Theo said.

"All of you are crazy if you think I'm going to let Pat boss me around. No way is that going to happen!"

Theo walked up to Patience and boldly looked her up and down, before he shocked everyone by spitting at her feet then went to sit beside his brother.

Violet was taken aback by this bold abuse. *Good Lord, how could her brother be capable of so much hatred? Star needs to banish that child.*

I know what Violet is thinking right now about Theo and I can't blame her. Marcus might be the only child who will be accepted out of all three of them.

"Theo, apologize or be prepared to face the same degrading treatment, three times fold." Star gestured and Theo was surrounded by drones. Theo wanted to rebuke Star but had no power or authority. He apologized but it sounded flat.

"I'm sorry Pat." Even though he apologized to Patience he was really apologizing to Star.

"It's Patience. From now on you'll call me Patience and Marcus will too!"

"I'm sorry Patience," He whispered. Theo couldn't look at her his head was bent downward he was breathing hard his hands were clenched tightly together by his side.

"You all must work harder at putting the love back into your family. There will be no animosity or discord in my kingdom. Right Patience, Theo and Marcus?"

CHAPTER FIVE

WHO'S IN DANGER?

As was their custom, Star and Violet held their morning council in the tower overlooking the valley.

"Violet, do you think they're ready?"

"Lord helps us if they're not. It's all on them to make a good impression with the colonies."

"Do you kids realize how important it is to be accepted by the colonies?"

"Yes, Queen Star! We do." The children were seated twenty feet away together on a couch Star turned to face them as she spoke. "Good because I can't keep you all here if you continue to contaminate our tribe with negative thoughts and emotions. We are pure in being positive and loving towards each other. So you must put a lot of effort into creating happy and positive thoughts. You must try very hard to show that you are positive in thought like us or they won't connect to you guys. Now remember what I taught you and I know the colonies will accept you."

Marcus surprisingly, took the lead. "Oh, don't worry, Queen Star. Well impress them. Right, Patience and Theo?"

"Yeah, right," Patience and Theo said.

Patience reinforced her own beliefs silently. *I cannot let my brothers' stress about me or Star. I can think positive. I got to only have positive thoughts. Lord help me.*

"Yes!" Violet agreed. She solemnly nodded at Star who looked at the children and then back at Violet, whose demeanor was one of disbelief. Everyone was frowning.

Suddenly Star, who had set the goals and expectations needed of them, felt drained due to the negativity. They'd all returned to the castle and the children were immediately sent to their rooms. Star and Violet spent the next ten days alone with them making sure they prepared for the introduction to the colonies. They left to get prepared for the showing and rejoined each other an hour later. Star, Violet and the children, were escorted out by her royal entourage, all of them dressed formally for the occasion. They were seated outside on elevated platform which made it possible for everyone to see the stage. The queen's colony had gathered directly across from the stage upfront. Star, Violet, Patience, Theo and Marcus were on a massive balcony low enough for the guests to see them it was semi-circled.

All seated semi-circled with about fifty rows, with one hundred guests on each row. It was as if they were in a great coliseum. The stage was impressive in size and design, with stage hands available to create the scene or atmosphere required for special events. It had custom designed Thrones for the Queen, Violet and the children that were miniature versions of the ornate large gold thrones. Star sat in the center while Violet was on her left and Patience on the right with her brothers beside her. Star first waved at her audience, then Violet and the children.

"Yes!" Violet agreed. She solemnly nodded at Star who looked at the children and then back at Violet, whose demeanor was one of disbelief. Everyone was frowning.

Star rose and went to the front of the stage and stood with both hands raised standing in front of a podium. She smiled and waved while the audience cheered excited to see their beautiful Queen. Her glorious eyes beamed with anticipation. She waved the crowd to silence before she spoke.

"Welcome, guests! I am blessed to have you all here to meet my new beautiful, extraordinary children that I have adopted. Patience, Theo and Marcus, will be a beautiful addition to our royal family and now in honor of all of you let me present them." Star returned to her throne while the audience cheered again.

"Oh my God, all those uju-inyasis' are looking at us," Patience whispered.

"Smile and look friendly. Don't be afraid, you don't want them to feel your fear," Star whispered.

She's right. I can't let all the uju-inyasis scare me. I have got to stay cool.

"Patience you're safe. Don't worry okay." Marcus whispered. "Yeah, Patience, It's okay," Theo said.

Patience stepped tentatively on to the stage and was terrified and apprehensive about being the center of attention. Although she was excited at first to wear the gorgeous gown she now wondered if it mattered; it was a stunning orangey gold tone, unique in coloring and billowed out like a ball gown. She wore matching gold-colored low heeled sequined shoes, a gift from Violet. She promised Star she would do anything to help. Violet escorted Patience to the center of the stage where she looked out at the audience then suddenly closed her eyes, imaging her Grandmother, Mother, and Father. Loud voices shouted questions as Patience stood there overwhelmed. "Why should we welcome her?" An unknown voice shouted from the crowd.

"What makes her special and what powers does she have? How can she be a Gatekeeper?" Her eyes widened in surprise when she heard her grandmother's voice in her head saying,

Patience, my brave girl show them the power that you have. That's my girl, sing to your Grammy.

Then Patience encouraged and as if in a trance, belted out her *Starlight* song.

Starlights in my Soul . . .

You will always shine in me, I will always look above to the light of your love . . .

Starlights in my Soul . . .

You are angels in the sky, although God called you home I will never be alone . . .

Starlights in my Soul . . .

You are "Stars" to light our way for all to learn and know how to light each other's days . . .

Starlights in my life . . .

I am grateful for your love, how you fill my lonely heart . . . Starlights in my soul . . .

You are everlasting Stars and will always be the Starlights in my life . . .

When she finished there was silence in the audience except inside of her mind. Patience heard the voices of her Grandmother and parents rejoicing happily. Unsettled, she looked behind her and saw Star, Violet, and her brothers clapping, all of them wiping at their tears while they clicked their antennas. Everyone went crazy, clicking wildly, jumping up and down and cheered for more. Patience stood there stunned.

Star was concerned from the expression on her face and went to her quickly escorted Patience back to her seat. Patience just sat there with her eyes closed breathing deeply, and trembled too. Marcus reached out and they held hands.

"You were amazing, Patience!" Theo and Marcus said.

"Good lord, where did you learn how to sing like that. I have heard that remarkable song before, right Violet?" Star asked.

"Girl, you sing like an angel and what a beautiful song. How incredibly strange, you reminded me of my Queen Tulip. That song, those words have a special meaning too." Violet said.

"What do you mean, Violet?" Star asked.

"That song was taught to my Queen who learned it from the Gatekeeper. It is a message from the ancestors to remember that stars are like faith. Faith should shine in all of us and we should always remember that faith shines bright no matter how dark or troubled your mind is".

"Thank you. I never understood why or how I know that song but the words are alive in my mind. Now I get what it means but still don't understand why I know it. I started singing it when I was four. My mother said she use to sing it and her mother too. Grammy said her mother sang it too. How can that be for real it's hard to believe but so is this world. I'm glad you all liked it I never sang it before like this it was scary."

Star found this incredible but even more incredible was how they were being received. There were loud whispers about how beautiful the children were, and curiosity too. Some thought they were a magical creation or some new species from a foreign part of their world. As fascinated as the audience was, still the colonies were experiencing a new emotion that affected their thoughts. They have never seen inyasis' like them before. Star was snapped out of her silent contemplation by Rosa. "My Queen, you have a visitor – your royal cousin, Adui, the Umuvi." Rosa her lady in waiting said. Suddenly out walked the largest, intimidating but humanoid-looking Wasp. He was an Umuvi, an ancestral relation to the Wasps.

Star rose and followed Rosa to where Adui stood at the corner of the stage. "When are you going to fire that rude creature?" Adui exclaimed as Rosa was walking out of the room "Hurry, don't take all night getting me something to drink." Adui sniped at her. Rosa looked at him smiling broadly as if she were in love. She walked up to him looking straight into his eyes with no regard or fear and then walked by brushing him aside.

"Adui, you forget you're forbidden to speak negative words while in my kingdom. I cannot stop your thoughts and am thankful Rosa treats you that way." Star said.

"Maybe Adui will grow a heart and be likeable one day." Violet said as she joined the children by standing close to them still seated on their thrones. Star laughed at Adui, chuckling but then realized his attention was turned towards the children. She stopped laughing when she saw how frightened Patience, Theo, and Marcus were. She heard them gasp when he stood before them, his expression scary.

Adui was a very large and intimidating Umuvi, a humanoid version of the pre-historic Wasps. He stood upright and looked similar to the inyasis' except his Torso was wider and more muscled. He was striped red, black and pink neon colored. He had long narrow face, exaggerated square chin, thin lips and large round eyes, ears and metallic red antennae's. His two arms and hands were exceptionally strong. The Umuvi's legs were long and muscular with large feet in black leather boots that matched the black fabric of his clothing. His wings had one set red and gold design and the other set were pink and silver. He had large eyes like big grey marbles but his pupils were bright red. He wore a half crown half helmet fitted tightly on his head.

The carefully placed holes freed his antennae and kept his helmet in place. He was immediately suspicious of the little freaky looking inyasis' who sat by his Queens's side. He watched her interaction with them as if he was invisible. *Those little freaks are making her smile more than I do. Who are they? The audience is completely captivated by them too.* As Adui examined the children more closely, he circled them repeatedly before stopping directly in front of the children. They sat but stared at Queen Star, fear in their eyes.

"What a bizarre looking little trio. They are very odd and weird. Why, just look at their colors. It's as if someone hung them on a tree and painted those hideous stripes of red, yellow, blue, green, and Violet. All those stripes in neon are gaudy and so tacky too. Do they look that way because they are from some evil tribe?"

I will not let them be popular or outshine me in any way. I will make everyone hate them too. He turned towards Star and Violet to see the effect of his cruel words. He walked over to Star his hand held to his forehead as if he was in mental agony.

"Dear Star, don't you feel a migraine coming on from looking at them. Those colors are screaming 'look at me' with such loud ugly tones.

What a horrible thing to have happened. My poor eyes cannot stand the visual abuse. Please get these freakish creatures out of my sight!"

Everyone was silent at his outburst and you would have heard a pin drop. You could hear a pin drop and then he faced the audience and started to bow. In response to Adui's presence the crown had moved closer to the edge of the stage and Adui was met with thousands of pairs of blazing green eyes. The audience was furious. Patience stood up from her chair, her mouth set tight and eyes blazing fire too. Star motioned for her to sit down but she refused.

"Hey, did you just call us ugly? You got way too much nerve for a freak like you insulting us since you're the ugliest bug on this earth. From now on when you look in the mirror you will really see what ugly is!" Patience yelled.

"Yeah, you're so ugly your Mama must have run away when you were born!" Theo yelled.

"What does his name mean?" Marcus asked Violet quietly.

"It means enemy because he is against everyone!" Violet said loudly. "I am against everyone's stupidity, which seems to be commonplace here!" Adui yelled.

"Oh yeah? As if anyone would want to be friends with you!" Patience said.

Patience and Theo stood up side by side. Marcus remained seated and watched. He gripped the chair arms tightly. Patience and Theo made the audience laughs so hard the chamber vibrated with their laughter.

Violet signaled to Star and this pushed Star into action. *Dear lord. Adui and the children are evoking too much negativity. I must stop this.*

"Now, now, children do not be like my cousin an negative thought minded Umuvi. Such conduct is unbecoming and not expected of you. Do you know how he got the name?" Star asked loudly.

Violet chimed in. "He is a double stinger. It's like his mouth and behind function in the same way."

"Yes, that he is! Adui hurts himself more than anyone else because of his nasty, negative thoughts. Isn't that true my loyal subjects?"

"Yes!" They all agreed loudly while clicking their antennas.

Star got up from her throne and came face to face with Adui. He took one step back when he saw the fury in her eyes. She slowly looked him up and down then suddenly turned her back on him and returned to her throne. She wanted him to feel her disdain as she sat back down. Star could intermittently communicate telepathically with Adui and hoped that this was one of those moments. *I resent that you are causing us to have impure thoughts. I hope you forgive me one day for what I'm about to say, but I must. It's time to make everyone re-focus on bonding with my children and cure the negativity that you bring.*

"He's just jealous of your beautiful colors when all he has are those big and ugly mismatched sets of oversized noise-making wings. He has no sense of style, either. Next to you, my little beauties, he is extra ugly because of his ugly thoughts and unkind words. Isn't that right, Adui?"

It shocked the kids to hear Star insult her cousin. The audience laughed out loud as steam flowed from his antennae while he breathed hard. He looked as if his entire system was about to explode. *I can't believe how she's stung my heart and insulted my style too. How could she put them above me? I am handsome to her or did they poison her mind.* His legs felt weak but he refused to buckle or stumble and managed to remain in front of her with his head still high. Before he could rebuke her he was cut off by Violet.

"Her Majesty's wisdom is why she will always be the Queen of all Queens." The apparent wisdom of her move however was short lived as the laughter turned to boos and insults hurled at Adui. The audience booed in a manner never before heard. Adui was shocked and couldn't face them.

"Silence everyone!" Violet demanded and the crowd fell silent. We cannot act negative or think negative thoughts. Now you know what your Queen expects from you, Adui."

Adui looked up at the children and strained his face to smile broadly but felt uncomfortable because he rarely did.

"Forgive me children for my unkind words and rudeness." *You ought to be sorry, you pathetic looking, freaky, twisted Wasp. I know my brothers' hate him too.*

Before Patience could vocalize her thoughts, Violet's hand on her shoulder stopped her. Violet, also an Empathic, knew what she was thinking and leaned in close to whisper, "Power and Honor come from respect not disrespect." Violet nodded for her to turn to face the crowd again. Patience looked at Violet and nodded her head suddenly held her head low to calm her thoughts. She shocked everyone as she suddenly smiled at Adui. As she did she found the Umuvi staring straight at her.

She smiled, but the way he looked at Patience sent shivers down her sides.

His eyes remind me of Trevor. I wonder if Marcus noticed this too.

Adui decided to switch his tact from brutal insults to pointed sarcasm. "May I ask where the little darlings came from? Obviously they're not from your colony."

Should I tell him the truth? Well, I'll bend it and remind them all how the Jefferson-Johnson created our world. Forgive me lord for lying but I'm trying to save them the best way I know how.

"Adui if you weren't so uppity, selfish and extremely negative today I would have told you about the children days ago. Can you recall ever seeing such beautiful colors? Don't their colors remind you of anything?" Star asked.

"Of course I have seen these magnificent colors before. The only living thing with these colors is on the sacred, Inhlakanipha. Well naturally the colors are beautiful on the tree, but a nightmare on them." Marcus pressed his back against the chair when Adui approached them. Star got up from her throne and called the children over. They quickly went and stood beside her. Patience held Marcus's hand. She knew he scared Marcus and enjoyed doing it too. Patience and Theo stood there and looked him up and down with blazing green and orange eyes. Their scary expression surprised Adui.

"Everyone, I am honored to introduce you all to my adopted children Patience, Theo and Marcus Robinson. They are the Grandchildren of our beloved Ms. Mable Jefferson-Johnson. You all know she was the human creator of our world and what she meant to us.

These children are precious, because their ancestors created our Mbaba.

Sadly, she has passed on so we must honor her memory by caring for her babies. They belong here with us. Our precious Gatekeeper, Ms.

Mable wanted her babies to grow up here. She gave them permission to eat the Inhlakanipha and now they are Inhlakanipha Inyasis'."

Wow, I can't believe this Queen's imagination. Our ancestors created this world. I wonder what my brothers are thinking.

Star, Violet, Adui, and the children watched as the audience started to click their antennae. They made a weird loud sound. The audiences' eyes that were friendly suddenly now looked scary, as loud protests erupted; some fainted because they were so stunned about this news.

"Never!" The crowd repeatedly shouted. The protests grew and the crowd surged forward again.

"Now hush. I command you all to be silent!"

Suddenly, it was very quiet and they watched and waited. Everyone stared silently at the Queen as she stood before them poised, smiling all bowed. '

"Remember our precious Ms. Mable Jefferson-Johnson? We all know if wasn't for their family, we wouldn't be here."

Now the audience upon hearing this bowed again in honor of these special humans, but some were too shocked to move. Adui was angered by their acceptance and public honoring and nearly walked off the stage. He was however convinced otherwise by the strong, powerful drones that stood at the exits meeting his gaze. He instead spoke out against the Queen as everyone has a right to a voice.

"How dare you try to shock me to death? You know that I absolutely loathe humans more than anything on this planet. These criminals are sitting beside you and you are treating them like special envoys. They broke our sacred law by destroying our sacred Inhlakanipha. We should put them in prison. No, what they did deserves a punishment of death. No Jefferson-Johnson relative would violate the most remarkable plant in the world!"

His words had some pull with the crowd and unrest rose again. Star was required to vocalize her position.

"I won't do that, Adui. You really don't get it, do you?"

"What don't I get? I get everything. I'm the most intelligent species on earth!"

She walked over to him and spoke directly to him. We have sacred laws that protect these children. If we destroy them, we risk losing everything; our homes, lives, and our world. We cannot destroy our creators' family. That would mean death to us all. Should we let your bloodlust be responsible for destroying our world?"

"No, no!" The audience yelled.

Star looked back at Violet who was with the others that agreed with Star.

Adui was quick to respond as he too had a place in this world. "My loyal subjects, humans living amongst us will destroy our world. We must protect ourselves before it's too late. Let them prove that they're Jefferson-Johnson children. They should know something about our world if they truly are. It just doesn't make sense that humans from that family could be criminals!" Adui yelled.

He wanted to prove that they were just Impostors, humans that were dangerous. He believed that humans' would contaminate his precious Mbaba because of their thoughts and emotions. He didn't believe they were truly related to the Jefferson-Johnson family too.

"Why do know about Mbaba and what doe's our species have in common with the insects from your world. Why do humans need bees to survive?"

"You're my cousin, Adui, but you're shameful. Treating these precious babies so badly and upsetting, scaring and terrorizing them too. How dare you create these horrible emotions for these positive thought loving children? You are contaminating them with negative emotions. You expect them to answer questions after attacking them!"

Patience, Theo, and Marcus looked at Adui defiantly. Suddenly, Star looked at Patience, Theo and Marcus then nodded her approval but still they looked frightened. Star spent time preparing them as well as for the story she made up about their Grandmother and why they ate the uhlamvu. Something in her spirit compelled her to withhold the truth about their ancestors and grandmother. Star believed she shouldn't reveal the truth. Patience, Theo and Marcus believed it was a fabricated story about their Grandmother. Star warned the children to remain silent and be careful, to always have positive loving thoughts. She then had the children escorted back to their seats.

"Queen Star told us it's because bees pollinate. Don't you know that fool?" Patience said. No sooner had she spoken did she realize that she had made a mistake. One glance at Violet and Star confirmed. "I am sorry and should not have said that!" *I messed up I insulted him. I know more than that. Who does he think he is? I won't let that ugly creature mess things up for my brothers' and me. He's bringing out the ugly in Theo and me.*

"Star, he's stressing me out. I can't focus." Patience said. "Yeah, he's confusing us too." Theo and Marcus said.

Adui scorned them further. "That's the best you criminals can do? And you claim to be Jefferson-Johnson children. You lying delinquents, expending on our Queen to give you answers. Do you think we're stupid?"

"Of course we are from the Jefferson-Johnson's family, fool. We just turned into bees, bugs, I mean inyasis'. We didn't plan this. Our Grandmother, Ms. Mable did. Honestly, I never would have eaten those Berries if I knew what they would do to me. Our Grandmother taught us that the most important job in the world is to love and care for all God's creations. She also talked about always trying hard to only allow positive thoughts and feelings live inside your mind. She said kind thoughts are what we need to have a healthy world. She told us about this place too. In fact, if you look up at that cloud, the smiling one, it's her," Patience said.

Suddenly, she pointed upward and everyone looked then suddenly bowed some in honor, most out of fear but Star was surprised and this made her eyes misty too. The Queen blew a kiss towards the remarkable image. The audience looked up and all of them pointed at the cloud, then applauded, and all bowed again. Marcus felt happy and he stood up on his chair proudly, bowed then stroked his antennas.

He was smiling broadly with his colorful teeth. Theo waved and Patience too. They stood on their chairs too looking up smiling.

Suddenly their Grandmother disappeared but Adui refused to look anymore. He spoke out loud his voice amplified by the chamber.

"No self-respecting inyasi or inhabitant from our world would ever claim to be human. That is the most disgusting species on this planet. They're nature destroyers and will cause the ruination of all of God's creations with the exception of the Gatekeepers. That species have lost respect for nature because of greed. Those evil creatures destroy the Forests and homes of animals. Humans have no respect for life. I refuse to believe that these criminals are Jefferson-Johnson descendants or had anything to do with our world. They say and express mean and nasty thoughts. They are infecting all of us with negativity. It's a dangerous lie. Just because they transformed into inyasis' doesn't mean that they are one of us too."

"Yeah those cool Berries turned us into inyasis', but we love it," Marcus said loudly.

"It's totally awesome!" Theo said.

"Listen, Umuvi, they are living with Queen Star so deal with it. The Gatekeeper, Their Grandmother, Ms. Mable Jefferson-Johnson told them stories about our world and they have been sent here to learn what you Adui still need to learn how to grow your thoughts into positive ones. Patience, Theo and Marcus must be here in Mbaba because their grandmother wanted them here, so you'd better deal with it." Violet said loudly.

"Adui, I have adopted these children and you hate humans too much to accept the reality of how our world came to be. Their ancestry gives them the privilege to live here and now they're a part of my royal family." Star said loudly.

Adui had no answer to this and the crowd behind him fell silent. Suddenly the audience cheered when Star stood up. She waived and as she beckoned the kids to come forward, they cheered louder. Adui looked at Star, then the children who stood in front of their chairs, smiling and waving then suddenly the Umuvi relented.

He turned to leave but then collapsed. They screamed some dropped to the ground from a thunderous loud sound then rain fell and within a minute vanished. Everyone slowly stood up wet and stunned. Star and Violet stared up at the sky which was not as bright. The sun looked different too.

*   *   *

Star dismissed the audience and had the children escorted back to their rooms. Adui was taken to his royal chambers. He decided to rest and stretched out on his bed. He sat up suddenly when he saw Star and Violet by his bedside.

"Well, it's about time that you came back to life. Right Violet?"

Unfortunately Adui is right for a change. I can't stand him I resent that fact that my negative thoughts surface around him I resent the way he affects my mind yet Star loves him.

"Star I fear these children are changing our world I cannot believe what happened. Never before have I experienced rain, clouds, and thunder. It is terrifying." Violet said.

"The children, Violet are not the reason as to why the sky was angry I believe our beloved Ms. Mable isn't happy with us and is making it known."

"Yes, maybe you are right Star but what if it's much more than we realize. Now we cannot banish the children it could be dangerous for all of us."

"Those children are dangerous and you must destroy them. Star you saw the proof. Our sky has never poured rain like that before! "He yelled.

Adui quickly scanned the room and was thankful they were not around. He was terrified by what he witnessed and became all the more compelled to separate Star from the intruders. "Human monsters transformed into inyasis will contaminate our species. They are the beginning of a dangerous invasion into our world.

Now it is changing because of them. Star and Violet we must remove them from here!"

"Star, you deal with him I can't stand it when reason fails his logic." Violet said.

"Relax yourself, Adui; you are really being over dramatic!"

"You want this allegiance with these monsters? Is it wise to allow for this?"

"Adui, don't you get that for our kind, having these special children live here is the opportunity of a lifetime. We'll get to learn and grow from each other. How you could not be excited about the benefits from this experience. We have no choice but to believe having them here will enrich all of our lives."

"Now you have lost your royal mind. A human is a human always. You have changed. Are you well, or did they infect you somehow?

Violet how could you let her do this? You know better. Talk her out of this before it's too late."

"Adui, don't forget who rules this kingdom. Star believes this is wise so we must respect her decision. I absolutely support her decision. You should too!"

Oh my God, maybe those evil humans have infected their minds and it might be contagious. I better get out of here and find a way to save our kingdom.

"Adui, don't make me choose between you and them."

Violet and Adui cannot know of the fear in my mind.

Patience had hid behind the curtain once she managed to slip away from the guards. She didn't trust Star, yet and needed to hear if she truly was committed to helping them. Suddenly, she sneezed and Adui spun around.

Reveal Yourself!

At his command Patience stepped out from behind the curtain then rushed towards her protectors and stood beside Star and Violet.

Patience reached out and grabbed Stars hand.

He hates us. I just pray that she can protect us. Oh lord what are we going to do if he changes her mind?

"How many of us have these so called harmless children killed insects in their world and what makes you think we are safe from them? If they are so innocent, why do they sneak around as thieves?"

"They're to be respected as a part of our royal family cousin. I command you to respect my wishes. How can you speak of thievery anyways when you come and go, unseen like a shadow in the night?"

He jumped out of the bed and quickly walked out to the balcony. As they followed him, just before he exited, Adui turned around his eyes blood red, displaying his anger and discontent. He bowed and then vanished into the sky.

"Are we going to be safe?" Patience asked. "Yes." Star lied.

Patience held her tightly. Star looked over her head at Violet, who shook her head with a sad expression.

CHAPTER SIX

CHOICES?

Adui laid down on his favorite tree branch, in his hidden garden. He needed to recover from the tribulation Star had put him through. He couldn't believe that he was close to crying for the first time, and it was an awful unexpected happening. It seemed that his beloved Star loved those humans more than him it was unbearable and terrifying too.

How could she care or want them in our world? Why did she need them when she had me? Why must I always compete for love? Driven by his anger and emotion forgetting to silence his thoughts, he spurted his sentiments out loud.

"I need an ally who could be almost as devious, wickedly brilliant, and be insane with jealousy enough to risk making an enemy of Star, and get rid of those monsters."

With voicing these thoughts it seemed as if their weight landed on him physically and Adui almost fell out of the tree spurred to motion from his sudden blinding genius. He stood upright after halting his fall to the ground. As he straightened to his full height, the extraordinary light of his plan took deeper root in his mind.

"Yes, of course, the perfect ally who is very dangerous. In fact she's lethal, the Queen of madness, my crazy cousin Enchantress. She would be the ultimate challenge to deal with, but I have no choice. Star will hate me, but if she truly loved me, she would have put those criminals in prison. That Formica Queen, Cousin Enchantress, is always competitive with Star and will destroy those infiltrators or imprison them because of their crime. I'll plan a secret meeting with her so that Star never finds out what I've done. Once those monsters are gone then I can eventually marry Star and become king of Harmony Castle."

Adui now relaxed, soared back to his perch lying down again with a smirking satisfaction of his plans to be brought to fruition with the dawn. He stretched out on the tree and finally fell asleep.

*   *   *

Adui was hanging out at his usual social dwelling, reading Queen Enchantress's publicity circulars. He was seated at the bar, pondering about how to approach the Queen Enchantress. She had special drones trained to write and report news that related to Mbaba and the human world. As much as he hated the Formicas, still his curiosity compelled him to read. He had also learned a lot from spying. The entrance to the human world was carefully guarded secret, privileged information known only to the Queens who ruled in Mbaba. Adui's spying had paid off the day he overheard the conversation that Star was having with Violet, speaking about how she was planning on visiting the human world and Ms. Mable. She couldn't believe that her cousin, Enchantress, still sent her drones into their world for food too. This always disgusted

Star and was reason for an excuse to decline Enchantress's frequent and repeated dinner invitations. Star did not want to bring negative thoughts or feelings into her beloved cousin's kingdom. Fascinated, he decided to follow her and was shocked by what he witnessed.

Star flew to a private garden he had never seen before and there was only one plant there. The massive bush appeared to be crowned with a bright red and gold halo all around it. The special bush tree appeared as if it was glowing. This plant was a guarded secret to all of Mbaba; the fruit was bright green, round and tiny and yet proficiently potent in its effects. It had stood alone too in Ms. Mable's private garden secluded and well hidden from sneaky prying eyes. Star picked one and made a face as if she was eating something distasteful, despite how magical it appeared. She then stepped back as the massive bush parted, opening from the center of it. Star immediately flew through it and in her wake it suddenly closed up behind her. Adui approached the plant inquisitively and stood beside it. In response to his presence its color suddenly changed to a dull grey, becoming darker and darker until the halo was completely black. He stepped back in surprise and awe.

The plant looked ominous but he fought back his fear. Slowly but determined, Adui reached out and plucked one of its fruits which turned black in color. With his attention focused on the fruit in hand, the Imfihlo tree changed back to its original color.

"Interesting, I've never seen any plant in Mbaba change color like this before! How strange! I must eat this fruit and discover what magic it possesses. I bet it will allow me to follow Star. I wonder where it takes her to. I can't believe I'm doing this but I have no choice. Star refuses to tell me where Enchantress lives just because believing that I'm insensitive towards her and would contribute to her low self-esteem.

My insensitivity is not rooted in anything to do with the Enchantress but only with Star and these children that she has allowed to come between the two of us. So what if I compare them and show Enchantress how inferior she is to Star? Someone needs to remind Enchantress that she cannot compete with Star." Despite the numerous questions, like the underlying beat to any song, his dilemma hinged on only one question.

"Should I eat one?"

Adui quickly picked the engorged fruit, shoving it into his mouth and swallowing it whole. His eyes widened from the shock of his exploding sense and the acrid taste of the fruit. He grabbed this throat in agony as he slowly fainted falling to the ground. He woke up and was terrified to discover that he was now on the other side in the horrifying human world. Adui got up, fearful of his unfamiliar surroundings. He screamed when a cloud suddenly loomed in front of his face. It was smiling and laughing with large pointy teeth and scary large black eyes. He was on his knees head held down covering his head trying to protect himself.

"Oh please don't hurt me!"

"Cowardly Umuvi, Why would we hurt you when we are here because of you? Now go!"

Adui flew off quickly out of the forest as if he was being chased by the devil himself.

*   *   *

"That forest, those clouds, so terrifying – why would it claim it has something to do with me? This is a first for me to experience the human world, it's terrifying, so dismal and dreadful too. How can anyone bear to fly – or worse, be a ground walker in such filth? So many humans, how can anyone from Mbaba stand being amongst these animals? There are no beautiful colors; it smells of pollution and garbage. How do they survive? These Formicas are truly the lowest of our species. No wonder they are comfortable with the low-life creatures that live here. I cannot believe that any relation to me could possibly love to consume that human food. Thank God our pre-historic ancestors' can't contaminate our world. That is why I must have those human inyasis' destroyed."

Adui flew high and low within in the city that was thriving with human culture, restaurants, hotels, and buildings too. He flew at a speed that made it impossible to see him clearly. He began to get discouraged when suddenly he spotted the two unusually large and unmistakable Argentinean Formica drones. Their markings were not the same. He frowned then his eyes widened – he noticed something strange, then gasped. He suddenly remembered reading something that terrified and prevented him from wanting to see the human world. Any humanoid visiting from Mbaba became transformed and appeared like their ancestors.

"Uh, on no I've changed too." He cursed this under his breath, realizing that he was no longer neon or adorned in special clothing. He looked like any large wasp, but still had his gift of heightened senses and faster flight. Adui was about to fly away and forget the whole plan when suddenly out of nowhere a large human hand tried to smash him. He escaped and landed on a nearby tree. Adui felt the urge to heave but held his mouth to fight the sensation. Fortunately his stomach was empty the loud thumping of his heart filled his ears. He sat up, tried to stay focused, and watched the drones down below walking slowly. He couldn't believe how big the humans were until he realized that it was he who had shrunk.

Attached to their backs was a basket full of human food but it was invisible to the human eye. The Formica drones were struggling to carry it. Adui was shocked when he witnessed a large creature with four legs and a long tail grey in color with black beady eyes attempted to approach them. The strong male drones threw a stink bomb that overwhelmed the creature's senses and sent it running in the other direction. They may have lacked special powers but their intelligence still remained.

"What a shocking display of intelligence. So that's how they avoid the danger of this world. It's incredible the powers they have here too.

However they are still disgusting and revolting. How am I going to not be revolted when I make contact with them?" His inner voice silenced and trepidations he had.

Adui you know what will happen if you don't. You must find Enchantress. I believe that you are smart enough to do it.

"Those evil children have ruined my life and filled Star's thoughts with negative ones. I will find my way into her heart even if it kills me." With this Vow he finally mustered the will power to force himself to fly towards the Formicas far below.

*   *   *

"Today for sure she's going to kill us, Uno!"

"Ah, Dos how many times has she threatened to kill us?" Uno asked. Uno and Dos were brothers who served the Queen Enchantress as personal attendants. They were humanoid Formicas, an advanced species evolved from the Argentinean Fire Ant family. Their heads were large and upright shaped like small eggs, with the pointed ends forming their chins. Their faces were human-like with small cheekbones. They had a high bridged triangular shaped nose that separated their large and round black eyes with red irises. Their lips were thin but deceptive because their mouths could open wide to full length of their bodies and held two rows of sharp pointy teeth. Two dark red metallic antennas that spiraled upwards from their temples were capped by two red caps.

Their skin was smooth and shiny dark red with bright green tiny dots everywhere. They had two arms and legs with fuzzy thin layer of fur and walked upright. In Mbaba they would have been adorned in Khaki green uniforms with sailor type hats with numbers on their sleeves. On their feet were black army-like boots. This was the standard look for all who served Enchantress. Here the nature of the human world revealed their raw muscularity and insect like behavior.

Uno and Dos were the Queen's most valued Drones being skilled in successfully voyaging to the human world and returning with her royal food. Their greedy Queen was so obsessed with human food, that she appointed them as her royal food gatherers. Uno was one year younger than Dos and the most intelligent drone of all from the Formica colonies. Uno tried to look back at his brother he managed to do so even though it was difficult.

"Every day Dos, you say the same thing,"

"But we are Drone males and males are estupido Uno,"

"What are you saying? We are like the other drones Dos! Clear your head, Enchantress has crowded it."

"If you think that we have brains, to think we are smart then you must be loco, Uno,"

"How can I be loco with a brain eh? We are still alive, yes? So one of us has intelligence and it isn't you!"

Dos suddenly stopped to think if he was right and Uno bumped right into him, moving him along.

"Ugh, I never thought about that before. How come I can think, Uno, and you don't?"

"You claim to think, but that brain of yours has no intelligence. Drones in our world are all inferior and subservient except me. I pretend to be as brainless as you and have as such learned the Enchantresses' reasoning. If you wanted to catch the hunter, you have to pose as bait. Your brainlessness is the only reason for you not seeing this. No wonder you're confused and forget that it's my brain that's keeping us alive. We are the longest living drones because I have a brain with intelligence, Dos."

"Uno, we are lucky that you alone are intelligent or maybe you're just lucky. I don't have the burden of your secrets. Only the Queen has a brain with intelligence. How come we are not dead, Uno? Would she not have discovered us by now?"

"We are still alive, Dos, because I pretend to not have a brain. Enchantress would go extra loco if she knew I had intelligence. My brain is smart enough to act estupido like you and the others. Remember it's my brain that saves our behinds all the time. Never forget that now be quiet!"

I will always fear her even though I am Uno the most wise as her madness knows no logic. She is also loco and love crazy. As such having her believe I am crazy in love with her helps. She is mad, worse than crazy. Oh, well maybe one day I will live to see my dream. My loco Enchantress will want me to be her King and I will rid the kingdom of her. It is getting harder to be Uno. I feel like my brain is going to break from so much stress. Today I feel more stress, like something very bad is going to happen. I wish I didn't have a brain so I can stop these terrible thoughts.

Adui unexpectedly interrupted their private thoughts. "Hey, you two Drones, do you know Queen Enchantress?" Adui asked.

Uno and Dos stopped but could not see who they were speaking too because Adui was too high up. He purposely tried to keep himself hidden until he was sure they could be trusted.

"Who wants to know?" Dos demanded.

Let me do all the talking, Dos. Stay quiet." Uno said.

"Adui, you imbecile I am her royal cousin Adui from Mbaba, the Kingdom of the North. I am known to all as the most notorious Umuvi of all Kingdoms. Adui means enemy so don't try to defy me as it will be to your ruin. I flew here on an urgent mission!" He looked anxiously around him but remained suspended high enough for a quick escape from danger.

"What do you want from my Queen?" *I do not like this royal Umuvi with his royal snobby ways.*

"How dare you use that tone of voice with me? I am Queen Star's cousin, a royal relative to both Queens, you lowlife Drone!"

"Umuvi, you are nothing, just another brainless Drone who thinks he's better than me!" Uno yelled.

Adui, outraged, incensed, and infuriated at being talked down to by a dirty, nasty ground scavenger Formica, suddenly flew low enough to face them, forgetting his fear and primary intentions. Uno and Dos were surprised by his massive size but they feared only their Queen. They walked again and Uno decided to ignore Adui but still the Umuvi continued to stay in Uno's path.

"Your Queen would destroy you for disrespecting her royal cousin, who came personally to save her life!"

This news suddenly stopped Uno, and Dos almost bumped into him. They stood side by side, looking up at Adui hovering just beyond their reach.

As Adui hovered Uno assessed his persona. *Perhaps I better listen to what this uppity Adui says. I know he is wise and evil. Maybe he was lucky to be born with a brain too.*

"Uno, this could be some trick do not trust him." Dos said.

"Dos, what if he is telling the truth? Should we take that risk? Better the devil you know than the devil you don't?" He looked at Adui again.

"Why is our Queen's life in danger?" "Drone that is none of your business!"

"Well, if you cannot talk to me, Uno, her number one Drone, then you cannot talk to her, you uppity, estupido Umuvi. It becomes my business, if you want her to know!"

"Okay, you silly Formica, but when your Queen is attacked and she finds out that it is you stupid drones who stopped me from warning her, it will be your time to fear for your lives. Do you fools know what she will do to you? Good luck you worthless low-life Formicas!"

Now I know why my brain is bothering me. This Adui is the cause of my suffering. I get this feeling whenever anyone tries to deceive me. Adui grew impatient.

"It's your life to lose, not mine! Your life and that of your precious Queen's too."

That foolish drone. I'll teach him never to mess with me. How dare he even try to? Adui turned to fly away. He knew they would have stopped him. His back was turned so they could not see the look of triumph on his face.

First, he heard Uno then Dos. They begged him to come back. He made them wait by remaining out of view when he returned; their heads were bowed as a show of respect.

"Let us apologize, amigo. Cousin Adui? You must be the most famous Umuvi we heard about. You honor our Queen by your loyalty and desire to personally warn her, flying all the way here to do so. She will be very pleased to meet you."

Uno tried to smile and prayed he looked sincere, trying to pretend that Adui's words did not frighten him. Dos looked nervously at his brother, unsure as to why the sudden change in direction. "Uno! Hey bro, she will eat you for lunch and then kill me for dinner if something bad happens because of this Umuvi. He could be a spy, our enemy." Dos whispered.

"Quiet! Remember who has the brain to make decisions. We will take him to our Queen. She will be pleased and entrust us with more duties, then we remain her Uno and Dos forever."

Adui heard the exchange and was fascinated by the idea that this Formica drone might have a brain of some intelligence; He knew that in Mbaba especially Formicas drones were known for being or acting brainless. *Their Queen wouldn't tolerate intelligence from drones.* Adui recognized this drone Uno was different but still inferior.

"Follow us Adui! We will take you there safely but you better not be lying. Never try to play games with our Queen! She always wins."

The Formicas, in spite of the weight they carried, travelled at a remarkable speed. Adui followed while deep in thought.

It's been decades since I've seen her. I succeeded in creating feelings of insecurity about her size and intelligence. Enchantress was young then, vulnerable and starting to want too much personal time with Star. I destroyed their intimacy, through fanning her competitive feelings which I knew would get in the way. Enchantress now feels superior to everyone and remains secluded in her own colony. No one has seen her for years. It was bad enough that I had to share Star with her colony. Enchantress would have demanded too much of her time.

Now she is an adult and no longer a teenager. Any memory she would have had of me, hopefully will have been lost with the years past. I must see her although we may be strangers. Why would I spend my valuable time with a disgusting, ground crawling, puny, greedy little human food lover? Even though she is a Queen her lack of intelligence must have her at a disadvantage, I will probably struggle at trying to dumb myself down to her level for her to comprehend what I am saying. It will be like talking to a child. Hopefully she won't be too intimidated or frightened of my powerful presence. After meeting me, she will probably beg me to help her rule her Kingdom. Imagine being King of two Kingdoms. That would be extraordinary.

Unbeknown to Adui, Uno and Dos had the ability to communicate telepathically. They were the only drones who shared this gift.

"Uno, does he have a brain with intelligence too. Is he like you? Yes, but I believe it is smaller than mine is, Dos. "

"Why do you say that, Uno?"

"His life is easy. His Queen is not loco, crazy; he doesn't need a brain to survive. What does he do, Uno? His is truly weird, Dos, we have seen him before. Remember that Umuvi with the strange hat and clothes? Any drone who can dress like that must lie around and do nothing all day."

"He talks strange and is big but he thinks you don't have intelligence, Uno."

"Let him think that. It will be fun to prove him wrong and watch how his brain deals with our Queen's madness."

Adui looked down at them when he heard them laughing. He refused to fly too close and tried to avoid the same air they breathed.

CHAPTER SEVEN

WAR OF BRAINS?

There is a dark beauty about this tribes land. How strange and different it is from the other parts of Mbaba. Adui circled the Enchantress residence surveying the grounds and circling several times before he landed rejoining Uno and Dos on the ground.

"Her home reminds me of something I've seen before." Adui said. "If you had a brain then you would recognize this grand home. It is so like the house of the human president, except our Queen picked a red house instead of a white one." Uno said.

"It is them that should have chosen red given all the killing that happens within the Human world. It is a stained land. That however is the downside to the freedom of power. You get to do whatever you want." "The White House? Are you telling me she lives in a house like the human President I read about? That's not being superior! Strange for a Queen from our world to want a home like that instead of a Castle." Dos rebuked him for questioning the Enchantress' choices.

"Yes, estupido Adui, our Queen knows only the most powerful should live like that."

Adui was incensed by his brazen insult.

"Watch your mouth; you're just a slave Formica. That monstrosity has three clashing shades of red.

You don't get power from where you live but how you live. Couldn't she pick one tone? It looks quite tacky."

"Shouldn't you shut your mouth? Enough with the criticism. You shouldn't talk with the clothes you wear. Right Dos?"

"Yes, brother, he's so funny looking." Dos laughed and Uno joined in.

Adui looked as if he wanted to attack them but reconsidered given the more pressing things he needed to deal with. Adui, annoyed, flew higher as they approached the massive awkwardly colored castle, seeking to get a better look at what lied ahead. On the grounds there was a Marigold-round, swings, teeter-totters, slides, and a large maze.

From above, Adui saw surrounding the central structure was a crazy mix of beautiful, colorful large statues scattered over the dark settings of the castle. It looked as if a large scary red mansion was dropped into the center of a massive amusement park. Hundreds of Formicas were visible doing a variety of tasks. The multitude of Formicas together comprised of a mélange of different shades of red, black, yellow and green bodies, whose colors shifted with their mood and location. They all however shared the same type of wings, large and solid black. The only other semi similarity was that they were all emblazoned with numbers which differed according to their rank and position. The children wore hats with numbers to identify which family they came from and their future jobs. They did not get their official number until they were old enough to work.

The fortress had several towers from which many armed guards stood watch. Adui remembered beneath the Towers, there were vast underground dwellings and caves that housed the thousands of drones in Enchantresses' army. A red brick Bridge served as a road to the Mansion. Beneath it, instead of water, was a beautiful bed of glittering red Ruby Stones. A tall gate standing about twenty feet high adorned with deadly looking pitchfork shaped spikes, served as the main entrance. The property and estate was twice the size of Queen Star's.

The plants and grass were in tones of red, green, black and orange. They were still some miles away from Queen Enchantress's castle, but from what Adui saw it was a massive amount of ugly and poor taste thrown together.

On the ground Uno walked with Dos beside. Glancing over at Dos he saw that Dos was following Adui's movements and not paying close attention to his own circumstances." Hey Dos! Estupido! Don't drop any crumbs. You know how much food we need to please our Queen." Uno said.

"Ah, that brother of mine, he is reckless when carrying and taking care of the royal food. If only Dos didn't talk so much."

"How can all that food get into her tiny body? She is Formica. I don't understand, Uno."

"Dos, I don't know. You always ask me the same question and I still don't know. Why do you always think you will get a different answer?"

"We had better find another way to please her. These constant trips to the Human world are killing my back."

"How will she feel after eating, this Umuvi? Maybe we will get to see her pop like popcorn and be eaten as such. Maybe she eats so much because she is trying to grow bigger than her cousin Star, Uno." Dos laughed so hard his basket was shaking and bits of food were falling out. "Hush that and watch the food. Adui might hear us. Keep your voice down. Don't be estupido, talking trash about our Queen, Dos. Quiet!" "Ah he cannot hear us flying way up there. We are safe from him." Adui could see the baskets in spite of the secured lid and tied to their backs still they bounced up and down, leaving a trail of crumbs on the ground. They went own a private alley and Uno called out to Adui who suddenly flew closer to him.

"Hey Umuvi, eat this fruit. It will take us quickly into the royal dining room."

"Really, that fruit can do that?"

"Yes. These are magical fruits from our garden now shut up and eat it!" Uno yelled.

Adui took the fruit and made a face while he swallowed it within moments all three of them were back in Enchantress's dining room.

*　　*　　*

"Truly I am growing so enormous in size. Why my three panel mirrors are almost too small for me. Maybe I need six more panels? I need to keep up with my increasing beauty. I also need new gowns and crowns – possibly larger, because I'm filling out too." Queen Enchantress said. She blew kisses at herself while her entourage of attendants watched.

The door keeper birth number ninety-two who suddenly interrupted her chain of thoughts announcing the arrival of Adui.

"My most beautiful Queen, you have a visitor from the North. Your cousin Adui, who thinks he has a brain and requests a visit with you."

She turned around to look at the Door Keeper, but then switched her attention to the trio of Adui, Uno and Dos behind him whispering loudly behind the door. Enchantress clapped her hands then clicked her Antennae as she jumped up and down like a happy child.

"How delightful, my cousin Adui the enemy is here. However he is a mere drone not worthy of that name. I must find out why he is here. Now after all these years wanting to be in my royal presence, how exciting yes, I will let him have the honor of my company. Bring him to me in hour I must continue to make myself more beautiful for his visit. I want him to see my beauty as my jaws close over his face."

"As you wish, my Queen."

The Door Keeper returned quickly to the guards who surrounded Adui. He stood still in spite of being larger than them. Those drones scared him. The Door Keeper motioned and they all followed him. They walked into the royal dining room which was more like a massive Ballroom. It had on the ceiling a large silver diamond that split the incoming light from the sun roof into a kaleidoscope of colors that illuminated the red walls. There was a very big stage that was oval shaped, twenty feet in dimension and stood about ten feet high. There were rows of seats like stairs set in the fashion of an amphitheater, in a semi-circle form. It was capable of holding about five hundred guests. They were high enough to give each guest an excellent view of the stage. On the stage was actually one enormous metal spoon that contained all the food that was in the baskets. There were hundreds of guests one by one mounting the steps to deposit food into the large silver spoon. It was big enough to hold about ten Formicas comfortably.

There was a mix of all types of food. Adui stood between Uno and Dos, who had ten large drones at their side. The platform was attached to the stage there was about three feet between the concealed structure and Adui. On the platform facing the stage, something large stood behind gold colored curtains, silently looking out at Adui.

Whatever the thing was, it had wheels and was heavily guarded too he thought.

Adui looked at the hundreds of Formicas of different sizes, shapes and colors that stared silently at the stage and waited too. *Well, now I am trapped in their seedy little world. I must win their trust by forcing myself to eat that nasty revolting human garbage and other rubbish. I hope it doesn't kill me.* Adui stared at the food and suddenly felt hunger pains. Driven by his desire for revenge and schemes he had forgotten to eat. Without thinking he tried to break away to get some but the aggressive Formicas blocked him from touching it.

"Touch that food and you die!" Uno said.

"I am a royal cousin. How dare you make me starve to death?"

A loud and powerful voice thundered through the room. The ground shook from the terrifying vibrations causing Adui to recoil in awe. He could not see what or who was so incredibly loud. Adui, shocked, grabbed onto one of the drones and tried not to lose his footing.

"Uno and Dos! You brainless estupidos!" Enchantress said. "Oh my God what or who is that?" Adui asked.

From the sides of the curtain, the largest heavily muscled Formicas Adui had ever seen, stepped out and blew trumpets before pulling on the red drawstrings. They stepped aside and the curtains split apart revealing the Enchantress. Adui was once more taken aback as by the enormous Formica. The largest he had ever seen or could recall. Adui did not recognize the entity but as everyone around him bowed, he knew it to be Queen Enchantress that stood in the center of twenty large, high glass panels. They were in a semi-circle around her. The first ten in the front were clear while the other ten in the back were mirrored.

Queen Enchantress was too beautiful to be real. Uniquely beautiful in humanoid structure from head to toe. With an oval shaped head, a high bridged triangular shaped nose, very large oval shaped eyes spread over almost half the length of her face. She had very thin antennae that maintained a curly wand shaped position on each side of her face, her mouth extended from one side to the other but her lips were shapely. Her neck was long and covered in chokers adorned with rubies, sapphires and diamonds that matched her crown. Her torso was hour glass shaped, leading up to large breasts and square, wide and graceful shoulders. Two slender but powerful arms extended from her shoulders which lead to her delicate yet strong hands and fingers. Her claw shaped nails were painted dark red. Adui falsely assumed this was paint, but to everyone else in the know she dipped her nails in the blood of her victims as a reminder of her conquests.

She stood upright in a shimmering dress with side splits that revealed shapely human like legs. She wore knee length black sequenced high heeled boots. A stunning crown encrusted with diamonds, emeralds, rubies, sapphires rested atop her head. The Impressive crown was almost six inches high and the tallest crown ever worn by anyone ever in Mbaba. Her hair was bright red and black, thick with curly waves that extended just below the shoulders. Her skin color was stunning in tone and texture. The color was reddish-pink but smooth, shimmery. Her dress was a glittering sensation, grey satin with red rubies sewn into it. Her eyes were the most sensational thing about her. They were large and oval shaped with a radiant Turquoise color. They were the most beautiful hypnotic eyes he had ever seen. She stood there, waved, and curtsied too. By far she was the most beautiful Formica Queen who had ever ruled the Formica Kingdom from her Queenly abode, Fantasy Castle.

Almost every insect was wary of the deadly Argentinean Formicas. They were the most formidable species in all of Mbaba. *Look at all my loyal underlings. How they adore me. They had better. I wish I felt happy instead of miserable and lonely. I hope that my cousin Adui will make me laugh.* Adui stared mouth open wide eyed at his cousin the Queen. My cousin grew so large and beautiful too, with a voice so manly, loud and deep. How is that possible?

"My loyal underlings we have a very special guest here; my cousin Adui from the North! Let us greet him kindly."

All the Formicas' clicked their antennae and approved of Adui and he appreciated the applauses. He looked back at the Queen, mesmerized by her gorgeous sea blue-green large eyes. Adui did not realize that he was being welcomed as he was set to be the next meal offering.

"Cousin Adui from the North, what pray tell would have you so desperate to see me after all these years? I really cannot blame you because you must have heard about my great beauty and came to admire it. I believe you brought gifts too."

Adui thought of approaching closer but remained where he stood a few feet away from the stage. She sat on her large throne that had been carried over, still looking very regal. Now he stared at her through the glass. *How odd that she would have her food placed in that large metal human spoon. I wonder why?*

"Dear Cousin, you have picked the perfect day to visit with me – or maybe not. It depends on whether Uno and Dos were successful on their royal mission."

Adui spoke answering on their behalf. "Your royal bewitching and stunningly beautiful Queen, you're drones were successful because I provided the help they needed to fulfill your wishes, in spite of my long exhausting trip. If it were not for me, they would have failed. I made sure they didn't lose one precious drop."

"Really and truly, my dear cousin, you made sure I got all of this delightful food? I adore you, Adui." Enchantress clicked her antennae so quickly they fired sparks. She began to rub her belly while she looked at her food. She smiled with anticipation but then frowned when she looked at her drones and Adui.

"Why should I believe you? How could you be capable of helping anyone? You are brainless! I am the most royal of all Queens. You wouldn't dare lie!" She cackled as she spoke, "Because here in this kingdom lie rhymes with die!"

Adui was about to respond but he was stopped by Dos' hand on his shoulder. He looked at Dos with eyes glowing in anger and shrugged off Dos' hand. He too had a quick temper and forced himself to keep his arms by his side.

"Humans just like this food, but I love it! Who would believe that they're allowed eat food fit only for a Queen like me? It's not fair the way humans get the best food to eat. I am royalty so I am privileged as well and should not have to pay for it. My clever drones' found a way to ensure we never pay for it. The Humans' choose to honor me by using special containers' they call it rubbish but it truly means royal food!"

I can't believe what I am hearing from this disgusting Formica. How could she believe she is more fortunate eating this mélange of garbage?

This time Adui could not restrain himself and voiced his disgust. "Don't you realize that you are eating the left over scraps of human rubbish?"

Queen Enchantress eyes suddenly changed color and her pupils hardened into emotionless, cold shiny black orbs, burning with her fury, as she stared at Adui. Uno and Dos looked at each other and started to slowly shake their heads knowing what was soon to follow. She ordered her drones to take her to her food. There was a ramp attached to the side of her platform and her drone servants carried her throne down the ramp. At the bottom of the ramp, Enchantress ordered them to stop and scuttled down off her throne. She walked down a smaller ramp towards the door that connected her throne room to where Adui, Uno and Dos now stood. As she neared the door she disappeared from view.

The double doors were flung open and she walked out from behind curtains straight towards them. When she appeared, Adui gasped aloud and looked around surprised. Hundreds of angry eyes stared at him and he realized he was in this alone. He shook his head to clear the shock of the unexpected visage before him. *She's an illusion; her beauty, size, and her crown somehow have been imaginations held above her head.*

Oh, my God, Her face isn't that beautiful just plain with a long pointy nose, ordinary, and tiny too. Her hair is black and spiked. How does she create the magic and the voice?

He rubbed his eyes then rubs them again harder, knocked himself on the side of his head, attempted to clear it. He wondered if he suffered from some kind of trauma.

"Is that the same Queen I saw behind the glass? How can this be?" "She is exactly the same Queen, just as powerful and more beautiful in person." Uno exclaimed.

Now Adui, you will know firsthand the price of honesty everyone in this Kingdom bears, pretending she looks the same to stay alive. I will have much fun watching you suffer." I told you Dos, my brain is much bigger than his. Dos, this will be the most fun we will ever have with this estupido Umuvi."

"Yeah Bro, I really like how you are letting him suffer! Let the Queen eat him piece by piece."

Adui still oblivious to being setup, still silently chastised the Enchantress. "Those drones must have been behind that glass holding her crown above her head, but I couldn't see them. That glass has magical powers or I am losing my mind. Her voice; was that real too?"

Queen Enchantress stood on top of the pile of food, still visible because she was beyond the average size of Formica. Two big, tall, powerful drones held her crown above her head. She waved at her audience as they clicked their antennae and clapped then cheered.

Adui watched, eyes and mouth wide from seeing how large her mouth was, almost the length of her body when opened two rows of pointy teeth were visible she smiled suddenly she began to eat with frantic speed.

When Adui saw her eating, he could only stare in awe. The manner in which she engorged her food was horrifying. She spewed food crumbs in every direction as she ate voraciously and insatiably.

The crumbs fell on them like rain. All of the drones present ducked behind their shields, preventing the mixed crumbs and spittle from striking them. She was like a buzz-sawing ravenous termite. Within minutes all the food was unbelievably gone. To add to Adui's shock and awe just as she finished the last morsel from her colossal meal she belched, a belch so loud that the ground shook.

Her Royal Crown holders returned with the main throne and placed it in the center of the empty platter. She then scuttled back up the stairs and rested her smaller frame on it. Beside her the drone Throne Carriers took a step back. They were freakishly tall giants larger than Adui, and so tall that they stood taller than her throne.

This allowed them to still hold the crown above her head, despite her elevated position. Settling in after her meal, Enchantress sat there and frowned, her eyes glowed an eerie red when she watched Adui who stood there eyes covered.

"Is she finished yet? I cannot bear to look at her, she is so un-natural, hideous, and reminds me of humans." he whispered.

"How dare you insult our Queen, the royalist Queen of all by comparing her to Humans?" Uno said loudly.

"Yeah, you have no class; you're just an estupido drone!" Dos said. "Brother, we should kill him now," Dos said.

When Adui heard their words, he uncovered his eyes and to his dismay everyone was staring at him, surrounding him, directly. He gulped silently, before dropping to one knee in submission, with his hands held together as if in praying. His face was ridden with anxiety.

He suddenly realized that he had been overheard remembering the powerful hearing abilities of the Formica.

"You my dear, sweet, cousin are my guest. Surely, you must be hungry from travelling." Enchantress asked.

Enchantress sat high on her throne. Her powerful eyes were now turquoise blue, staring at him unrelentingly as she waved and smiled.

Suddenly she belched so loud it echoed in the room. She gestured Adui forward and he was bumped from behind and stood up.

"Yes, yes, I am famished, simply starving!" He looked at Uno and Dos with a smirk on his face and moved towards the eating area.

"Well then I will let you have the honor of serving me your food. You did bring me food? There is no better way to demonstrate your true devotion to me than by starving yourself for your new Queen."

At this invitation the guests made additional gift offerings. Her "guests" always had food and were prepared to offer their gift for their mighty Queen's bottomless pit appetite. The invited guests ate prior to accepting their invitation to dine with her, wanting to avoid the revulsion Adui was now faced with. The guests knew and they acknowledged their visit as a privileged honor to watch her eat it was the only entertainment in the colony.

"What, how dare you ask that of me?" Adui said loudly. "I will not be starved!"

"No, you will not be starved." She gave a nod of her head and two powerful drones seized him, pulling him forward to the feeding spoon.

"You will eat till your fill and then I will eat you!"

He looked at her, flabbergasted. He held his hand to his mouth, shocked. Suddenly, he went down on his knees and could only stare at her. When he looked up at Uno and Dos, they had knowing smirks on their faces again. "My royal and most beautiful cousin, as your guest and royal relation, your hospitality would surely be generous towards your cousin?"

"Which is more Important, my appetite or yours?" she asked quietly. "Dear cousin, I have suffered much during this treacherous journey. Naturally, I expect you to provide me with food I need to eat, and deserve too, as much as you do."

Her massive drones, while using one hand to hold the crown above her head, used their other hand to support the Queen who suddenly stood up on her throne. Everyone in the audience had their heads bowed. Uno and Dos on their knees looked at each other, frowned then looked down on the ground.

Dos he is not so smart eh?

No Uno, I could almost feel sorry for him if I did not hate him so much.

Uno, I think I feel pity for him. Do you? No, he isn't worth it. I want him destroyed!

Suddenly, Enchantress screamed thunderously, releasing an eardrum shattering fury. Her eyes were now glossy black orbs, shining with madness and mad intent. She struggled to not say the words that would make her drones tear Adui apart. Gaining control she admonished Adui, cackling before she spoke.

"How dare you expect me to share my food with you and want hospitality too? That's not the proper way to treat a guest in my kingdom.

You insult me. Is it not your duty to care only about my hunger and wellbeing, Umuvi?"

The guests watched, fascinated because no one had ever spoken to their Queen like Adui. Their conversation would become unforgettable and gossiped about for many years to come.

"You don't have intelligence but you do have eyes and can see that an enormously beautiful Queen like me needs to eat as much as possible to maintain my status. You mindless drone should realize that there is not enough food for the both of us!"

"You are so tiny. How can you possibly eat so much?" Adui asked in shock.

"Tiny, you called me tiny? My underlings, my poor cousin is demented. He is brainless so he doesn't realize what he is saying. We all know that I am the largest and most powerful Queen in the world!"

Enchantress maintained her rule not only physically but telepathically as well. She had chosen her royal crown holders single handedly for the trait of being able to communicate telepathically. It was through this communication that they obeyed her every command as if led by an invisible cord. The consequences of not doing so would ultimately be tragic and final, having been advised their heads would explode if they ever disobeyed her. So when she suddenly flew back to her throne behind the glass panels, they stood at her side, crown in place. Adui once more recoiled at her larger than life size and shook when her eyes met his, being bright red and full of fury. He noticed how Enchantress eye color changed with her moods.

Adui tried to back away but Uno and Dos lifted him up and placed him in front of their Queens' glass panel. Uno held his neck forcing

Adui to face her until his face was within one inch of the glass. He was mesmerized, captivated by her gorgeous eyes. When she saw him before her, she got up from her throne and walked towards the glass until her face was also within one inch of his. Her beautiful painted red full lips smiled gently, her now dreamy blue eyes gazed at him.

"Dear cousin, do you know what I expect of you?"

"Yes. I am willing to give you whatever you want to make you happy." "Does that include your own self? Ah, I am pleased that you want the honor of letting me eat you, but I don't think my royal belly can stomach the taste of you!"

Uno and Dos gasped and looked at each other, surprised that even he could suffer the same fate as them. Adui tried to pull away but they were too strong and held him tightly. When his eyes rolled upwards, they stepped out of the way and let him hit the floor. He lay before her unconscious.

Drones dragged him backwards at Enchantress' beckoning to their platform while Enchantress laughed and danced before her audience. A drone quickly threw a strange, smelly wet substance on him making Adui suddenly wake up. He sputtered and then pulled out his handkerchief to wipe his face. He blew his nose as he tried to clear his nostrils. He sat there until Uno and Dos gave him a vicious kick, yelling at Adui to get up.

-*Oh, so she did not do it this time, Dos.*

What, Uno?

Scare him to death. We have seen her do it before. I cannot believe he is still alive, Uno.

Yes, our Queen will torture him some more and hopefully succeed the next time, Dos.

Enchantress eyes when blue made everyone feel loved and adored. She knew and always used the power from her eyes to control her colony. "Adui, dear sweetest of all cousins, help me to understand why you are capable of sounding intelligent? Is it because you might have a brain?"

"Yes, I am sure I have a brain. I know that I have a brain bigger than anyone in the world and universe, my precious Queen!"

"How delightful. Shall we crack your skull open and peek inside to see if you do. May I remove what I may find? You are a drone and don't deserve to have one. What shall I do with a brain from a drone like you? Shall I eat it, everyone, if he has one?"

"I am no drone and my brain is not yours to eat!" Adui bravely responded but felt a growing inkling of fear that if he did not sway her Favor, he would indeed be her next meal.

"Oh, Adui, I was so depressed until now. Now that you have invited me to crack your skull open to see if you have a brain. I love you and you may not survive, but I know how much you adore me and want the honor of being my next meal. Sadly dearest, Adui, my guests didn't bring enough food. I know you will understand."

Oh my God, she is going to eat me.

Adui suddenly dropped the handkerchief he had used to avoid the nausea of her smell being unaccustomed to it. He stood there eyes and mouth tightly pursed staring into her cold black orbs. Suddenly she gnashed her amplified teeth and rubbed her belly, with one hand. The other hand slammed the glass pane beside her causing it to splinter. Strong hands seized Adui before he could take to the air and as he desperately struggled in vain, the Enchantress sang and danced her way back to her throne. He was brought to the edge of the steps leading to the throne a short distance from her.

Enchantress sat calmly back into her throne, looking down at everyone with her turquoise eyes, and blowing kisses. She pressed a button and suddenly the glass panel slid to the side creating an opening. Enchantress stood up and slowly walked toward the opening, which emitted a light that projected her image off of the mirrors everywhere. She stood two feet away from it and sang. She stared at everyone her brilliant, radiant eyes were like blue light that enveloped the audience and Adui too. They all stood there smiling dreamily at her. Seeing everyone completely hypnotized, she began to sing and chant. They were all completely hypnotized except Adui, Uno and Dos.

Come into my . . . love, Come into my love so it is the nurturing soil for your seed to . . . grow, Come into my love let it be the sunlight for your flower to . . . blossom, Come into my love for all to see your beauty on this . . . earth!

Suddenly a boy child appeared alone without his mother. He flew onto the stage and landed in front of the Queen, regarding her with loving amazement. He raised his arms upward and she bent down and picked him up. She kissed him lovingly on his forehead and held him close before staring into his eyes. He stared smiling; nodding his head then suddenly almost as fast of a blink of an eye, her enormous vice like jaws enveloped his head, snapping it off at the neck. Her Jaws cracked and ground the bones of the boy's skull.

A grotesque crunching sound could be heard as the bones of the child skull broke within her jaws giving way to the soft brain underneath. She spat out the bone shards and with one gulp ingested the whole child brain into her belly. She held the headless child until the drones quickly took away his body removing all evidence of the horrific crime.

The audience cheered loudly while Enchantress cheered back loudly hooting and hollering as if she was at a pep rally. Her powerful eyes froze their brains, making it impossible to react or remember her actions. The child's parents wouldn't remember what happened or that they had a child. All memory of him would be wiped clean from all their minds. Enchantress believed that if you consumed an innocent mind the purity of youthful loving thoughts would permeate her own mind, making her mind empowered because her brain was made up of young brain matter too. Her brain now rejuvenated enough to always be learning keeping her youthful and mentally sharp.

Adui was not hypnotized and fought to control his horror from the incomprehensible horror that had happened. A part of his mind tried to recall what he had seen but the image was being pulled into another part of his mind that needed to protect him from it. He shook his head to recollect what had happened. He knew he saw something but it was snatched away from his memory. He was shaking, terrified but still in a dreamlike state, in the wake of the calamity. Adui continued to stare not understanding why he was shaking. The colony was scarily docile as if like silent sheep, lost on a hill. The blue light faded within her eyes and was replaced with bright red. He looked around him and saw everyone was seated quietly and smiling while Uno and Dos stood beside him frowning, immune to her manipulations just as he was.

So this rumored nightmare of the Enchantress, being a mad Queen is real and there is no way to save myself from her madness. Now I know why others call her that. I will have to play the cards I have for leverage now as this is the best opportunity.

"My Queen, I am here to help and serve you, but most importantly save your precious life!"

"Estupido Umuvi. Your life may be over within the next few minutes." The Enchantress replied curtly. She cackled still licking her lips from the memory of the child's brain she had eaten. *He is a lot of fun, my cousin Adui. I love it being so evil and scary. I will scare him so much that I will crush his pride into dust. If he starts to act too smart as if he has a brain, I will eat it. His deceptiveness alone makes him disgusting and is repulsive because it is capable of dark ugly thoughts. He could be dangerous if he has a brain with intelligence.*

"I won't take the chance; I will just eat you now." He was dragged kicking and screaming towards Enchantress. She watched, smiling as he struggled in vain. Adui stopped struggling as he was brought to his knees. Uno and Dos held him tightly one foot away from the glass. "Please, please, my royal beloved cousin, there is a conspiracy plot to destroy you and your Kingdom!" Adui pleaded loudly.

"A conspiracy? Who would dare to conspire against me, the most beautiful, largest and powerful Queen in the universe?"

Everyone held onto each other from experiencing the most powerful vibration her voice had ever caused. Her unexpected reaction shook everyone from their stupor. The audience started to whisper to each other speculating about who it may be. Now some left their seats and gathered closer to the foot of the stage. Hundreds of powerful guards formed a barrier. Most stood up in their seats while some sat rigid with fear, all desperate to hear everything Adui had to say. Adui was enjoying the drama and curiosity, knowing the distraction created by their attentiveness and curiosity would be his means of escape. He knew this lie had to be perfectly expressed with utmost sincerity.

"It behooves me to say this." he whispered. "Say it and try saying it before tomorrow!"

Adui sighed loudly, wiped his eyes now looked directly at Enchantress sadly.

"The traitor is your cousin, Queen Star from the North!" he yelled. Her scream was so piercing; all present covered their ears falling to the floor except the royal crown holders who were hearing impaired.

Enchantress recomposed herself and she sat once more on her throne reflective but agitated. Rising slowly she walked over to Adui and looked at him. Her eyes were a bright eerie red as she rubbed her chin, now doubting if he truly had a brain. Her logic couldn't permit her to think star would attack her.

"My guests, his head must be empty to say such a horrible lie against my most beloved cousin Star. This foolish drone forgets I know everything. He's a pathetic Umuvi in love with a Nyuki that would never want him!"

The Drones all laughed loudly at Adui and he stood their fuming. Adui tried to control his rage but he couldn't. Uno and Dos' eyes widened from surprise, as he shrugged them off.

What does this crazy air head, brainless of a low life drone know? Star loves and admires me. That's why I can love her and believe that she knows I'm more beautiful. She would not harm the sacred tree she gave me the Inhlakanipha. I have not seen her in years but I can't because my great beauty would cause her to have a mental breakdown. I stay away because I

153

love her too much to let that happen. Our cousin Adui is a treacherous drone who's supposed to be loyal, brainless, and devoted to her. He is not worthy to live.

"Okay, it's time to eat and I am starving. Drones open his skull to see if there is a brain worthy of my royal appetite. You are a crazy liar and deserve the death of a mindless traitor!" she yelled.

Adui suddenly backed away from Uno and Dos but was cut off by other drones. All on the large platform, the audience cheered loudly as the drones encircled him. Prepared to attack, two grabbed him while two other Drones appeared and moved forward. The others on the platform looked then waited for her command. Adui was shaking, struggling to free himself then suddenly stopped when he saw her dreamy blue eyes. He quickly closed his eyes and stood still, before erupting in a booming voice that almost matched the Enchantresses'.

"There Humans are here. Star has commanded them to attack you!" This stopped the Drones. They suddenly froze as if dipped in ice. Adui spread his Iron clad wings and spun around knocking those who surrounded him to the ground before commandingly stepping forward. "Three humans who will bring you to your doom, in the same way they destroyed the Inhlakanipha tree!"

Everyone was motionless, stunned by the word, humans for they were the most dreaded of all species. The Formica colony all read about them and thought they were nature destroyers. Enchantress grabbed onto her royal crown holders to save herself from collapsing.

"What humans? How . . . how can that be true?" she asked.

"My Queen, it is true head reporter agent sixty-six confirmed this with me. That Umuvi is telling the truth!" Agent sixty said.

My stomach is hurting. How strange.

When Adui saw her expression, her eyes now orange, she looked shocked and frightened. He knew she had forgotten about eating him, for now.

I must keep her eyes orange, as that shows the state of her confusion . . . I can control her if Enchantress is frightened. Shock is the best way to stop a nut case like her. Thank God it worked. I hate what I am doing to Star, but I cannot stop now. I must save myself. "Star has not only betrayed you by having Humans, she let them break her oath to you too. Allowing them to eat all of your sacred unlamvu and now they have transformed into 'Inhlakanipha Inyasis'. They are hideous looking creatures and dangerous too."

"My Unlamvu, my precious Inhlakanipha is barren? She let humans eat my sacred fruit and now they are in her colony? " Enchantress screamed and held her hands in front of her face, frantically shaking her head then she looked up laser beams of red shot out at everyone. The audience covered their eyes until they changed back to orange. She stood in behind her glass motionless. Every one watched, as she now stood before her magic glass suddenly pounded on it in fury. Then she dropped to the floor and crouched on her knees. She struck great blows into the floor causing large cracks to appear in the staircase, simultaneously yelling "I want my unlamvu! I want my beautiful unlamvu!" No one dared touch her as her enlarged image was like watching a naughty, spoiled child on a big screen TV having a temper tantrum.

"Can you believe it, Dos? She loves the sacred fruit from Inhlakanipha so much that it's the only thing that she would not eat?"

"The Queen Nyuki, Star, was supposed to guard it with her life, Uno!"

That cousin Adui, he is dangerous. Maybe I should not eat his brain; it could destroy the superpowers of mine. I know what I should do. I will use him against Star!

All of them watched as she returned to her throne and sat on it while she looked at her audience with beautiful turquoise blue eyes, smiling and relaxed. "Are they beautiful, those human inyasis'? God only created two beautiful living things in the world; the Inhlakanipha and me. Now do these human inyasis' have the same colors as my Unlamvu?" *Star can never become more beautiful. She is my best and only friend but now*

I need to destroy her too. I hate you Star for being so selfish and keeping the Humans. I must own and eat these humans which will make me more beautiful.

"Why did she keep the humans? Is she is trying to be more powerful than me? Can they make her more beautiful?"

It dawned on Adui that he could kill two birds with one stone. I must be very careful with this answer and lie well to Enchantress. *I can have Enchantress dispose of the children and then meet her end at my hand.*

"Why nothing on this earth could be more beautiful or powerful than you, dear cousin, not even Star. Those humans' are repulsive and torture to look at. Worst of all is that female one who is the most revolting of them all."

"You mean, dear cousin, that by some miracle someone could be uglier than you?"

The audience laughed loudly with Enchantress as she pointed at Adui. Suddenly his eyes glowed yellow and his mouth puckered. He looked terrifying. When he turned to look around, his eyes silenced all but Enchantress.

Adui makes me uncomfortable. I need to destroy him but at a later time.

"We both have red on our bodies so we are alike in some ways dear cousin Enchantress."

"Are you blind too, Umuvi? You do not have any colors on you that are beautiful like mine. However I do like the combination of pink and red in your eyes. Maybe if I eat them, my eyes will have that color too." "Eat my eyes? I need them to see. If you want the same eye color, you can have these."

Adui bent his head down and with a trembling finger; he quickly plucked out his contacts. When he looked up at everyone, the solid light grey made his eyes even more frightening. His colorless eyes were like windows of death. Grey was the color of death in Mbaba and extremely frightening too all. He heard everyone scream too, when Enchantress did. In his trembling hand the red and pink orbs just sat there. Some of the males and females fainted from shock, even the big strong guards.

Uno and Dos grabbed onto each other and backed away.

"How dare you! Put your eyes back in, you disgusting Umuvi!" Enchantress yelled. She feared his new look as all in Mbaba had been taught that to see gray was to see death.

With shaky hands, he popped the contacts back onto his eyes then looked up at her smiling. Enchantress lost her appetite.

"What does Star think of the human inyasi?"

"She believes they are the most beautiful of all Gods creations. Especially that despicable female one."

Uno, bro, he really hates those human inyasis'.

Yeah, look at his face. It's pretty scary, eh Dos?

Uno looked at his brother, who shrugged his shoulders as the audience leaned forward, gripping the seat handles tightly. Some who were standing backed away as they watched their Queen get off her throne. Suddenly, Enchantress pressed her face to the glass. Everyone looked at the largest black glittery orbs ever seen. Her lips were squished against the glass. Her eyes narrowed then she began to pound on the glass again.

My plan is working. I can see the insanity building in her eyes. I wish I knew what kind of madness I would be dealing with before I came here. I must find a way to leave and have it deliver vengeance in my wake.

Enchantress stepped back and danced around the stage singing off key as she danced back to her throne. Her eyes made her singing sound beautiful to everyone but Adui.

"Umuvi, you believe that another female has a beauty that Star envies more than mine?"

"Yes. She said that female is by far the most beautiful of all God's creations."

He watched her eyes return to their hypnotic blue and she blew kisses into the camera.

"My beloved Star has found a way to make me more beautiful by creating these human inyasis' for me to devour. She wants me to become all the more bewitchingly gorgeous Queen of all. I will conquer her Kingdom, eat her humans, and you too. I believe by some miracle you have a brain. Guards take out that brain for me, my appetite is returning."

They grabbed Adui and held him down while one large drone held the axe in his powerful arms. Slowly the drone raised the axe but suddenly stopped just before it sliced off his head. The drones looked up at their Queen and bowed then left. Everyone rose from their seats protesting, angry that he wasn't beheaded. Adui grabbed his neck as he sat on the stage trying to catch his breath.

"Oh my God. I am still alive!" he whispered.

"Lucky for you, I just remembered why I cannot eat you now. You are devious, evil, and nasty too. I like that. Therefore, I will spare your life for now and use you to set the trap to attack Star's kingdom. Your fantasy stories better be true. Now get him out of my sight!"

"I swear I am telling the truth. Please believe me."

She laughed as he shouted for his release in protest as they dragged him away.

*   *   *

Queen Enchantress watched the ongoing pandemonium from the heights of the castle. The colony was still reacting about the Humans.

Some had to be revived while others were crying or arguing about what to do. Her antennae, when clicked together, created a bright green spark when she transmitted information and didn't want to talk. Within minutes there was silence.

Good, they are all looking into my eyes. Now I will make them do what I want.

Everyone stared into her glowing, hypnotic eyes lost in her spell except Uno and Dos. They knew what was coming and guarded themselves against her spell. They watched the audience, blindly following her every word.

"I intend to punish that painful-in-the-mind Umuvi for upsetting us with his lies. It is not possible for that horrible lie to be true. Now go home to your families and forget you ever heard that story. Now before you leave make sure that you have deposited all your food onto the royal dining spoon. Now leave."

She blew kisses and smiled with all of them as they were leaving. All smiled and left quietly as if they were returning home from a fabulous party. Now alone, she looked at Uno and Dos and they stopped smiling. Uno pinched his brothers behind to prevent him from leaving. Uno and Dos then followed her to her private chambers. After the meeting, Uno and Dos left in tears and pain. Enchantress was smiling dreamily into her magic glass while she danced and sang. She loved the praise and approval she was receiving from the reflection of herself.

CHAPTER EIGHT

WHO IS RUNNING?

"My little Inyasi, where are you?"

"I'm right here, Queen Star, hanging out with the flowers, sharing some petal love with one of my petal pals, the Calitu. In this world it's so unique because of their shape, looking like a Calla Lily and Tulip. This flower's petals are so beautiful such delicate snowflake designs on the petals, and the colors are incredible too. Aren't they amazing? Now that I'm an inyasi, I appreciate nature like seeing it for the very first time. I get to pollinate to help this amazing flower to grow and spread more beauty. I never thought I could feel this powerful connection to anything like this, but I do."

Patience looked tiny next to the flower. She caressed the large petals gently and rubbed her cheek against its softness, smiling. Star and Violet flew side by side, now comfortable enough to give the children the opportunity to explore and trusting they would stay within the parameters. While out with the children, the guards gave them all their privacy by staying out of sight and protecting Star, Violet, and the children.

"Can you believe what that child just said Violet? She is learning to see beyond herself and her own woes."

"Star, I never thought I would hear those words coming out of that child's mouth,"

"You're telling me it feels like a miracle that Patience is starting to embrace her transformation? Violet, the boys have come a long way too. Still there's a lot of healing needed between them, especially Patience. Ever since I've met her there's a very different vibe I feel that I don't like."

"What kind of vibe? Is it because of how she was when you first met?"

"No, it began when I first looked into her eyes. It's a feeling that still won't go away no matter how nice she is to me."

"My love, I still have my reservations about them. I worry about if we might regret this decision to raise them. I just don't trust the situation."

"Relax, Violet. The colony seems to have partially accepted them."

"I just don't like this feeling that I have. That something very bad is going to happen."

"I'm not worried. Now, let's go check on the boys. That Marcus, I just love that boy with his gentle, compassionate nature. Theo, that child, is trying so hard to be a man before his time. I can see that he is slowly learning how to enjoy just being a child. Thank God."

"Amen to that."

Marcus and Theo were having a contest to see who would pollinate the most flowers. They would quickly fly to a plant chant quietly then touch flower than fly on to the next. "Theo, I can't believe it. Queen Star was right about work being fun. I feel like in this world work means fun."

"Yeah, Marcus, I thought she was playing us, trying to turn us into slaves, but being a drone is not so bad. I can deal with it as long as Patience doesn't get to mess up our lives by power tripping."

"No she's cool, although she's not totally cool about being an inyasi yet. Okay Theo, you win. You always win, but one day . . . you just wait." Marcus was flying belly up in circles around his brother who stood in the center of a Calitu laughing. Suddenly they heard Star and flew off together to find her. Patience, Theo, and Marcus found Star sitting in the center of the largest Daismar they had ever seen, with Violet who sat alone on the petal. Star motioned to the children who came and sat with them. They each found a petal and seated themselves and smiled, looking at Star.

"Okay, my children. Tell me what you all learned today."

"I use to think that only people made flowers grow, and insects had nothing to do with it. Now that I know this, I have so much respect for insects." Theo said.

"I realize that we all are Important and need to take care of each other no matter what species we are," Marcus said.

"I'm learning about harmony. It's amazing how so many different kinds of flowers and plants can live together peacefully. Even if they're different, still they know how to co-exist together. I think I understand what my Grammy was trying so hard to teach me about nature, and even in life unity makes the world beautiful. It's like if plants had thoughts they wouldn't think about hate, war or jealousy. Maybe they can't have thoughts and that's why they're so beautiful." Patience said.

Star and Violet looked at each other and then at Patience. Patience expression went from happy to sad. Even the boys looked sad as they listened to their sister.

"Patience, Theo, are you feeling what I'm feeling?" Marcus whispered.

"Yes, guilty." Patience and Theo said.

"Now, it's too late to show Grammy how much we appreciate the lessons she tried so hard to teach us," Patience said.

"I feel bad she tried so hard with us too," Theo and Marcus said.

"Patience, Theo, and Marcus, she is proud of all of you. You have got a witness. Just look up at the sky. Violet and the children suddenly looked up pointing, smiling, and waving. The children on impulse soared into the air and flew as fast as they could towards the cloud that resembled the face of their Grandmother but she vanished. They returned to Star and Violet once again and sat on the petals, heads held low with disappointment.

"She's gone," Twins said.

"It hurts so much when she disappears. I miss her," Patience whispered.

"Patience, Theo, and Marcus, she is always with you. Do you know why she appeared? It's because she was confirming what I was saying.

Do I have a witness?"

"Yes." the children and Violet said.

"I have never seen Ms. Mable but Star would tell me stories about her. God in his infinite wisdom found a way for her grandchildren to know that she is watching over you," Violet said.

"God took her and my parents away from me and ruined my life," Patience said.

"Patience, I believe that all of us are on a journey on this earth. We are born to learn and serve a special purpose and when we learn those lessons and fulfill that purpose, then we are called home to God." Violet said.

"What are you saying? That earth is like school and when we graduate we go to heaven?" Patience asked.

"Patience, you are a very smart young woman." Star said.

"Gram told us that heaven is like paradise, the best vacation anyone could ever have, but I miss her." Theo said.

"God had no right to take her from me and destroy my life!" Patience yelled. Patience gasped loudly as she looked as the flower's color lost its neon light. It looked dull without the radiance then is flashed back to neon she looked around her and could tell no one else saw it. She touched the petal nervously and then swallowed hard frowning. *I think I'm losing my mind – is that flower changing color? I must be going crazy.*

Patience suddenly flew away and Star told everyone not to follow and to give her space. Star pointed out things, teaching Theo and Marcus more about her world. Patience returned and sat down, frowning, everyone ignored her but she listened.

"Queen Star, I was wondering if flowers and plants have brains because they're a lot smarter than us." Theo said.

"Yeah. There's no racial problems, property, money, greed, or hate wars going down with them," Marcus said.

"They all live together in harmony. It's like Plants are the only ones that are not dumb, like people and animals," Patience said.

"We believe they have souls because they live and die too. Flowers and plants are the most incredible creations from God and his greatest gift. I learn from them every day about harmony and peace. They have remarkable intelligence in how they live amongst us. In the world's Oceans and Rainforests and here in Mbaba we have oxygen and can breathe because of their existence. We can exist because they provide food too. They are life, have life's wisdom and watch us but still their thoughts. Imagine how conscious plant life is. Plants are the most conscious of all species.

Plants live peacefully among thousands of species without being destructive towards themselves and others. They are quiet, still, and only move by wind or growth. They serve us, provide for us more than we provide for them. Because they still provide sustenance, regardless of the mental noise and destruction we create. I just sit and watch them to learn about how to not let thoughts get into my head that will make me not feel peaceful. Thinking and thoughts can make us lose peace, harmony and even love. I always try to remember what I should or shouldn't do so I can be like the flowers; beautiful and peaceful.

Plants get how to live right. I believe they should and can be our Shepherds that can lead us into consciousness. Patience you are becoming so wise and funny."

"Queen Star do you think that in this century humans and other species will learn to live together in harmony like flowers and plants. It's so sad that I didn't get why my Grammy loved plants so much until now." Patience said.

"Honey child, I pray about that every day. I choose to believe that we will just wake up become conscious before it's too late."

"Your right, Star we need to wake up and be conscious. It's like we appear to be awake but were asleep, walking through life. Not seeing and doing what's important, we need to become just like flowers, sharing our beauty without messing up the world." Patience said.

"I can't believe the thoughts that these kids are capable of I am learning so much from them." Violet said.

"Yes see Violet I told you they were special."

Star instructed her drones to set up the picnic lunch. They ate, laughed, and told jokes, but Patience became quiet again. She sat there forcing herself to remain calm as she watched the plants blinking on and off like flashlights.

*   *   *

"Violet that was some outing. Ever since these kids came into our lives, something remarkable always happens."

"Yes, they are very interesting, although still that child Patience worries me."

"I still don't like this feeling when I am around her, but I try to overcome it. I wonder if it's because she is a female. I hope that's all there is to it, Violet."

"Maybe that is so. Wasn't it fascinating seeing Ms. Mable Jefferson-Johnson as that stunning cloud? Seeing her validates my belief that these children are related to her."

"I wish you'd met her Violet. She truly represented innate spiritual beauty, and you would have loved her too."

"You know, why I never wanted to go back to that world after what happened to your mother, Star."

"If I didn't meet Ms. Mable, I wouldn't have." Star said.

"These kids are a blessing to me. I finally have my own family. Kids to raise, love, teach, and learn from too. I have you, Adui, and the kids I know it's a challenge, as it is I wouldn't give it up for anything. I love my new family."

"Today was another success they're learning and growing. We all are. I hope that when Adui returns he will have a different attitude. He has been away for a while and that is surprising. I am exhausted love. Good night, Star."

CHAPTER NINE

YOU DID THE RIGHT THING?

Star, Violet, and the children were once again on the royal balcony celebrating a holiday. Star's birthday was the only day that the colony celebrated. It was their one day off and everyone wanted to visit and honor their Queen. They the royal family and guests all dressed for the occasion and enjoyed the live entertainment. It was festive, exciting with the decorations, music and entertainment.

Star and Violet were laughing as they watched the children enjoy performing as well as the other artists that entertained too. Suddenly as fast as lightening, Adui appeared, surprising everyone into silence. The jugglers dropped their balls startled by his unexpected appearance. The guards suddenly stood between Star and Adui. She gave them the signal and they stepped aside. Violet insisted they needed guards when Adui came into their lives. Adui now stood in front of Star's throne trembling and looking nervous. Star, Violet, Patience, Theo, and Marcus sat and watched him silently.

Violet observed the children, who looked upset, but sat quietly. Patience suddenly got up and went to stand beside Star's throne, her eyes now red and green as she crossed her arms and glared laser beams at Adui yet he ignored her. Star and Violet looked at Adui and frowned at his appearance his clothes were ripped and dirty and he was not groomed. They noticed he constantly looked nervously around him.

I wonder why Adui looks like that. He actually looks scared. I wonder if my brothers notice that too.

"Oh my god, Star, thank heavens I had the strength of will power to survive the most treacherous of all journeys. What a miracle that I have finally come home to you!" he exclaimed.

"Well, now that you have finally come back. You must explain your disappearance. You've got all kinds of nerve, making me worry and stressing about you, Adui. In all the years we had our issues, you would "Yes I am too. It will be another day to conquer tomorrow so we need all the rest we can get. Good night, Violet."

They kissed each other goodnight, got up, and left the royal dining room. The castle was quiet. Everyone slept except Patience, who quietly returned to her room after eavesdropping.

You never stay away this long. You've been gone for two weeks over a disagreement just because you didn't get your own way. Adui, I ought to disown you!"

The crowd heckled him and as he looked back at them, his eyes brightly glowed. Their Queen clicked her antennae and they became silent. Star stood up and everyone bowed. Patience returned to her seat and looked at her brothers. She could tell they were scared too.

"My honored guests, I must apologize about having to leave but I must have a private meeting with cousin Adui. Please stay and enjoy the festivities. I thank you all for your well wishes. My children will also stay and continue to enjoy the festivities too. God bless you all. I love you. Take care."

Star, Violet, and Adui, were led to a large chamber that was another elegant dining room with a sixteen-tier chandelier. It was impressive and a circular shaped gold with a purple and gold spiral painted on its surface. The round table had eight ornate high back chairs, pictures, and spiral purple, gold, black rug on a black marble floor. Decorative gigantic planters with a lot of foliage were in each corner of the room. The guards seated everyone and then left the room. Adui sat alone on the right hand side of Star while Violet sat on the left.

"Adui, it is childish for you to hold a grudge. What kind of example are you setting for the children?"

"I was captured, held hostage, and worst of all almost made into a royal meal by our lunatic of a cousin, Queen Enchantress. I cannot believe how insane she is and why weren't you worried about me?" Adui yelled.

Can I do it? Can I deceive her again? Everything that's happened is all her fault, but I still love and adore her. I hate this war of thoughts, but she missed me so much. What am I going to do?

Adui, are you all right? Star asked, sensing something was amiss. "Honestly, Adui, you must stop the dramatics." Violet said.

"You shouldn't believe the vicious rumors about our dear cousin Enchantress Adui!" Star said loudly.

"They are not rumors! You don't know what I saw. I don't know what I saw!" he cursed his blank memory Adui looked up at them, his fist pressed against his mouth. Now looking at Star and shaking his head he sighed in frustration. Violet and Star looked at each other wide-eyed surprised to see him so openly upset.

"Adui, I'm getting the impression that you did something so bad that the guilt alone might kill you. I know you cousin, what's up?"

"Star, I have horrible news. Enchantress knows of the existence of the humans and about the barren Inhlakanipha tree. She knows all of it. She has spies, large drones that kidnapped, tortured and subjected me to the most horrible of terrors imagined. Inflicting starvation for days and worst of all threatened to make me into a royal meal too!"

"She knows about the children? What a mess this is now!"

"Star, I warned you that I had a bad feeling. This is it," Violet said. "Yes, Enchantress knows everything. Remember that she is an imperialist and has spies and reporters everywhere. She tortured me, trying to force me to reveal what I know about them. She was no match for my strength of will power, not even her threats made me betray you. I was positively unbreakable and clever enough to escape too."

Physically he stood straight being good at cloaking his emotions from Star. Internally however he felt pain as if he was being struck from the inside out. He held his head down low struggling to endure the pain he was inflicting on his beloved Star. It saddened him to share this news to strip her of her happiness. He closed his eyes, wanting to conceal his fury about her lack of concern for him too.

Because of those kids, she will always withhold her heart. How could she not love and adore me again. Oh, how she tortures my soul. His bitterness was too heavy and he voiced his frustration. "I must say that the peaceful existence between our Kingdoms has been sabotaged by your miss- placed devotion for those criminals. Thanks to you, Star, we are now at war!"

Oh my God, I told her we are at war. Adui, you fool she wasn't supposed to know that.

Star and Violet rose from their seats, exchanging disbelieving looks and started to pace the carpeted floor, back and forth, heads low and deep in thought. When Violet and Star stopped at Adui's side, he looked up at them both.

"War! Oh my God, would she do that? What was I thinking? I should've gone to her weeks ago and explained what happened. For years I have always found a way to prevent her crazy mind from getting out of control. Now she will think that I was up to something devious and I was keeping a secret. She will be furious that her Inhlakanipha is barren and the human children committed this crime."

Violet responded half criticizing and half advising. "Star, this is the worst news to receive and a most dangerous circumstance, knowing how mentally unstable she is. Now you have jeopardized our kingdom to save these humans. We can't possibly win a war against her army!"

"War, did I say war?" Adui tried to cover his tracks."The stress of what happened to me is playing tricks on my mind. Enchantress wouldn't declare war on you. I told her to expect an invitation from you to come to the castle to meet her new family your children."

"No! I know her too well. She is clearly up to something. Perhaps, we should leave and go into hiding at once?"

"If that is the case, we could surrender the troublemaking brats?" Adui suggested.

Surprisingly violet agreed with his proposal. "Yes, for once maybe Adui is right, Star. Let's not sacrifice our kingdom for these children. Star do not forget we are not sure if Enchantress is capable of heinous crimes. There has never been a threat to us and we have co-existed peacefully. We are a colony that never allows for wars. We represent peace and harmony. We cannot fight any war or possibly win."

"No, we can't leave. Listen to Violet. We know that Enchantress would not harm you or the kingdom. She knows that your army is no formidable threat to her. Why not invite her to visit and explain what happened. You have always been the one that she enjoys spending time with, and she loves you too. Once she learns of why you have them, she will be thrilled that you were planning to give them to her as presents. Star, your relationship with her is strong. No one else can relate to her the way you do. Let that be our shield and pray it is not too late!"

"Don't tell me you're going to listen to that lying ugly bug. He probably set you up just to get rid of us. Queen Star, he hates us and we hate him too!" Patience yelled.

No one had been aware of her presence. Star, Violet, and Adui, suddenly turned around to see Patience emerging from behind a very large potted plant, where she had been hiding and stride forward from the corner where she had hidden. Patience had noticed the entrance to the room when she was leaving for the celebration. She managed to sneak away from the festivities and quietly entered the room unnoticed in the midst of their discussion. She had only heard the last twenty minutes of the conversation but she'd heard enough to realize they were in danger because of Adui.

"Patience, you have no business being here!" Star said loudly.

"Oh yes, I do! It's my business when it comes to whatever that lying Umuvi has to say. I don't trust him, and you shouldn't either!"

Violet reprimanded. "You are an ungrateful, little brat. How dare you interfere in adult affairs that are not of your concern? We have this situation under control and my Queen knows what she must do. If you delinquents stayed in your world, our kingdom would be safe!"

"Patience, be still! You don't know my cousin Enchantress, but I do have a very strong and good relationship with her. We share a very powerful and unique bond and I know that once I invite her here and she meets you guys, everything will be cool. The last thing I need is a war zone going on in here between you and Adui, so please return to your room, Patience, and trust that you will be safe. It is best not to worry your brothers' about what you heard. I promise you there will be no war. Patience, we are your family and you need to trust us. Now go to your room. Good night."

Star blew a special horn and, within moments, the castle guards appeared and at Star's command escorted Patience out of the room. Star gave the guards instructions to return her to her room and not let her out of their sight, under any circumstances. Alone in her room, Patience laid on her bed looking up at the ceiling. One of the servants brought her tea. She thanked her and after drinking it she fell asleep. Star, Violet, and Adui, were sitting down and having tea and honey cakes. This time the bodyguards stood watch outside of both doors.

I thought I could be happy here but this place, this world is turning out to be worse than home. I am starting to hate my life again.

Back in the other room, Adui, Star and Violet continued to discuss the developing situation.

"I can't believe the nerve of that female criminal! Interfering in our private affairs! Star, those humans are nothing but trouble."

"Adui, if you were not so emotional, dramatic and not prone to immediate brash action, none of this mess would have happened. Instead of staying here and trying to get to know them, you had to go off in a huff and get captured." Star said.

"Yes, Adui, when are you going to grow beyond your mistrust?" Violet asked.

"You are long overdue to achieve removing negative, dark thoughts from your mind how is it after all these years you seem to have become darker in thoughts?" Star asked.

Adui looked at them both, eyes and mouth wide open in frustration. He sucked in his lips and narrowed his eyes. He gripped the arms of the chair hard he pounded it with his fists. Suddenly, he stopped after he noticed Star and Violet drinking their tea. They looked at him, their eyes were glowing red. He forced himself to smile and began to sip his slowly. Their eyes changed when he calmed down.

Oh that Star. She really deserves what's going to happen to her. How I hate that Violet, how dare she criticize me? That female human criminal always finds a way to make me look bad. I can't wait for Enchantress to get rid of her.

"Star the only way to resolve this is to invite her here. I forgot to mention that I told her how excited you are about the special party you are going to have in her honor, which thrilled and excited her. Enchantress cannot wait to attend and be welcomed. Just knowing you are having a special event for her has nullified any potential repercussions to our colonies. She is strangely excited about those humans, not angry."

"Really, Adui, do you really believe she will understand and that they and our Kingdom is no threat to her?"

He could not look away as he stared into Star's beautiful eyes. He noticed his heart was racing and his began to thump in his chest harder. He put down his teacup. They stared into each other's eyes with passion aflame and he could not look away. He was once again captivated and so was she.

"No, I don't. None of us are safe here anymore!" He whispered, burdened with emotion

Oh my God, what have I done? Her eyes are my weakness. I can never lie to her when she looks at me that way. Now I am doomed.

"Adui, we will leave in the morning. We have no choice but to go into hiding. As your Queen, I command you to tell no one and come with us. Retire to your guest room and be ready in the morning at first light, Adui!"

"Yes my Queen."

Adui slowly rose from his chair, brow furrowed. They watched him walk slowly to the door. He looked back and bowed his head with a nod before leaving the room. Their goodbye seemed to have reignited the previous fantasies of a life shared in marital bliss.

*   *   *

"Violet, do you remember when Adui came into our lives?"

"Yes. You were in your early teens Star. I had never seen a drone like him before. It was said that out of all his siblings, he was the most handsome because of his unique wings. However that was before he spoke. With so much vanity and attitude, it's no wonder I dislike him so much. There are other male species in Mbaba but he seems to have a mindset that is different than other drones. His mind is too negative and barren of any positivity in spite of being a drone. Males here are more subtle in thoughts and behavior. He causes negative emotions too."

"Yeah, he's quite a character. What a sense of style too. He is colorful from the inside and out. That's one of the reasons why I love him so much. From the moment we met, he always made me feel special and accepted. Maybe it's because we have that in common, being so different from everyone else."

"I have always and still do believe he is in love with you,"

"What? That's crazy Violet! He wouldn't consider any another species other than his own!"

"Like that's reason enough to stop him from feeling the way he does. Don't pretend you do not see it. He tries so hard to please you. Has no interest in anyone else. He talks differently with you and even his attitude isn't abrasive or sharp towards you. Thank God you don't feel the same way."

"Well there was a time when I wondered if he could be the one for me I thought about marriage. Adui made me feel smart and beautiful. Then I forced my mind to let go of such crazy thoughts. I have had romantic feelings towards him in the past. However, even though Adui is handsome and charming, most of the time; His mind and mental thought patterns are the reason why I didn't let my heart go there or want more with him. Sadly he doesn't have pure love thoughts or recognizes how important it is too. He is family like a brother now. Violet, still he is mysterious the way he shows up and seems to know things before they happen. I don't understand why he refuses to live at the castle."

"Well, love, hopefully he never will. This castle isn't big enough for the both of us. He had better not try to run off again. I would personally go find him and make sure he won't be able to fly again. I agree, Star. We should leave in the morning. It's best to have an early night. We are going to need all the rest we can get."

"Amen to that. Good night Violet. I love you and thank you."

They stood up and walked hand in hand out of the royal chambers. Unaware that once again they were being spied on, Uno hid behind the massive potted plant. Uno waited until everyone slept then he pulled out his map and re-entered the secret underground corridor. Dos ran to him when he saw his brother and together they left quietly.

CHAPTER TEN

WHO NEEDS COURAGE?

The children were escorted to the Royal dining room to have breakfast together with Star and Violet. They left Patience, Theo and Marcus, on their own after twenty minutes of conversation. Rosa stayed behind to observe them quietly and they pretended she wasn't there and enjoyed the selection of food.

Should I tell my brothers? No, Rosa is watching so I better not accuse him directly. I just know it that Adui is up to something. "Has anyone seen Adui lately?"

"Do you think he's the reason why we are taking a vacation from our lessons?" Marcus asked.

"Well we know he hates us. Isn't it weird that knowing how he feels he would be coming on our vacation?" Theo asked.

"I don't know. Maybe Queen Star and Violet planned this so that we can all learn to be friends with Adui. I think that's a good idea." Marcus said.

"What? Me tolerate him? Never! First Trevor and now him no way." Patience said.

"Patience, remember what Queen Star said? We have to think in harmony in order to live in harmony. We got to get along with everyone here and have no haters." Marcus said.

"I believe that only plants can live in harmony." Patience said. "Patience, you can't run things here, and don't let that ugly dude Adui get to you." Theo said.

"Yeah, if you do, he wins, so just ignore him," Marcus said.

"I have no choice but to try, even if it kills me." Patience said.

"How many days did Queen Star say we would be away for?" Theo asked.

"She's not sure because we're going on a journey to a place she would not say." Patience said.

*　　*　　*

Rosa, accompanied by several large female guards, unexpectedly awakened Patience. Rosa made it clear that she had ten minutes to get herself together because the Queen wanted to see her immediately.

Rosa was a very strong, commanding presence and Patience immediately obeyed not wanting to challenge her. Once dressed, she was led to another unseen library with many books, art, and plants. In this room there were ten large comfortable Daismar shaped chairs all in a semi-circle and a large throne in the center. Patience was surprised to see Star, Violet, Adui, Theo and Marcus there along with two very large male drones that stood at the entrance, guarding it to insure no interruptions. At Rosa's direction Patience sat across from the group.

"Patience, I have a wonderful surprise. We are leaving today for our family vacation. There are so many special places I still want to experience with all of you and now's the best time to do that."

Why me lord? Are you trying to mess up my life again? "How could you include that nasty lowest of low insect on my vacation?"

"We are a family and must try to get along, human. I will try because our Queen insists!" Adui said loudly.

"Okay, cool it! Let's all do this for Harmony. We must accept the challenge to face and overcome our differences and shortcomings." Marcus said.

"Marcus, you think you can run things now because you're in this world? Don't forget who makes the decisions. Umuvi, don't try to play us for fools. You be straight and we might be too." Theo said.

"He's not capable of honesty or decency. It's going to be extra hard on us to enjoy this vacation. Do I have to go?" Patience asked.

"Your brother Marcus seems to have learnt more about what Mbaba stands for than the two of you combined. I expect everyone to make an effort to treat each other with respect and try to enjoy each other too. You'll be surprised at what can happen if you try." Star said.

"Remember that Star is our Queen and we must try to be a family as much as possible," Violet said.

"Adui, Patience, Theo, and Marcus, you'll have so much to learn from each other." Star said.

"Me, learn from criminals? Why, those brats – I mean human brains – can't possibly relate or teach me anything!"

"See! He's always talking trash about us." Marcus said.

"Oh man, Adui, try to give us a break dude." Patience said.

"The only thing I want to do break is his neck!" T h e o said. Suddenly, Adui jumped out of his seat walked towards Theo but Rosa stepped in front of him. He stopped and looked at her angrily but Rosa met his gaze unflinchingly Adui retreated back from Rosa. Rosa then turned her attention to look at Theo directly. "Words of war to easily cause wars for no need!" Theo in fear and ashamed avoided her gaze. *Those eyes of hers! If looks could kill I would be a pile of dust!*

Adui watched them glowing eyes blazing hatred. *I can still win the war, but for now I must pretend to want this vacation. I still have a chance to get rid of them.* Adui realized his mistake at being so easily provoked by Patience. He stepped back and quickly returned to his seat.

He took two deep breathes then adjusted himself to appear calm, then smiled. "Vacations are supposed to be fun and I am willing to learn how to be fun, "Adui said.

Violet addressed the three kids directly. "Children, you can go and explore but only after we are settled at our camp site. You must listen to the guards when it's time to return."

"Cool." They said quietly, quickly exiting the room. Six guards, including Rosa, went with the children to prepare for their trip. Star watched until they were out of sight. Within two hours, they all left with about twenty guards for their vacation. They flew for eight hours resting in between. When they arrived at their destination everything was set up. It was a lovely campsite. It was still day light and the children were so excited by their surroundings. Star had her own tent while Patience shared with Violet. The boys were together, but Adui preferred his own. Star allowed the children to go exploring with ten of the guards and to return within two hours. Star, Violet, Adui, and Rosa, were in the dining tent having tea and talking.

"I can't believe were at war after all these years of living in peace. What a mess. I ruined our relationship after years of convincing Enchantress that she was more beautiful, powerful, and the most regal Queen in Mbaba. All that effort working on her ego and helping her to believe she is the most remarkable Queen was worth it because it kept the peace. How am I going to win a war ruling a kingdom of peace loving uju-inyasis' when pitted against the most ruthless Formica army?" Star asked. They talked for two hours and agreed to meet again when the children were in bed.

Star, Violet, and Adui, had a late dinner in the royal dining tent and the children were in bed. Star was pacing again while they sat there eating and watched her walking back and forth. Suddenly Violet stood up and she quickly went to Star. Excited, she grabbed then hugged her while smiling broadly. "I've got it. Why fight a war with uju-inyasi when you come from the most powerful species of Nyuki in the world? You can return to the kingdom you were born to rule, claim your birthright, and have your own powerful army of Nyukis' to win the war!"

Adui suddenly jumped to his feet and marched over to them. He stood face to face with Violet while Star went to sit down. She just sat there and stared into space, ignoring them both. Adui thought it was best to support the idea but under his guise of normal negativity. "How dare you, Violet, suggest the very same idea that I thought of too?" *That Violet, how I loathe her for being so smart. With an additional army Star might win and save those brats, who would forever be my curse as they have been before.*

Violet stared him down then put up a hand to his face to stop his tirade of words. She went to sit down, picked up her cup of tea, and left him standing there. He looked at Star and noticed that she was not paying attention to them so he returned to his seat too.

"I need to be alone. Can you please give me some space?" Violet and Adui nodded their agreement and left the room; they exited the tent and with a disdainful look at each other, parted company, both going their separate ways. Star sat there silently when they had left, perplexed and heavily contemplating the days to come.

*   *   *

Everyone slept peacefully except Violet. She left the tent and went to be with Star. Star was asleep and so Violet sat by her bedside and watched her, frowning. Star was having another one of those restless nights; she was tossing, and turning, sweating and mumbling. Violet used a damp cloth to lightly dab Star's her forehead fighting the urge to wake her up.

Ever since those children came into our lives, she started having the old nightmares again. Maybe tonight will be the night my precious Star will remember everything and begin to heal. I must be patient like her mother was and let Star's mind decide when she's ready to face the truth and finally stop blaming herself for what happened to her mother.

Violet got up and started pacing back and forth while she watched Star then she returned to her bedside.

How I wish her mother was here to help me deal with Star's feelings about her memories. What am I going to do if I can't?

"Mama!" Star cried out loudly. She tossed and turned and before Violet could move to wake her up, she violently screamed in anguish and bolted awake. Suddenly Star sat up wide awake sweat and tears streaming across her face. Violet in earnest quickly went to her bed and reached out to her while she sobbed. Violet held her for what felt like hours until she was silent. Star and Violet did not realize they were not alone. Patience almost ran into the tent but forced herself to remain still.

"Queen Star, are you okay?"

"I remember. I remember everything. Oh my God, she died because of me."

"Your mother died doing what any mother would have done to protect their child."

"If only I listened and never left her side. Oh Violet! I killed my mother!"

"No you didn't. It was that human female child who lived in the big white house." Violet cursed herself. She had blurted out the one thing she had wanted Star to remember for herself.

Star looked at her, eyes and mouths wide open. "Patience!"

"Yes it was Patience!" Violet admitted . . . "Oh my God, she killed my mother!"

"It was Patience! I can't believe it but it all makes sense. Now I know why I had to struggle so hard to connect with that child," Star said. She sank backward on the bed and Violet was to stunned to bring her to sit up again. Violet needed to sit down on the side of Star's bed. Her legs were weak and just stared wide eyed down at her.

"Oh my God, Patience murdered my mother! What am I going to do? I can't let her stay in the colony after what she did. Violet, I think I'm going to be sick."

"Lie there and don't move. I'll get something to help you."

Violet returned with a special tea and sat beside her. She held Star's shaky hands as she slowly drank it, and then lay back down. Violet stood up and got a cup for herself. After she finished it quickly, Violet returned and sat by Star's bedside.

That murderous child killed my beloved Star's mother. I must convince her to banish those children. Finally, maybe now she will do the right thing for our colony. These children are affecting our minds in a destructive way. "Star, you must banish them. We can't protect the human that murdered a Queen. Nobody will support your decision if it becomes known."

Star stared blankly into space so she never saw Violet's tears or Patience's as Patience backed away from her hiding place. Adui almost blew his cover but silenced himself when he saw Patience. He held his hand over his mouth as he danced away. He had the one thing that he would need to forever banish the children and convince Star to abdicate to Violet and escape with him.

*   *   *

Patience flew frantically away, almost smashing into a tree from being blinded by her tears. She finally managed to find a low hanging branch to rest on. She looked at her hand with the ugly scar and suddenly started to punch the branch harder and harder. Patience looked at her bloodied hand and wiped it on a leaf. She stared at what she realized was not a typical bee sting but from a Nyuki sting from Star's mother.

"I wish Star's mother's sting had killed me too. All these years I hated bees because I thought a bee stung my hand. Now I hate myself because I killed the mother of a Nyuki I love. Oh, lord, why do you always make my life so hard? When is it going to stop? All the stressing and worrying? I feel like I was put on this earth to get hurt all the time. Oh no. No way. It's not fair to make Star hate me when she worked so hard to show me love. She will never forgive me like I haven't forgiven the woman that killed my parents."

Patience flew higher tried to reach the highest branch way up far but her wings were not strong enough. She lay down on the branch then stared up at the stars, exhausted. This time she wasn't enjoying the unique orange, yellow, green and red stars that twinkled in the dark pink night sky.

"How am I going to fix this for my brothers and me? It's just not right making them suffer too. It's like I'm not meant to have a family. Everything always gets messed up."

Her eyes were like faucets that opened to release all the tears in the world. She wiped at her eyes with her uninjured hand.

Stop it Patience, crying can't fix things.

"Grammy, I finally get it about family, this world and everything. Love makes a family no matter how different you are or where you came from. Family is about love, being loved, and loving what's inside and out too. So I learned to love myself again even though I'm half human and insect. I have gone to a higher level of thinking because it doesn't matter what I look like, not letting my brain get in the way of love. It's about thinking with a mind full of love. I must try to be beautiful from the inside to share beauty on the outside. I get what you love about plants they're just beautiful not spreading hate but beauty. I am trying to be conscious of my thoughts and actions. I know it's so very important to just stop with the judgments and talking junk. It's so tough but I'm trying, trying to have a mind like yours that puts love first. Grammy, I get it now about loving yourself and others with a love-filled Soul. This news ruined it for all of us. I'm so sorry, Grammy. I have to be strong for my brothers and find a way not mess up their lives too. I better get back before someone comes looking for me."

Adui hidden watched Patience fly away from the branch above her. After Patience left, he glided down to the branch she had previously occupied staring out after her disappearing form. He should have been elated but was a bit irked and frowned at this.

"Perhaps I will be more elated when my deception has run its course. So Patience is finally going to get what she deserves. Now I know what to do to get rid of those brats. She ruined my life with my Mama and there's no way I'm going to let her destroy my relationship with Star too. Well now, Patience, you have always under-estimated me. It's just a matter of time before I make you pay."

Adui relaxed on the branch and fell asleep with a smile on his face.

*　　*　　*

Patience, Theo, and Marcus, were having breakfast with Violet until she excused herself to visit with Star in her tent. Star remained in bed, emotionally drained from the shock of what she'd discovered about

Patience. The children were informed that Star was not well but would be better soon. Patience joined her brothers' and went out to explore their new surroundings while Adui watched them from a distance he lounged on a branch and read his newspaper.

"Hey, Patience, were going on an expedition with the tough girl warriors. We'll see you later." Theo said.

"Patience, you've been quiet all morning. Are you alright?" Marcus asked.

"Yeah I was just thinking." "About what?" Marcus asked.

"About how much our lives have changed for the better. You really like it here, Marcus. Are you really happy?"

"Yeah, it's great now that were not fighting and Trevor's gone. I feel like we got a new family and we are family too."

"Yeah, I agree. I never thought that I would feel like we belong or happy here but I changed into something I used to hate, and now I love what I've become. Crazy, huh?"

"No, not really. When you think about it our Gram has always tried to show us that when you give love you get love right back at you. In this world, we get to see how much better it is to do right by others and for each other. Give me love over hate any day." Marcus said.

"Marcus, come on man, let's get going. Those warriors are waiting on us."

"Patience, it makes me happy to be a family again. I gotta go but I'm glad you're happy too."

"Bye Marcus. Have fun." "Thanks."

She watched Theo and Marcus as they played and laughed then flew off with the drones. Then Patience went in search of Adui. It didn't take her to long to find him. She remained out of sight and watched him lounging on a branch with his newspaper on his belly sleeping. When she called out, he sat up so suddenly that his newspaper went fluttering to the ground. Patience kept a comfortable distance but stayed suspended in front of him. Adui sat there with his arms crossed like an angered child and stared at her.

Lord give me the strength to deal with him. Grammy if you're watching help me!

"Hey, Mr. Umuvi, Adui I've got good news for you,"

"The only good news is that you little criminals are leaving,"

"I know how much you hate me and I can't force my brothers' to leave. I'm tired of this situation and I want to move on by myself."

"Yourself? I don't think so. Why should we be stuck with those hoodlums?"

"No, I need to be alone. I don't need the headaches of them too. Or maybe I should just forget the whole thing and stick around?" She watched his expression and it confirmed that he really wanted her gone. She slowly turned and started to buzz away.

"Wait!" "Why?"

Thank God he stopped me.

Patience turned around and slowly returned. She was not smiling as she stayed suspended in front of him. Adui sat there, legs swinging back and forth on the edge of the branch like an excited child, and tried to smile too.

"Really? I could be rid of you and you know how much I despise and absolutely loathe you more than anyone or thing in this world. I would do anything to free Queen Star of you. It's about time you do the right thing. What took you so long to realize that your presence here is causing a war? Now we had to abandon our kingdom to save our lives and poor Star is so depressed she is bedridden. This disaster is your fault. It's ridiculous and selfish for you to try and pretend you are a real inyasi. You're a criminal and never were meant to be in our world."

"War? Wow, really – a war might happen, too?"

How I hate him more than Trevor.

"You know this vacation is just an escape to save you criminals from the mad Formica Queen Enchantress. Sadly, Star's misplaced devotion to you humans broke the truce that existed between our kingdoms. Now her life is in danger too."

"First, I caused the death of her mother and now a war? I've got to get outta here."

"I will help you to find a new home that is far away from our kingdom, and then finally we all will be safe!"

Patience suddenly flew closer to make direct eye-to-eye contact with him. She wanted to look deeply into his. Adui looked at her and tried to cool the fire in his eyes. He feared she might recognize him. Her eyes narrowed then widened. She gasped and backed away as he watched her and then smiled maliciously.

Oh God, he reminds me of Trevor. He's not lying but can I trust him? I have no choice, I have to.

Good, this is turning out to be much easier than I thought. She still doesn't know who I am.

"Okay, cool. I accept your help but I'm not taking the boys' with me. So Umuvi you get rid of me or none of us. You choose."

I've got to make him take me alone. I have to be alone with my worst enemy.

"All of you criminals must leave." "Forget the whole thing."

Patience felt weak, landed on the same branch, and sat there with her head hung low. She wiped at her face, took big gulps of air, and tried to control the waterfall of tears. Adui's eyes widened as he looked around him nervously. He touched his stomach because he felt queasy.

As much as I hate her, I can't stand her waterworks. What is happening to me? I almost feel sorry for her.

"Okay, stop it. I will help you but we must plan this out carefully. Star, Violet, and those brats, must think there is nothing going on. Star will most likely leave to get help so we must pretend to get along creating a false sense of security. You and I will sneak out of the camp but you must promise to never return."

"I promise."

Good now I can redeem myself with Enchantress by helping them to catch her then eventually her brothers too. Enchantress will be blamed for their demise and I will have my Star.

"Okay, human, I will help you. Now leave me alone. I need my beauty rest."

He flew away to a higher branch. Patience stared up at him as he flew off; still trying to figure out if he was up to something. Reluctantly she too flew off, returning to the camp after she had calmed down.

* * *

Adui almost fell off the branch when he saw Uno and Dos looking up at him.

"So, Umuvi, you thought you escaped us, eh?" Uno said. "What are you two fools doing here? I mean you found me,"

"My brother has a brain large enough to deal with you," Dos said. "Yeah, estupido, you are not smart enough to outsmart me," Uno said.

"You always find a way to save your behind. Now I have to wait to destroy you because of your plans to bring the humans to Enchantress. She expects all the humans, Umuvi. She will not be happy with one. Right Dos?"

"Yes!" Dos roared at Adui. "I gave you the map, and tricked and lied to my Queen. Naturally I have a plan that will make my new Queen very happy. So be quiet and listen carefully," Adui commanded. He flew up to and floated at a distance where he could speak openly to them just beyond their reach.

Adui watched from his perch on the branch as they left, satisfied that he was once again safe from his cousin Enchantress. Suddenly he grabbed onto the branch, shocked as the tree he sat on began shake violently. He gasped when he saw the entire tree color change to an ominous grey. The leaves of the tree then all fell off like stones to the ground leaving the tree barren and exposed. Frightened he flew away returning to the camp and immediately entered his tent, pondering on what this meant.

Grey meant death in Mbaba and the death of this tree in this fashion shocked every fiber of his being. A tree does not die alone. Was this a foretelling of death to come? He pondered what this meant going forward and fell asleep with this on his mind. Unbeknown to him and everyone else, as they slept, Mbaba was transforming every plant and blade of grass color began to ever so slightly fade. Patience had a restless night she tossed and turned as the visions filled her mind of an Mbaba that had plants crying for salvation.

CHAPTER ELEVEN

WHO'S SAVING WHO?

"Star, you're up early and well-dressed looking much better, "Star smiled slightly weary. "Violet, these past two days was the most difficult of my life. I'm so grateful for your help,"

"There is nothing I wouldn't do for you."

"Good. So you have forgiven Patience too, Violet?" "Never!"

"Violet, she was a little girl not more than four or five years old. How could I punish an innocent child for something like that? She did it out of fear not malice. Remember."

"Yes,"

"Would our Queen Tulip see it the way that I do?" "Yes,"

"What does a true Queen's mentor do?"

"A Queen's mentor makes decisions with God's guidance and forgiving ways," Violet whispered.

"Are you living up to that code now? Violet, I have never had a better mentor than you. Do not fail me now!"

Suddenly, Violet went into the open arms of Star and cried. Star held her as Violet voiced her concerns.

"Star, that child has always been so difficult to know because she caused your Mama's death. You have suffered all your life from horrible nightmares and guilt too. However, it's not your mother's death I'm struggling with. I have forgiven her. You are right. She was acting as a frightened child. I am angry because of how much those children have impacted all of our lives and well-being with new emotions. I believe the struggle is with my faith. Faith in that it will all work out. I am so frightened for you. I don't know how you do it."

"I have to give thanks that I was raised to have a heart filled with God's love. Violet, you taught me about forgiveness too. Remember when I struggled to not hate my sisters or myself because I was different? I learned the only way to grow my mind and spirit is to learn how to love. We both know God can heal any sting to the heart. Violet, Patience isn't the same bitter, broken, disrespectful child anymore. Her heart has grown because of the love we put into it and we just keep on doing what we're doing. Enjoy watching it expand large enough to embrace all of humanity. Remember, she is next in line to become our future Gatekeeper too. Everything we do for this child will influence our worlds. She is no ordinary child Violet."

"Your wisdom never ceases to amaze me. Yes faith. I must believe in the power of love too. You always remind me of why I am so thankful you're our Queen,"

"Remember, Ms. Mable and Patience both have Jefferson and Johnson blood in their veins, let's not forgot Patience great grandmother Isineko Kuleni. Patience is the fourth generation Gatekeeper. We must always be grateful that they gifted us with this world."

"Yes. True. I must remember that and it's best if we do not tell Patience about what she did to your mother."

"I agree. Now let's go join them for breakfast."

As they getting ready to leave one of the guards raced into the tent with the news that sent them sprinting outside. As they looked around them and the outlaying lands, Star held onto Violet. Both were frightened and shocked by what they saw.

*　　*　　*

Star and Violet entered the breakfast tent but saw no one there. They immediately went to find Adui who was sitting on a tree. He looked miserable. He had heard their conversation the night before and was depressed about it.

"Adui, we have bigger problems than Enchantress! Have you noticed anything different or strange happening? Where are the children?"

"Yes. Last night I experienced the terror of a tree shaking me so violently, then it changed to a color I never seen before – grey, the color of death. Now our entire world appears to have changed as well – the colors are slightly different, dim and lifeless. Those humans are the cause! Now you see what why we must give them to Enchantress." *How can Star not be frightened enough to get rid of them Violet better help me to convince her.*

Oh my God! What if he is right? I pray that Star's does what is best for all colonies and our world.

"Adui, no need to get overly dramatic about this everything will be cool. Our plants are a little sensitive so calm down now where are the children?"

"They are safe out with Rosa. Is that all that matters? You no longer care about my well-being too."

"Adui, stop being a big baby. You know I do."

"Star, you stopped caring when you poisoned our family by including those criminals in it."

"Adui, I've got one war to deal with. Let's not make it worse. I am sick and tired of your jealousy. It's shameful!"

"I agree you are shameful. You claim to be intelligent and still don't realize that Star has enough love for everyone. Your mind, heart and soul should have learned by now to trust in the power of Star's love. You allow your feelings of insecurity to corrupt everything!" Violet said loudly.

"Really? You're destroying our peaceful lives for your selfish needs. Everything in our world is in danger. Isn't that shameful too? I am trying to save our world and you are doing the opposite. It's not too late. Let me take those criminals to Enchantress as presents from you. She will be appeased and then we can get back to living a peaceful existence," "No! You will do no such thing. I've decided to return to the Kingdom I was born to rule. I know they will help us."

Adui spat back. "What. Have you gone mad? Why would they want to save humans? They loathe them too and destroyed our sacred tree. Star, you are not thinking clearly."

Why am I trying to help her after what she has done to me? My Mama picked Patience over me to be the Gatekeeper. Now Star will let her rule her Kingdom one day. Do not help Star, she is not worthy of your loyalty.

"Adui, cousin work with me, I not going to tell my tribe everything, but I need your help. Don't bail on me now."

He got down from the branch and approached them. He went and stood before Star but avoided her eyes. Crossed his arms on his chest and then he turned his back on Star and Violet. Star walked around to face him and looked deeply into his eyes. He didn't want to see Star but she placed her hands on his face and forced him to look at her. He couldn't look away for her eyes were the most beautiful he had ever seen. They were why he had fallen in love. She stared deeply into his and felt something stir in her soul. Her eyes widened in surprise, her brows furrowed while he watch then Adui's eyes looked downward. He feared his feelings would be revealed. He looked up tried to smile to break the tension. She caressed his cheek then reached up and kissed it.

Adui put his hand to where she kissed him and held it there. He looked at her, his eyes widened and lips pressed together. She held his hands facing him, smiling.

"Star, if anyone can do this, you can. I know you can convince the Nyukis' tribe to win this war for us. Just remember to come back. I, we need you,"

"Do you mean it, cousin? If you believe that I can do this, then I know I can. Now I need you to help Violet to take care of my kids. If anything happened to them, I wouldn't be able to live!"

"What. Your kids? Those criminals, humans, how could you call them that?"

"Love! Love is the foundation for family, unity, and empowerment. Loving them has presented me with the opportunity to enlarge my heart, mind, and soul. The gift of love is to know fulfillment and completion.

When you love someone or something you have a chance to feel happy. It's no different from when you came into my life and I still love you. I'm a better Queen because of you too. Adui love opens your world, frees your mind, and makes grow a beautiful soul."

"You love them, yet these humans are not only are criminals but would bring about the end of our world dependent on plants? Our world is threatened by their presence. You truly feel love after everything they have done to destroy us and your mother?" His eyes opened wider as he put his hands on top of his head shaking it too.

Patience always wins no matter what she does! How does she do it?

Patience killed a Queen and ate from the sacred unlamvu. Am I losing by continuing to try and destroy her? Should I try to grow my mind and heart too?

"How do you know that? You've been listening in on my conversations again? It was an accident, Adui, with a frightened, innocent child. I don't get why you hate Patience so much. It's like you have a personal vendetta that goes way back."

Wow she is perceptive I must be careful. Now I must lie and be convincing.

"Star you can trust me to take care of your precious humans, just don't expect me to love them too."

"I need them almost as much as I need you!" Star said.

Oh, Star does care about me still. I have done such terrible things to her. Wow can I live with myself if anything happens to her.

"Adui, why are you so troubled?" "I feel awful, just terrible."

She hugged Adui for the first time in a long time as she spoke passionately about her love for all of them. How she wished they could be a family. Slowly his arms rose he hugged her having never touched her before and felt un-comfortable. He cleared his throat.

I can't believe she is this close to me. Just imagine how she would feel if I protect those brats. Maybe she will finally realize I am the love of her life and make me her king. He held her at arm's length and looked into her eyes. She was smiling. He stepped back to put distance between them.

"So, we're cool now and I can leave knowing that when I come back, we can get to work at being one big happy family?"

"Yes, of course. Go in peace knowing that your precious children will be safe with me."

He watched Star as she returned to her tent. He turned around and found Patience watching too. Suddenly, she flew away.

"Patience, I will break you if the last thing I do." he whispered.

*　　*　　*

Uno sent Dos to get an update on what Adui was up to and if their plan was working. Uno was napping on a Sungold flower, dreaming when he suddenly sat up, shocked out of his sleep by the frantic screaming and crying of Dos. He was terrified to tell his brother what he seen and heard. Uno quickly got down as Dos was running his way fast.

"Dos, stop the noise. What is it?"

"That Umuvi, Adui! He has a brain with intelligence, Uno. He scares me."

"Yes. How does he always find a way to save his neck?"

"He acts smart. I don't like this still. He cannot be trusted. He is in love with his Queen, Dos."

"Oh, yes, Uno. I can tell by the way he looks at her. It's almost like you when you look at our Queen."

"Dos, you are not capable of knowing how I feel. That Adui wants to rule her heart and kingdom too. He cannot have both. If he helps us to capture the children then he will lose his chance at love. But if he saves them from Enchantress, he will win Star's heart. He is clever and realizes he must please his new Queen Enchantress."

"Uno, you can see how much he hates those humans who are so beautiful. Why does he hate them or is it fear?"

"Dos, hate is a powerful thing. It is like an infection; disease in the mind that will make you do terrible things. When you do terrible things sometimes you can feel bad. That Umuvi is very hateful and values his life more than anyone. He will follow our plan. Now, let's find our Queen, I miss her so much."

They quickly flew in the direction of their Queen.

*　　*　　*

They ran into their Queen as she was on route to Star's castle with her small army of two thousand. Big powerful Formica drones were marching and some flying above Enchantress. She had a special platform built for the occasion with a roof above it as she lounged in between six panels of glass in a semi-circle. It had private chambers that allowed Enchantress to hide and a beautiful throne for her to sit on. It was unique in that the platform could be removed and carried on the backs of her drones. She had custom designed wheels for the long journey. She wore a fuchsia colored gown and her crown had matching jewels. Her eyes shone the exact same color as her ensemble. As they approached her they communicated telepathically. Enchantress was still unaware of Uno and Dos telepathic abilities.

Dos, we must pretend that Star is still at the castle with the Umuvi.

Yes. I will act extra estupido, Uno.

That is hard for me because I have a brain, but easy for you, Dos.

"My Queen, we arrived just in time to escort you the rest of the way to the castle. Everything is working out as planned."

"Splendid. You must tell me how extraordinary I am looking today."

"Beyond beautiful, my Queen. Right Dos?"

"You are truly captivating!"

"Dos, do not speak to her that way!"

"Thank you. I am truly beyond beautiful. I can't wait to see how jealous Star will be."

Behind the safety of her marching army, they arrived at Star's castle to discover they had escaped. Enchantress sent her drones to search the castle and they discovered that everyone was gone and the castle was completely abandoned. The Enchantress was furious!

"I don't believe it. They escaped with the humans! How dare they leave and ruin my attack. I went to so much trouble to make myself more beautiful and this plan my sneak attack was perfect, and she leaves!"

From her army of two thousand only five hundred entered the castle with their Queen. The remaining Drones in Star's castle covered their ears when she released an ear-shattering scream. The foundations of the empty castle shook so viciously forcing Manfred and his personal guard from hiding. He had stayed behind to protect the castle and pretend nothing had changed. He was immediately seized and taken in front of the Enchantress for questioning. She clapped her hands, delighted to see him. Manfred managed to smile while the other few inyasis' drones beside him looked terrified.

"Oh, Manfred! I remember you, dear! How are you?"

Manfred was visibly shaken and stunned by Enchantress's enormous size and voice. He wiped at his forehead quickly and tried to smile. He cleared his throat to reply with composure.

"Welcome your Royal Highness Queen Enchantress. I am well and thank you, your majesty. Welcome to, 'Hope's Mountain'."

"Thank you. Now, where is the Queen of the castle?" "Our Queen it appears has decided to take a vacation." "Where?"

"I am not privy to that information your highness."

"Well, maybe I would be privy to that information if I were to open your skull and devour your brain? Now where is she?"

He stepped forward from behind the other drones, as they were not charged with his duty. He stared into the large blue shiny eyes. He left his desk, started walking towards her as if in a trance, and stopped two feet away from her. He opened his mouth before the whites of his eyes were visible then passed out cold.

"Leave him. Get me out of here. I will find them!" She yelled. "That traitor the Umuvi. He lied to us." Uno said.

Enchantress immediately looked at Uno and Dos and Dos nodded his head in agreement nervously.

"He said we should get lost because if we are seen it would ruin his plans," Uno whispered.

Star dares to make me starve and still control those humans too. I want their brains, I must consume their powers. Maybe I should eat those estupido's brains for letting them escape. No, I cannot! They are brainless.

Uno and Dos stood before their Queens platform heads bowed low enough to touch the ground, trembling. "My incredibly beautiful, Queen! That evil Umuvi lies very well he tricked us into believing him. We will make him suffer for betraying you!"

"Uno you use to be remarkably lucky but now that seems to have vanished. This disaster and humiliation should not have happened to me!"

"Please forgive us, my Queen!"

"You know how much I need to eat those humans' brains. I want their power, I need it. You are lucky that my royal appetite wants nothing else!"

As Queen Enchantress and her army left the castle, she sang off key torturing everyone with her horrible sound. Manfred recovered was so overwhelmed he needed the aid of one of his assistants to get up.

Suddenly he screamed when he looked around him all of the plants in the castle colors changed they were fading some lost the vibrant Neon glow. Manfred ran to the front entrance and opened the door he grabbed onto his aid for support as he watched horrified by the transformation that was happening to his beloved land.

CHAPTER TWELVE

SURVIVAL OF THE QUEEN?

Star flew for three days and two nights south until she saw signs that told her she was now near where her powerful tribe lived. Her foster mother Queen Tulip long ago gave her a map to guide her back if she ever wanted to return and she had her mother's blessing to do so.

Star felt guilty about returning to her tribe because of all the sacrifices Queen Tulip had made to get her colony to accept her, in place of her own daughters. The uju-inyasis were her family and she never wanted to leave them.

After all these years, what if they don't accept me because I chose to rule a kingdom of a tribe deemed inferior? What if I come from a tribe that is racist? I have always wondered why they have stayed separate from everyone else. How will I deal with that? Mother believed that family always forgives. Lord, please help me to be strong enough to do what I must do.

Star was tired and saw a lovely old house. She landed and approached it cautiously. She knocked on the door and no one answered. Exhausted, she knocked again on the door and tried the lock.

It opened. The house looked recently vacated not being dusty or smelly. It was old but beautifully decorated. She walked towards the center of the house where several pieces of furniture were covered with sheets. She pulled the satin sheet off of one revealing a large black and gold couch. She stared up at the unique ceiling above it admiring the spiral design and its color of purple and gold. Light shone through the multiple windows allowing Star to see within the interior. She explored the entire house and smiled as she admired it's ambience before returning to the couch, where she lay down and pulled the sheet over herself. Resting her head on the pillow, she stared up at the ceiling and reflected on the current state of things . . .

"Okay, I made it this far. It can't be more than a few miles from the land of Taboo. I hope that that name won't represent my experience. I wonder what their Queen is like and I pray she is cool with me and helps to save my family."

Within moments, Star was fast asleep.

*   *   *

Star felt a hand on her shoulder and slapped it away, annoyed at being disturbed from her slumber. The hand was persistent and shook her shoulder again.

"Good lord Violet, can't you see I'm sleeping!" "My name isn't Violet, it is Storm."

Suddenly, Star's eyes opened wide and she sprung upright to look upon the stranger standing by her side. She found herself staring at a large muscular Nyuki, adorned with a silver domed helmet, fashioned with a unique emblem in its center. The Nyuki was clothed in a leather vest that bore a similar bronze emblem centered square in the middle of his chest. Below his waist the drone was enshrouded in long black leather like kilt that extended below his knees. His calves were covered by golden grieves that stretched from his knees to feet upon which leather sandals were fastened. His eyes were a beautiful turquoise that matched the color of the markings on his body. The emblem that adorned his helmet and chest matched the tattoo like birthmark that Star had kept private and revealed only to her closest confidant, Violet.

The Tattoo Birthmark and emblem was the mark of the Queens of the Nyuki tribe. She knew instantly that he was from her tribe – a Nyuki, a very large powerfully built male with strong arms crossed against his chest. He was all muscled, chiseled, beautiful, and proud, standing at his full height looking down at her his gaze unwavering.

"Who are you and why are you here?"

Oh lord, have mercy am I dreaming? Is he for real? Star sought to recompose herself. "I would ask you the same!"

"I am commander Storm from the kingdom of Taboo; I serve the Nyuki Queen Sunshine. Why are you here hiding in this summer house?" Star stood up seeking to meet him with level gaze but despite her posturing internally was unsettled by the male in front of her a position she had never been in.

"Are you lost? Where did you come from? Do you need help?"

So this is what the Nyuki males from my country look like. How they would tower over any drone from my own kingdom. Star felt flustered and blushed and unable to name the emotion and feelings of desire that swept through her, drawn to the bold brazen stranger in front of her.

May the creator have mercy on me; he is too beautiful to be for real.

I have never seen this Queen before. I know of not what kingdom she may come from but royalty is still royalty no matter what setting one may find oneself in. No Queen has ever looked at me like that before.

Why is she staring at me so? What if she cannot understand me?

"Beautiful Queen you are trespassing by being here without a formal invitation."

"Oh, I am sorry. I have never seen a male like you before. You're amazing!"

"What do you mean?"

"Where I come from there are no Nyukis' like you."

A Queen never spoke with such direct candor, a tact that seemed to have escaped this visitor. What a tragedy that such a beautiful Queen like her could possibly be demented.

"Whose Kingdom am I trespassing on?"

I cannot stop looking at the form of this being in front of me. From his stoic, bold face, sculpted chest, shoulders, arms and steely mesmerizing eyes, I can't stop myself from feeling drawn to him. A fleeting fear of the unknown feeling tinged her spine but instead of pain she found the sensation appealing and quickly realized it was her response to his allure.

Storm found it hard not to smile at the stranger, who was acting like a young woman experiencing her first crush. He had not been oblivious to her symptoms, having seen the same response from many other women. He was half surprised but half excited that he was able to evoke this response from the Queen in front of him. He smirked trying desperately to maintain a serious expression but the way she kept looking at him made it harder by the minute.

"I am the General Storm of Queen Sunshine's army. We are from the land of Taboo."

Recomposing herself to match his demeanor. "My name is Queen Star. I am from the far north; the land of Harmony and Queen of Hope Mountain Castle. General Storm, I have come here on urgent, serious business."

Storm's seriousness returned in response to her declaration. Duty came first to Queen and country. "I have never heard of such a place or of you. How strange. What do you want from my Queen?"

He can look fierce and scary, but that is not what frightens me about him. I'd better remember why I am here.

"I seek her aid and that of those who follow her to stop a war that could destroy us all!"

His sharp blue turquoise eyes narrowed while he massaged his chin watching her intently.

Why haven't I heard of this Queen, and how is such a remarkable looking queen unheard of? She resembles our own lineage. Could this Star really be one of us or is this another of the Enchantress infiltrators? Could she be trying by some trickery or magic deceive to me, her beauty being a tool of distraction to prevent me from seeing her true purpose? Her beauty is mesmerizing and her eyes are incredible. They show much feeling but are they genuine? I will not be so easily swayed and her appeal will not have any impact on Queen Sunshine. Before I present her though I must learn more about this war she speaks of.

"I am not aware of any war. How is that possible? You claim to have travelled from a foreign land to protect our kingdoms. Who has declared war on our kingdoms?"

"The Argentinean Formica, Queen Enchantress!"

"That is a strong and large army, but we are much more powerful and Queen Enchantress knows that. This cannot be true and you are trying to play some game with me."

"You are aware of our sacred tree, the Inhlakanipha?"

"Yes! We too protect it although due to matters within my Queen we have not been there for a while."

How strange this Queen is, that she knows so much of us and yet no one from our colony has encountered her or her colony.

"Storm, the Inhlakanipha has been destroyed and Enchantress has declared war on us because of it. Although it is all of our responsibility to protect it, she is blaming our kingdoms."

Storm's passion for what he was sworn to protect and had been laid to waste enraged him and he reacted rashly suddenly grabbing her shoulders, his eyes blazing with green fire. "The sacred Inhlakanipha destroyed! How did this happen without our knowledge? Who is responsible for this terrible crime?"

Thinking of her wards that she had left behind she responded with a half-truth. "I don't know, but my kingdom isn't powerful enough to fight Enchantress on our own. We must unite to ensure the safety of both kingdoms. We must hurry. Time is running out as we speak. She is on her way to destroy our Kingdoms and other Formica colonies have joined her ranks seeking our destruction too."

"Then time is short. Follow me. I will take you to my Queen. This is a decision best made by royal council. If this is the start of war then it must be planned for! Before that however the blood of the perpetrators of this act must be brought forth to wash the ground where the tree stood and soak its seeds so that it may spring forth again."

Shocked at the revelation of how the Inhlakanipha was re-propagated Star remained silent. She pondered revealing the truth of the matter rather than risk the children's lives in the event of words carried over the wind. She then realized however no words would come this way and no member of any Kingdom crossed into the land of another's without official reason. Violet would ensure that no word of her departure or the kids' actions would reach beyond their borders.

She would deal with one worry at a time.

Storm took her silence as acquiescence and immediately turned around, motioning her to follow. He went to the entrance of the house, holding the door open for both of them to exit. Once outside he gave orders to his Sergeant who in turn gave orders to the lieutenants. Star smiled at Storm as she emerged from the house. She was surprised when she saw about fifty drones in the air above them. Storm flew up to them and gave orders. They then dispersed flying off ahead of them.

Turning back he beckoned to Star. "Queen Star, please follow me!" Star soared into the air and they flew quickly towards his Queen's castle.

* * *

Storm decided to take the scenic route back to the castle. As scenic as it was, still it provided the quickest way back to the palace. Duty came first! It also provided distraction to the still unfamiliar companion he had at his side. This would allow him to study and see if any tale revealed that she was not who she claimed to be. If that was the case, her head would swiftly be parted from her shoulders to join those of the other infiltrators that adorned the outpost fences at the farthest outposts leading to the kingdom. The message they sent was simple. If you came here to bring harm, the harmful plot you carried would be your undoing. For this very reason Storm wanted to spend as much time as possible with Star before he introduced her to his Queen. He had doubts about this war and wanted to learn more about Star and her position and unknown nation.

Although it was the land of Taboo, it was uniquely beautiful in its vegetation and colors. He smiled, which was rare, and told jokes – but for Storm, each joke and laugh was actually a question that Star answered through her jovial responses. They laughed with each other and behaved like two love struck kids enjoying a camping trip. It was their last night together before Star would meet his Queen. His guards escorted them to a spectacular garden to dine. There was a lovely dinner prepared for the two of them. The guards watched over them and gave them much privacy as they sat and dined.

"Oh, my goodness! This is so beautiful, Storm!"

"My team never ceases to amaze me. This is a pleasant surprise."

He seated Star and then sat down and picked up a glass, pouring her some exotic nectar and some for himself. He raised his glass to salute her and drank. Star smiled and did the same as she watched him over the rim of her glass. Her long lashes framed the most remarkable eyes he had ever seen.

I never want this moment to end with Storm, but it must so I will enjoy it for what it is.

My Queen would be furious if she knew of what I was doing but I can't help myself. Star is extraordinary.

"We will soon be arriving at my Queen's castle. Tell me more about your childhood."

"Like I said, my colony is so small and far away it is probably why we never connected. I had a very loving family and three wonderful children. Their father passed away years ago and my sisters are real characters. It's funny how were so different from each other. You know the usual family issues when there is jealously and stuff. My Aunt Violet took excellent care of me when my mother passed when I was a teenager. It was a very difficult time."

He is easy to talk to and so beautiful. I wish things were different.

She is by far the most beautiful of all. How I wish things were different.

"You have children but no husband to return too?" "No, he passed."

"Interesting how someone like you would have no King and raising children on your own still."

"Yes. What about you with no wife?"

"No. I have no time for that. My career is very demanding."

"Tell me more about your colony Storm. It is such a lovely night." They talked for another two hours until it was time to turn in and they said their goodnights.

Storm escorted Star to her tent and then left her to join the others in final preparations for tomorrow. Star got ready for bed but felt restless and could not sleep. She lay there smiling up at the ceiling. Storm sat above her tent on a Tavo branch looked down at the roof of her tent, the laughing smile gone from his face, frowning his brow deeply furrowed in deep thought.

*   *   *

"Her castle is so beautiful. It looks like an Egyptian Pyramid. How extraordinary. The massive gold statues with Phoenixes carrying large female warriors of our tribe on their backs. I like the way they're positioned around the castle. I thought my home was amazing, but this definitely outshines mine."

"Yes, my Queen has exceptional taste. She loves African history, has a passion for her culture, and celebrates it in all that she does."

"Wow!"

"Yes, you will see she's really quite the historian."

"I hope she will do the right thing and stop Enchantress from getting hurt and destroying her own kingdom. Our poor cousin doesn't have the mental capacity to realize she is making a terrible mistake."

"She must be crazy to want a war with us."

"Yes, unfortunately she is. Crazy is as crazy does."

"My guards will escort you to our meeting room. Please wait until I come to take you to meet Queen Sunshine." "Thank you, Storm."

"You are most welcome."

They lingered there staring at each other, neither one of them wanting to leave. Storm took a deep breath, bowed, and forced himself to walk out of the chambers. Star went to the window to look at the beautiful View. Storm walked down the secret corridor leading to Queen Sunshine's chambers nodding to the herald who struck the gong signaling his return. He paused at the bottom of the stairs and when two sharp drumbeats sounded in response he ascended the chairs to her residence.

Queen Sunshine was always one to test his vows and from the moment he walked in to her chamber he knew this day would not pass without such an incident. "Oh, baby, I can't wait to give you some more of your Sunshine. I just know you how much you missed me."

Oh no. She is back to that nonsense talk again. Hopefully it's fleeting and will stop soon.

"My Queen, I have returned but I am not alone. There is another African Queen who claims to be from our tribe yet reins over one unknown kingdom and she has come her seeking your help. I would have not brought her here except for the reason she made the long journey which if true is extremely dire to us. Her name is Star and she needs to meet with you."

Sunshine was about to return to her mirror to have her attendants complete her regalia, but waived them off abruptly when the weight of Storms words resonated in her ear.

"There is what? Did I hear you right, Storm?"

"Yes. Her name is Queen Star from the northern part of Mbaba. She rules a kingdom called, Harmony and is here on an urgent matter."

"You did what? Oh no, you didn't bring another Queen into my kingdom, Storm. You better explain everything to me now!"

"Yes, my Queen."

He cleared his throat and recanted the details of how he had encountered Star and their journey here and specifically what he had learnt along the way. He thought Queen Sunshine would be mostly keenly focused on ingesting his recollection of events but instead she seemed to be fixated with an uncontrollable anger. Sunshine threw her brush at one of her mirrors and shattered it, commanding her attendants to disperse. They immediately left, needing no additional encouragement. She went into another dressing room and stared into the mirror checking her appearance, hands on hips then she smiled.

She turned around when she heard the door open and stayed in her dressing chambers.

"Storm, sit down. You just ruined my good mood because of what you said. How could there be another Queen Nyuki from our tribe and why is she here?"

"My Queen, I never knew of her. I am just as surprised as you are when I discovered her on our land in a vacant summer home. She is from our tribe but not like us. I brought her here to tell you about the war she claims we are about to be involved in."

"Bring her to me now!" "Yes."

Sunshine started to pace back and forth and Star one level beneath them was doing the same when Storm returned to her. His expression had changed. Now he looked stern, serious and there was no smile in his eyes. At his beckoning she followed quietly to the Royal chamber that was more lavish than hers. They were silent as they strode up quickly to meet his Queen. His eyes avoided hers, and she tried to do the same as he buzzed into her suite and they entered. Star's eyes widened in surprise and she smiled at how extravagant this Queen's suite was but still she was nervous.

Storm announced her presence. "My Queen Sunshine, Queen Star from the land of Harmony is here to meet you."

"This so called Queen Star had better wait till I'm ready to deal with her!"

A brash attitude was something Star did not expect and she responded in kind. "She's your Queen? I do feel sorry for you, Storm."

Star responded in anger unaware that she was being tested.

How dare that imposter insult me? "Storm you tell this so called Queen that my kingdom isn't big enough for the both of us. I don't care about why she came here. She'd just better get to leaving and buzz herself back to where she came from!"

With so much animosity this might need my intervention but I dare not offend my Queen. Storm stood unsure of whom to reproach or correct and decided it was better to let them argue between themselves. "Now hold on, Queen Sunshine, I didn't come here to try to interfere with your kingdom or your court. I don't want any part of it. I came here seeking your aid to save my kingdom and in turn save yours.

Though you may not know it, I have my own beautiful kingdom. I'm no threat to you!"

"You're in my kingdom with that attitude! Just who do you think you are?" *The nerve of this Nyuki who for all I know is from some other species trying to pass as one of us. Most probably an infiltrator as Storm suggested.*

Star turned and was about to leave when she sensed another presence in the room. Sunshine marched over to her and suddenly they were face to face. Both Queens suddenly took a step back, a distant long-forgotten memory returning.

"Oh my God, I can't believe what I'm seeing," Star and Sunshine said.

They just stood there less than a foot apart and stared wide-eyed at each other with mouths opened. Now they looked each other up and down as they circled one another twice then stopped face to face.

Though being far from identical to each other, there was something familial about Star that resonated within Sunshine. Both simultaneously placed their hands on their hips as if they attempting to mirror each other.

"The Enchantress has definitely out done herself this time. You must have seen some picture and used her magic to look similar to me. You're an imposter. Storm, how would you dare believe her to be one of us? She will die an impostor's death."

At Sunshine's threat Star responded challenging her authority." I am no impostor. There may be only one Queen Sunshine, but there is also only one Queen Star! I came here for your support not suspicion of criticism."

They circled each other again, both surprised by their similarities, which were further augmented by their differences. Storm stood behind his Queen and tried to remain indifferent. He positioned himself so that only Star could see his face.

Thank God I can see in his eyes that he is still on my side. I must quickly convince her or I will lose everything. Lord, how many tribulations must I be burdened with to protect what is just and right in this life?

"I am really from the same tribe but born elsewhere. You are my family, even though I am unbeknown to you. We must fight together to save and protect this land, all inyasis' and our kingdoms!"

"What fight? You speak of fighting others yet you have come here with demands instead of pleas! Do you want to fight me? Never have I encountered any other Queen, brazen to come into my sanctum and attempt to dictate my affairs. You claim to be one of us but cannot explain how you became Queen of another kingdom? An unknown Queen and an Unknown land, heralding news of an unknown war! Is this how the Enchantress would seek to unseat me?"

"Whether you believe me or not, War has been declared against our tribe the Formica Queen Enchantress is marching with her army of tens of thousands vowing to destroy all of us."

"What? Impossible! That crazy scavenger Queen declaring war against me? What a sad ruse to draw us away from our sacred home, to leave it under protected and vulnerable to attack. Enchantress would not be able to save you if you are lying and one of her infiltrators. A fact we shall soon determine." She motioned to Storm who moved purposefully to the hallway. "The scouts would have seen and reported any movements towards our borders. For your sake you'd better be telling the truth, otherwise your head will join the lines of others adorning the outposts!" "It is not my death that I fear but failure to act to prevent the deaths of others!" Despite the circumstances and Sunshine's skepticism, Star's response rang true. Before she could reply in kind, she was interrupted by commotion at the entrance. She spun round to see Storm striding hurriedly back with two scouts in tow as they entered the royal suites. He handed Sunshine a scroll which she unraveled and began to read in earnest. Knowing the rules by which she lived as a Queen, seeking to save her face, he made her apology to Queen Star indirectly. Bending his knee before he spoke, he rose and met her gaze. The other two scouts remained kneeling.

"My Queen, I have just received verification that the sacred Inhlakanipha has been destroyed. It is possible that Queen Enchantress would believe we are responsible and in such a state, she would not hesitate to declare war."

"Do you know of Queen Enchantress' movements?"

"No she is hidden to our scouts, but it is believed that her troops maybe moving through the underground tunnels. The Fire gate has been broken apart."

Queen Sunshine not letting surprise overwhelm her contemplated the revelations. "How did they break through the Fire gate? It was designed to be impervious to these Formica and all other species.

Regardless they will only get as far as the underground tunnels which will be unsurpassable. It is there that they will be forced to the surface and it is there that we must meet them and halt their march. It will be a few days before they reach that boundary. Send the scouts out! I would know more of their exact location, numbers and direction! Also send summons to all the regiment commanders."

Storm tapped the Scouts beside him and they hastily departed taking flight through the chambers windows. Upon their departure, Sunshine turned back to Star. "It would seem these revelations add plausibility to your tale."

"I told you in all truthfulness of the danger. Enchantress has declared war against our kingdoms and we must unite to protect our colonies."

"You may fear her army but I don't! I will take your statements under advisory! You must be crazy as well to believe that we fear that army. She's no match for us. She's crazy, but she isn't that crazy. I can't believe that you, a so-called royal Nyuki, would fear her army."

Sunshine suddenly started to laugh at Star and Storm chuckled despite his self-restraint. "I mean come on. You ought to know better than to think we would tremble at her footsteps. We host the deadliest army in all of Mbaba. Your blatant fear speaks to the heart of a girl rather than a Queen! A fear I would not have your bleating spread within my walls and borders. Storm, take her to the cells!"

Now Storm looked at her, uncomfortable, but at his Queen's behest moved forward towards her . . . Star looked down at her feet then back up at them. Storm and Sunshine's eyes narrowed and he cleared his throat. Star coughed. *Okay Star, you've got to tell them. Your plan isn't working.*

"Enchantress has good reason to declare war on us because my kids are responsible for what happened to the Sacred Inhlakanipha. Her spies informed her about what happened then she captured our cousin Adui and tortured him, but he escaped and told me about her intentions."

"What?" Sunshine and Storm said.

"My army is too small and not large enough to defend my kingdom and protect my babies. I need your help!" Star watched Storm and Sunshine unnerved by the expressions on their faces. "We are family and I would fight for your kingdom if you ever needed help!"

"What? Your brats destroyed our sacred Tree? They caused destruction and now you seek salvation on their behalf? How and why did they? Oh, lord! Storm, you're relieved of your position. I can't confine someone who carries the burden of such news. With what this so-called Queen is saying, she is better destined for the spikes! Storm as my war council, can you believe that a true superior Nyuki would be capable of that?"

"No, no I cannot believe this. No it doesn't make sense."

"You know it means death to anyone who dares to violate the Inhlakanipha. They should be destroyed or better to let that crazy Queen punish them. How could you want criminals in your tribe? I don't get it or you. Are you crazy too?"

"No one's going to take or hurt my babies even if it means war. I will fight alone for their lives if I have to."

Stars eyes blazed with the brightness of their natural color. It stopped them from talking. No one had ever seen Star's eyes so powerfully a blazed. Sunshine and Storm instinctively guarded themselves their own warrior instincts coming to the forefront. "This war has been declared due to the destruction of the sacred tree. We cannot be said to harbor the precipitator of this calamity." Turning to address Star directly, Sunshine continued her proclamations.

"None of you deserve to live because you failed to raise respectful, intelligent children. You lack what it takes to be a proper Queen. They're from your colony and may create future drones that can be poor examples of us. No, I can't let you live and destroy our powerful reputation we have. Storm if you destroy her and those brats then we can contain the situation. In the same action, their blood will restore the sacred tree. No one needs to know what this so-called Queen and her hoodlum kids have done. We are the most respected in Mbaba; her tribe is fortunately unknown here. We can't let anyone find out about them. We must destroy these Northern Nyukis'!"

"Never!" Star shouted and leapt forward at Sunshine but was immediately tackled and restrained by Storm. Storm held her at bay, his position fixed between both Queens. Despite her restraints, Star did not let her voice be silenced! "You think fulfilling Enchantress's intentions for her will save you! She has called countless others to her cause and all the Formicas' nations. You will not survive this without me!"

Sunshine scoffed at her. "We will survive anything and everything Enchantress throws our way."

Storm at this moment unexpectedly interceded speaking against his Queen. While their army was the most reputable and fierce and the Queen rightfully had faith in their capability, Storm knew all too well that the greater numbers carried the day. If the Enchantress had doubled her forces it could spell their doom. If the fictional Northern Nyukis did exist than they would balance the scale. "My Two Queens, Queen Sunshine and Star! We must resolve this peacefully. You both rule and represent the kingdoms of the most powerful species of Inyasis'. In the shadow of this threat, neither one of us can ignore our mutual plight. United we remain powerful." he said.

"No. She deserves to be sentenced and it ought to be our army that does it. After we've finished with her, then we to go hunt down her tribe and destroy them all!"

"No." Star and Storm said.

"What if she is right? Ignoring her request for mutual aid would be condemning us to our own end, my Queen. Divided, we will fall!"

Sunshine was silenced and looked at Storm, mouth wide open and Stars too. Both were surprised about who he was defending.

Lord, help me find the words to calm these two powerful Queens down and not let my feelings cloud my judgment. "My beautiful Queen, I believe it is wise for us to get involved and aid Queen Star with her predicament. Why implicate us in this disaster and destroy our reputation? Enchantress knows who is responsible for the destruction of the Inhlakanipha. We can never allow for a Queen from our colony to run from a fight. She is here because she needs our help to win. I say we help her and let the Formica Queen be reminded never to march north. This way we will keep our reputation as fearless warriors and not be implicated as being responsible for the disaster because we refused to get involved. However, the blood of the desecrators of the Inkhalapia tree must flow".

Recomposing and reasserting herself, Sunshine replied. "Storm, this plea for negotiation could well be a stalling tactic. If she does have a tribe and army who is to say they don't stand with Enchantress? There is still too much mystery about her! What if she and her tribe survive by some miracle and win this war, will any partnership end then? What if this inferior tribe attempts to become a part of our colony? If we do find them to be true and open our borders to them they will make us weaker internally. We are perfect. To let that happen would be contamination. I won't take that risk. I want her destroyed!"

"I am no threat to you. I rule a kingdom of peaceful uju-inyasi. There are no other Nyukis' in my kingdom, only me."

"You rule a kingdom of uju-inyasi? How is that possible?" Storm asked.

Oh no, Star, I wished you'd told me. I never would have suggested what I did. You cannot win and you will not survive an attack from Enchantress. I cannot let you be harmed but I serve a Queen who will do worse. What am I to do?

"It's a long story that I don't have the time to tell. I need to get back to my tribe now!"

"I can't believe she is capable of being more shameful. Uju-inyasis' you rule over an inferior tribe. You are a traitor to our tribe too. Oh lord, help me survive this nightmare!"

"You might as well let me go back to where I come from. It's very far from here. I will surrender myself to Enchantress. We both know what she will do to me and my colony."

226

"Storm, I command you to destroy her now!"

Star backed away while Storm just stood there. Finally he moved towards Star she raised her fists, ready to fight, but he just stood in front of her. His eyes were almost brimming with unshed tears. He cleared his throat his back facing Sunshine.

"My Queen I cannot!"

"Storm, I command you to attack her!"

"My Queen I cannot! Her Uju-inyasis will balance the scale and strengthen our reserve. Under the power of head of the war council, I place my life in her stead until we ascertain the truth of her kingdom."

Both were taken aback by his action, but none more than Star. "Then it will be your life forfeit if you are wrong Storm!"

"Yes, Queen Sunshine."

"Take her to the cells and summon the rest of the council. Dispatch additional scouts in the direction of where she came based on her map." Storm turned with her to the door leading to the cells. Not wanting to be imprisoned but not wanting to condemn Storm to death, if she escaped he would be forced to follow and bring her back. He would bring her back but return with proof of her Kingdom and Uju-inyasis.

Star realizing an opportunity sprung forward to escape but was seized by Storm once more! As they struggled Sunshine turned to the sound of the commotion, responding as did several guards who burst in to the room weapons drawn. They were set to pounce on Star when Sunshine released a powerful piercing scream. "STOP!!!!!"

Everyone froze and remained still as Queen Sunshine moved forward pointing at Star's back her eyes fixated on her Mid Back Shoulder. In the struggle that part of Star's back had been exposed. Sunshine unapologetically pulled the garments further back revealing more of the birthmark that covered Star's back. A tattoo that could not be mimicked by any magic being magical itself.

"This cannot be!" Sunshine's face was unusually paled in shock and Storm could never remember having ever seen her like this! "Oh my God, It's you. I can't believe it. I knew it was strange how much we looked alike. You have the same hereditary birthmark identical to my deceased twin sister. Look at her neck Storm that big star and sun intertwined. Oh my God, she's my fraternal twin sister!"

"What?" Star and Storm said.

"Look at the back of my neck. You see? We have the same birthmark!" Star stood there frozen and Storm had to take her by the hand and lead her over to examine Sunshine's neck. Then with shaky hands, he examined the back of Star's neck too. Both Queens' wore their hair up and the unusual birthmarks suddenly glowed. Her neck felt hot from his touch. When she turned around they all stared at each other.

Sunshine and Storm were smiling.

"We are sisters? I can't believe it," Star whispered.

"I was only told of you when I first became Queen and I was told that you had died at birth with Mother!"

"If we are twins you should know that your Mother did not die at my birth."

"But she did die! So why was I told of her and your death? Why the meaningless lie?"

Sunshine was cut off by the voice of someone unseen. "Because at the time the truth would have not served you well and be unbearable for you on your journey to become the Queen and Queens that you are both!" The voice that uttered these words was new and not familiar to Star. Shrugging off Storm's hold she pulled her garments back in place, Star turned to look at the old wizened face of the Nyuki who had uttered these words.

"Who are you?" Star demanded.

Sunshine started to reply, "He is . . . ." but was cut off by the elder Nyuki. "I am your Father." "Father?!"

"Yes. I can see you know the circumstances of your Mother's end and so will your sister in time. Now is not the time for past revelations, which will be postponed until the appropriate time.

Sunshine know that Star speaks the truth and her Kingdom and Uju-inyasi will be our salvation. I had cast you out to them in anger at the death of my wife and your mother. Upon my anger and bitterness waning. I sought to bring you home but found you had a new one where you have resided till now. It has taken all this time for me to come to terms with your Mother's loss. You are the identical image of her. I would not have been able to bear the daily reminder of seeing you in her. However now that you are both here, I realize that we must unite again as a Family so we can save both Kingdoms and I as your Father can ensure that what both of your mothers left behind is protected."

The revelations were too much for Star and she sank to her knees crying! Sunshine moved swiftly to her side, picking her up and embracing her. "You're my twin sister and my family! You have finally come home. Thank God you found your way home!" Sunshine embraced Star who could only stand there while her sister, Sunshine, held her as she cried. When Star looked at Storm and her Father, she saw tears swelling in his eyes, and tears flowing down her Father's cheeks! Both men had been moved by the circumstances. Star suddenly pulled away to look directly at Sunshine. The twins were happily wiping away each other's tears while smiling.

Star spoke breaking the silence. "I now remember you. Something happened in my mind. You use to hug me like that all the time when we were kids." *Lord, you always gift me with a miracle when I need one.*

Thank you for Sunshine, Storm and my Father and Mothers.

The sisters embraced each other again then their elderly Father joined in on the hug.

"Welcome home Queen Star!" Storm said.

CHAPTER THIRTEEN

THE BEST ALLEY IS?

"I don't trust him, Patience. Star has been gone for days," Marcus said. "Yeah, being left alone with Adui is like being protected by a two faced Jekyll and Hyde. We both know that now that's she's gone he's more dangerous," Theo said.

"Yeah, I agree. But Star knows him best and believes in his promise to protect us," Marcus said. "We should trust in her judgment."

"We all know how he feels about her," Patience said. "Yeah, he's in love with her. Poor Star," Marcus said.

"Oh man, that's crazy. I would be tripping and so mad if I were her. Having to deal with an ugly dude like him being in love with me would make me nuts." Theo said.

"Well we can use this to our advantage," "How?" Twins asked.

"We can make Adui believe that by helping us, Star will fall in love with him too."

"Your brilliant, Patience, and it might help if we could suck up to Adui and make him think we like and respect him too," Theo said.

"Now that's what I call an amazing plan. There's nothing we can't do if we work together," Patience said.

"Yeah, cool, let's do this!" Theo said.

"Now we will have to be extra careful now that Violet's left to go home because she's sick," Patience said.

"Too bad she's not around now. It's us against him," Theo said. "Patience and Theo, that's an amazing plan. Why should we use it though? We can't earn peace with lies and head games. I learned that forgiveness is like house cleaning. You must constantly remove the junk and trashy thoughts from your mind. Cleaning your thoughts gives you a positive mind."

The children sat on a tavo branch high above Adui and looked down at him keeping a comfortable distance. Marcus and Theo decided to take a nap while Patience sat there thinking. *I don't have to run away anymore because Star has forgiven me for what I did to her mother.*

Why shouldn't I believe her? She's right. I was so young and scared and didn't know what I was doing. How she figured out that I knew about our past is amazing. She has the biggest heart in the world next to my Grammy Mable. Star is like a mother to my brothers and me.

Since Star's forgiven me, I learned to forgive my brothers, and maybe Trevor, and even Adui too. I want to make her and Grammy proud of me. I plan to do it by protecting my brothers and getting along with Adui. I will do whatever it takes, so help me God. Patience decided to relax too and lay down stretching out then yawned. She was fast asleep within moments. Adui was now watching them from a Seiko directly across from them. He leaned against the trunk and stared at the sky.

Everything is ruined. Now those brats are staying and worst of all, Star had a private meeting with Patience which formed a deeper connection between them. If only I'd forced her to leave before Star left. That brat is sure to stay because she was forgiven and having heard the word love shared between them she sees this world now as her home. Now Patience has no reason to leave thanks to Star who convinced my niece that she wasn't to blame for the war too. I am doomed! He sat there frustrated with directionless anger and fury.

Suddenly he jumped up and stood on the branch, smiling broadly another devious plot springing to his mind.

What if I accidently left a trail for the Formica drones to help them to find us? This is perfect timing with Violet gone. I know that I can get rid of the drones that are here to protect us by suggesting we go treasure hunting. I can pretend to lose our way while I lead them to Enchantress. Once they are caught, I pretend to escape and was injured from trying to save them. I'll make myself cry buckets of tears making Star console and comfort me. She will realize how much she loves and adores me while we are healing from the tragic loss of the children. Oh, Adui, you are so brilliant!

He returned to the camp and had the drones prepare lunch for them in the dining tent. He went to wake the children and decided to be friendly too. "Younglings, it is lunch time. You must return now. We're in the middle of a war, not a playground. There's no time for fun when your lives are in danger!"

I need to scare them into leaving with me, but how?

Patience, Theo, and Marcus, suddenly sat up on the branch and looked at each other, rubbing their eyes. They all yawned at the same time then smiled at each other. Patience whispered quickly. "Now remember our plan. We have to make him our friend no matter how tough he is. We must focus and think positive thoughts. Let's do this. Okay?" Patience said.

"Yeah, we got your back Patience." Twins said.

The children flew down from the tavo and were surprised to discover Adui was having lunch with them in the tent. Since Violet had left, Adui never joined them but this time he seated himself at the head of the table and was sipping on some nectar from a very tall glass. Patience, Theo and Marcus, entered the tent smiling and sat down. The guards were outside.

"Mr. Adui, we thank you for looking out for us. We know we are safe because you're so smart and will protect us because you promised Star. We know that you would never let Star down. She told me that about you and I believe her," Patience said.

"Yeah and being an inyasi is much better than being human. I really want to be the best Drone ever. Someone like you can teach me a lot," Marcus said.

"I'm glad that you are a part of our family, because you are the sickest drone I know. In our world, 'sickest' is a serious compliment that means the best of the best." Theo said.

Patience, Theo, and Marcus, kept their eyes on him, smiled, and nodded in agreement. Adui was about to take a sip from his glass but suddenly stopped. He looked stunned, eyes widened in surprise as he looked at them.

I can't believe it. Those brats are finally appreciating what my Mama tried to teach them. Imagine, after all those years of loathing my niece and nephews. Especially Patience who always disrespected our heritage by hating what our ancestors valued the most. Their mother wasn't worthy and then to have to deal with her daughter becoming the next Gatekeeper was a twist of cruel fate. Mbaba belongs to me, not her. I am the only one that deserves to be in this world. If only my Mama would have given me the opportunity, but she insisted that the, Gatekeeper can only be a female. Her gifts, powers will transfer to me when her life ends. I am the only one capable of continuing our legacy. I have to get rid of Patience to preserve our heritage. I will play their little game and see where it leads.

They ignored his silence and told jokes, laughed while they took their time eating and watched him too. He looked at them eyes narrowed and yawned then put his head back against the chair as if he was exhausted. "We now get it that insects and inyasis' are more intelligent than humans." the Twins said.

"Yeah, I feel smarter as an inyasi and I don't think I want to be human again. It's just not cool to be a species that doesn't respect our planet. Humans are so destructive I never realized how bad they were with nature," Patience said.

"I don't know if it's because you're an umuvi that makes you smarter than everyone else. Theo and Marcus, you remember what I told you Ms. Star said that I shouldn't be surprised if she decides to merry Adui because he is brilliant and saved her children. She said we not only need a mother but a father too."

His shock made him collapse he hit the chair, his chair fell over and he laid there breathing hard. He suddenly got up smiling and ran to Patience he picked her up and swung her around as if she were a doll then put her down. The boys stood there watching, smiling and nodding their heads. Patience quickly stepped back and went to stand beside her brothers. Their mouths and eyes widen from seeing the pupils in his eyes glowing pink hearts, and his goofy smile.

"My Queen wants me to be her king and recognizes that I am the most brilliant and intelligent species in the universe?"

"Yes!" they said.

"Oh my God, my dream is finally coming true!"

"Yeah, but only if you protect us and make sure that nothing bad happens. Adui, you do realize that we are her kids now?" Patience said.

"Yeah, Adui, no more hating on us and we'll do the same," Theo said.

"No more insults. Let's commit to stopping the nasty thoughts and trash talk. We'll be decent towards you because you're going to marry our new mother," Patience said.

"Yeah, you'll be a very cool dad and we'll hang and do cool stuff," Marcus said.

"I only want her!" Adui yelled.

"Without us you can't have her right guys?"

"Yeah, she will be your worst enemy if anything happens to us," Theo said.

"You know you can't break a promise to Queen Star. She'll hate you forever," Marcus said.

"Wow, I cannot believe what I am hearing but it's true. Okay, you got a deal!" Adui said loudly.

"Great. All right, we really appreciate all that you are doing for us. I use to think that you were just bad, ugly and a miserable sad excuse for an umuvi, but I have no negative attitude towards you now. I think you're a pretty cool dude." Patience said.

Patience, go seal the deal and give him a hug.

Patience frowned then suddenly smiled as her brothers' mouths and eyes widened when she went over to Adui and quickly put her arms around him, hugging him. Adui arms remained by his side then he watched his niece return to her brothers. He stared at them wide eyed and mouth opened too. He took a few steps towards her then suddenly stopped deciding to return to his chair. The children stood at the other end of the table watching him.

She hugged me. I can't believe it and I let it happen. My niece touched me for the first time in years. I feel different now. They want me to be a part of their new family. I can't let that happen. They are supposed to be my enemies and I ought to loathe them. I put so much into planning their destruction. Mama would be so shocked to see what's happening. She always wanted us to love each other. Star would be so proud of me if I open my heart and accept them. The ones that I love most would want me to love them but how can I give up becoming the, Gatekeeper? How can I continue to let my mind and heart deny them the love they deserve? What's happening to my mind I am thinking like a conscious, caring, being that's not right or is it?

He held his chest because it started to hurt. He sat back with his head resting on the back of the chair, his eyes closed, but they still watched him silently.

"I feel different. I don't feel comfortable. I might be coming down with something," Adui said.

"Maybe you're feeling what I felt when I started to care about more than myself," Patience said.

"What's that?" he asked.

"Love. I learned so much because of this world how to love, respect, and care again. This place works miracles on you if just let it happen.

Living here has transformed me making me care about what I think and how others' feel. Adui you should let your mind and heart grow as well. Mbaba can do that for anyone. Mbaba helped me to become a conscious, caring being." Patience said.

"Yeah, you got a witness, sis!" Twins said.

Theo and Marcus approached her then hugged Patience. She embraced them too. The three of them stood there hand in hand watching Adui and smiling. He stared at them, his expression cold.

Suddenly, he put his head down on his folded arms on the table. His shoulders were shaking and he looked pitiful.

Oh my God, is he crying? My brothers and I made him cry. Maybe his heart isn't made of stone.

They quickly went over and started to pat him lightly on the back as a show of support.

"Hey now, Adui, we always knew that you were a very cool dude. You must be if Ms. Star loves you so much!" Patience said.

Adui looked up at the children with watery red pools of tears and his bottom lip was quivering. He was taking big gulps of air, trying to claim down. He dabbed at his eyes and blew his nose again. Now he was calmer and breathed deeply. They stood by him and realized they no longer had to fear him.

All these years wasted hating my orphaned niece and nephews, when they have always needed me too. I can't let them know who I am. I've done too much to be forgiven. Patience, Theo and Marcus are transformed in more ways than one from becoming inyasi. Is it wise to reverse their transformation? They are trapped here. We are all better off staying in Mbaba but they can never know I am their uncle. Now I can transform my mind and heart there is no need to hate or have destructive thoughts it will only make my life miserable. Now I have a second chance at happiness. Having Star as my wife and my niece and nephews love me is far better than being a Gatekeeper. Hate can serve no purpose.

"I have never felt that special before. Thank you humans you are royal inyasis' now. We will be the most incredible family in Mbaba but you do have names, don't you?"

"I'm Patience."

"I'm Theo, and he's my twin Marcus. Ya, he's bigger than me, but I run things."

"Well, we all stay here until Star returns. You are now safe with me!" It's time to make my Mama and Star proud of me. I got to do this for myself too.

"Hey, Adui, what's that sound?"

"Yeah the ground is vibrating like hundreds of marching feet," Theo said.

"Oh no, she found us!" "Who?" they asked.

"She's the most terrifying creature that ever lived, the Formica Queen, Enchantress!"

"Oh my God, you set us up!"

Patience flew at him pounding him hard on his chest while he tried to protect himself from her blows. He grabbed hold of her arms and picked her up so that they were face to face. Her eyes were brimming with tears she struggled trying to fight him.

"Put me down you lying, awful bug. I know it's your fault why this is happening!"

He put her down quickly and ran outside to the guards but they were gone. The camp was empty everyone vanished. "We have been abandoned. No one is here to protect us!" Adui shouted. *Oh my God, I have got to save myself and them too, but how?*

"No way am I letting any bug mess with me again. Come Theo and Marcus, let's get outta here. Forget him, he doesn't care. Adui isn't capable of caring!"

"No. Yes I do. Please trust me. Be quiet and follow me."

Patience, so tall, marched over to him, reached upward and grabbed him by the lapels she pulled him down so that she could look into his eyes. His eyes narrowed as he grabbed her hands then freed himself. He stepped back and the children stood there watching him.

"Okay, what's the plan?" Patience asked.

Adui peeked out of the tent then tiptoed quickly over to a very large Seiko tree. He flew up on a branch and picked four very odd looking flowers. The children remained in the tent hiding under the table. Adui entered the tent and called out. They quickly went to him. In his hand he had three small neon yellow flowers. He told them to eat it and then follow him as he quickly flew to a very high Kaugee tree. All three sat on the branch and watched silently.

"The flowers will make you invisible to the Formicas' eyes. Now eat this pink one too. It will give us time to escape and save Star from being trapped."

Patience held the flower up. Her brothers looked at her and she nodded her head. They all ate the flowers and then flew up to a higher branch and sat there with Adui and waited.

"How do we know you're not playing us? Can we really trust you?" Patience asked.

"Yes. I am trying and will protect my new family. We must leave. We will fly south then rest when it is dark. Follow me," Adui whispered. The flowers have taken effect. We cannot be seen. Let's go!" They flew off but although invisible Adui had forgotten about the Formicas sense of smell. Enchantress and her army were tracking their prey by their scent.

"I can smell my yummy, Funky-Inyasis' and when I catch my scrumptious, delicious little pretty inyasis', I will eat them and become more like a human in my thoughts and smarter too. First I will devour that treacherous Adui, consume his knowledge making me extra devious. Just wait. By the time I have finished my breakfast, lunch, and dinner, I will be the largest, brilliant and most beautiful Formica Queen in the entire universe!"

"Oh, my Queen, you are most terrifying and beautiful. What will you do with that traitor, Star?" Uno asked.

"I cannot harm my precious cousin. She has always been kind to me so I will only bury Star in a hole and leave her head exposed for the rest of her life. Naturally I don't want her to be lonely, so I will visit and let her tell me how much more beautiful I am. Imagine how she will feel knowing that her incredibly beautiful, smart cousin is ruling her kingdom of Uju-inyasis'." Enchantress said.

They applauded and cheered for their Queen marching on in search of Adui, Patience, Theo, and Marcus.

*   *   *

"He's a mess. I can't believe Ms. Star put him in charge of us, with all that bragging and talking junk that he did. He's just a big old punk!" Theo yelled.

"Yeah!" Marcus said.

"He is making it hard to have faith in him but we got to trust him." Patience whispered. The children were sitting close together on a branch. It was nightfall but the sky was clear because of the stars. It only rained for one minute every night at midnight since that terrifying day

Adui came into the children's' lives. They had been flying for nine hours and rested during their journey.

"Whisper, Theo! We don't want him to hear us." Patience said.

"I don't care. He's a good-for-nothing punk. I'm more of man then he'll ever be," Theo said.

"He is dead weight slowing us down. We've got to get rid of him," Marcus said.

"If Trevor were here, he'd know what to do!" Theo said.

"What are you, crazy? Don't ever wish that evil man back into our lives. I'd rather be stuck with the cowardly lion than the evil warlock. Now we got to get him to pull himself together. We can fix this." Patience said.

"Yeah, let's work together. He needs us more than we need him," Marcus said.

"Okay, Patience, It's time for me to man up and take control of this mess," Theo said.

"Hey, Adui, shouldn't we hide where Formicas won't want to go or hate? Like some plant or tree, they stay away from? Think of something. You're from here!" Patience said.

"Yeah, Adui, she's right. They can't fly or crawl onto everything here." Theo said.

Adui suddenly jumped up and walked over to the children. He stood before them and smiled feeling more confident. "Child, being in my company definitely has a very positive effect on you because you suggested the exact same plan I thought of!"

"Ya right," the twins said.

"They hate the Pudgy-Tickle Bushes. It tickles their bellies and they can't stand the smell. It is one of the tallest tree bushes in Mbaba." Adui described how it looked and they went in search of it. Theo in a few minutes flew back to them excited. "Okay, I found it! It has bright blue leaves with fuzzy yellow and orange stuff on its trunk, and wow it's very tall too!" Theo said.

Patience, Adui, and Marcus, followed Theo. They were now on the ground and looking at the tallest plants they had ever seen. It was bright with fuzzy fur instead of bark and the branches were curly without leafs but pretty blue flowers. They had to bend their necks back to see its top. "Oh man, how are we going to get up there? It's way too tall for my brothers' to fly up to!" Patience said.

Oh, my, I had no idea it was that tall. There's no way that I can fly that high. I'm already exhausted from dealing with these kids. Maybe I should escape and save myself.

"Child, you are mistaken. It's that much smaller tree over there! Now follow me," Adui said.

"Adui, are you blind and lost your mind too? I know you can see that taller tree is the one you described. Now you're trying to play us for fools because you're afraid you can't fly that high. You would risk our lives because you fear heights, or you're just pretending to help us?" Patience demanded.

His eyes blazed red at her. Theo and Marcus backed away but Patience stood still. Her eyes glowed too as she determinedly stood with her hands on her hips. Adui shook his head then rolled his eyes, frowned, and suddenly smiled. *That child will be the death of me. I know it. She has fire and is so much like me. I never noticed that before.*

"Oh, I get it. He's too old and scared to fly up to that tree!" Marcus said.

"Yeah, it might kill him, trying to man up. He's all washed up!" Theo said. "Yeah, he's a coward, a no good punk!" Theo said.

Patience took the opportunity to make use of the situation. *My brothers are smart. I'll play along too.* "Stop it. What's wrong with you guys, picking on poor uncle Adui when he's trying to help us. Don't listen to them. I know you can find a way for us to make it up there. You guys leave him alone. That's not cool. We're family remember!" Patience said.

Patience has faith in me still after all the pain I caused her too. I keep messing up with her. It's time to redeem myself. Adui, you can do it. Imagine what Star would think when she hears of what I've done.

Adui turned around and faced the children smiling. He puffed out his massive chest proudly as the children were looking around them nervously. He decided to take charge.

"A responsible father wouldn't let his children fly up to a tall tree like this one. I am very strong and capable of getting us up there!"

"Yeah, that's why you are going to fly my brothers' up there one by one. That way we all will be safe," Patience said.

"Hey, that would work, Adui. You take us one at a time. You're our ride piggy-back style – that's going to be sick, dude. I knew you would man up!" Theo said.

"Truly you children are trying to kill me. You want me to fly up there back and forth twice? You must be mad!"

"I knew it. It's your fault were in this mess, now you fix it. I know you're the reason why they are after us. If you mess up Star's going to want to kill you and I will too!" Patience yelled.

"It's my fault? I never told you criminals to come here and destroy our lives. How dare you!"

"Good luck. I don't have to take any abuse from you brats." Suddenly he flew off way up high to the tree out of anger. His rage gave him the energy to reach the third largest branch. He sat down and discovered Patience sitting on the branch too, eyes blazing her fury.

"Wow, you made it, Patience. Get him to help us!" they yelled. "Yeah it's amazing what you can do when you're pissed off enough, Adui. I expect you to help my brothers, or Star will make you pay!" "I'm exhausted I need few minutes to rest." He whispered.

"Adui, we don't have a few minutes. Help them now before it's too late. Please, I'm begging you, please help my brothers!"

He slowly sat down and leaned against the trunk huffing and puffing, trying to catch his breath. He was furious and wanted to push Patience off the branch, but was too weak to move. "I can't. I need to rest. I am exhausted."

"I can feel the ground moving like those ants is getting closer. Please don't let them get me!" Theo yelled.

Suddenly Adui stood up he took a deep breath and flew as fast as he could down to Marcus. Marcus ran into his arms frightened and hugged him quickly.

"Marcus, climb onto my back and hold on!" "Okay."

Up they went. He quickly flew as fast as he could for he could hear the marching Formicas too. Halfway up he was straining because of Marcus's weight but by some miracle, he managed to make it. He returned to get Theo. Fortunately he was much lighter and quickly returned to the branch. Adui feeling exhausted slowly crawled over towards the large tree trunk and rested his back against it. The children looked at him and went over to thank him. He saw genuine gratitude in their eyes and surprisingly smiled.

"Adui, you look pretty scary. Are you going to be alright?" Patience asked.

He could only nod his head just barely while his eyes were closed. They watched him struggling trying to catch his breath too. He was pale and sickly looking. The children went off and quietly talked. "Oh, man, he looks so messed up," Patience said.

"Yeah, I wonder if he'll be strong enough to save us," Theo said. "He'll be alright. He just needs to rest and get something to drink too," Patience said.

"Patience, I hope he'll be okay. We all knew he was in no shape to fly up to this tree," Theo said.

"Let's just pray for Adui to recover. Grammy said pray for the helpful and the weak."

"Yeah," the twins said.

All of them bowed their heads in prayer. Suddenly they looked at Adui when they heard him scream as he fell from the branch. They could only stand there and watch as his body bounced from one branch to another.

"Children, stay where you are and wait for Star!" he yelled as he fell. He was too weak to break his fall or fly. He fluttered a bit to prevent himself from getting injured. Adui tried to protect himself from smashing to the ground. They saw him lying there, unconscious.

"Adui!" they yelled.

"Adui get up!" Patience yelled.

CHAPTER FOURTEEN

WHO'S WAR?

"Oh how I've missed you my Sister. Finally, my prayers are now answered. I can't believe this miracle has happened!" Sunshine said.

"My Sunny, I remember calling you my Sunny!" Star said.

"You were always the better half because you never got into trouble, Star."

"I wish I had happy memories about our parents. I just remember what happened to our Mama I feel so guilty about that. I'm sorry. Can you forgive me?"

"Of course Star, you were just a child. You can't blame yourself for that. Our Mama wouldn't blame you. No one would. How sad that you lived with that guilt all your life and it prevented us from being together. I was sick that day and Papa stayed home with me. When the guards returned without you or Mama, he went in search of you both but returned alone. They had to confine me to my bed because I became hysterical making my illness worse. I was so ill that I didn't even know papa was sick too. We were both sick, I think from a broken heart. I was ill and couldn't attend Mother's funeral. We believed you died. Father ruled for as long as he could but sorrow overwhelmed him and as soon as I came of age, I took over leadership. He retreated in to himself and I was raised mainly by our royal stewards, Auntie Beryl and Lena. They were our Mama's older sisters and true Queens. Sadly they passed on when I was barely twenty."

Sunshine paused to look deeply at Star who in turn spoke of her own sentiments. "I missed all those years and I couldn't return. I was afraid to try and reconnect with my tribe. I felt guilty for Mother's death, not heading her word and straying from her side. I was practically a baby when I was adopted but could not forget the overwhelming regret. I truly loved my new family, especially the Queen Tulip. God blessed me with being adopted by the most loving Queen you could ever imagine.

How many Queens would adopt another species?"

"A Queen with a heart much larger than mine, that's for sure, Star!"

"Sunny, you've welcomed me back home. I have been here for two days and what amazing place this is. The colony, your palace – everything!"

"You mean our palace, our colony, and Storm!"

Star suddenly held her head down and blushed then she looked up at her sister. Sunshine smiled and held her hands.

"Good lord, you're in love. I knew it. I bet Storm feels the same way about you, too!"

"I don't know much about that, but that's not why I'm here. I still have my kids and a Kingdom to save."

"Oh that, Sis, stop your worrying. You can't go back to a colony like that. Why, it's shameful. I feel a whole lot better about the whole thing knowing that those criminals aren't your real babies."

"I adopted Patience, Theo, and Marcus. They are my children and I love them."

"Sis, you're not from that tribe and a Queen like you can't associate with uju-inyasis'. Now you got a whole new life here with me and Storm. This is where you belong. Stay here, I insist!"

Looking to change the subject and recollect her thoughts, Star asked. "Why didn't you look for me?"

"Father did not tell us that you were alive." "He said I was dead?"

"No he didn't say that, he just let me believe that. He told me last night as to why he never came for you. You reminded him so much of Mother and for the longest time he blamed you for her death. To see you constantly in the wake of her passing would have been too much.

The Anguish of the memory of your loved one's loss and her living memory and perceived cause of death constantly hounding you daily in the face of your own daughter was not a sorrow he could tolerate. He knew you had been taken in by Queen Tulip and at that young age, memory of her death passed to your dreams as I have been told."

Star sobbed at this revelation.

"As you grew to womanhood he forgave you, but to bring you back and rip you again once more from the family that took you in and raised you to the person who you are felt selfish. Guilt affected my decisions and I knew you were happy, safe, and loved too. It would have also been too much to witness what he had missed out on."

Turning to her sister Sunshine tears in her eyes she pleaded bond and share memories, catching up as they enjoyed some honeycomb cakes and nectar. It was as if they were never apart. They liked the same things although Star was more conservative, still there were very similar in actions and personality.

"Star, my Sister, I'm going to throw you the biggest home coming party ever. You will have real drones to serve you. The best looking drones in town, Big, strong, handsome ones." With mischief in her eyes, Sunshine quipped, "How many you want four, five, ten, or maybe just Storm?"

"You are funny the way you live having fun all the time. What about children Sunny, are you not ready to settle down?"

"Me. No way. Not when there are so many males who want to worship, adore, and pamper me. I will hold out for as long as I can before becoming a Mama. We're too young and have plenty of time. You should forget about that adoption."

"I've got to go. My babies need me. I must protect them from Enchantress!" Suddenly, Star got up and rushed to the door but the guards appeared and blocked the entrance preventing Star from leaving. "Once you left and never came back. If you think I'm going to let you leave again to fight some losing war you're crazy, Star!"

Sunshine's eyes widened in surprise and she quickly put down her teacup when Star stood before her crying. "So I'm your prisoner?"

Sunshine watched Star as she sat down then held her sister's hands on the love seat. "No. You just won't be fighting this war by yourself!" Star wiped at her eyes calming down and now looked intensely into her twin's eyes.

"Sunny you need to listen to me, please, just listen and say nothing, cause what I'm about to tell you is going to blow your mind. You'll think it's not for real and that I am making this up but it's all true. I need you to help me to save these children because they are the descendants of the Jefferson-Johnson family. They created our world."

"What? That's not possible. Inyasis' can't be ancestors from humans. That's crazy!"

"The kids are Ms. Mable's grandchildren. They transformed into inyasis' when they ate the fruit from the sacred Inhlakanipha tree. They had no choice. It was the only way to protect them. Her grandchildren had to come here to escape death at home and needs us save them."

Suddenly, Sunshine jumped up and stared at her sister as if she had just grown two heads.

"Oh my God the Inhlakanipha tree destroyed by humans. They ate the sacred fruit but that's against the law!"

"Yes. Ms. Mable, our Gatekeeper's grandchildren were transformed into unlamvu colored Inyasi. There are three of them Patience, Theo, and Marcus, who are fraternal twin boys too. They are young and her grandchildren. They didn't plan to eat the unlamvu or become like us, but now they are dealing with it. They have learned to embrace their transformation."

"So we have human inyasi living amongst us and twins too here in Mbaba. I heard of Ms. Mable but how can you be complacent about them eating our sacred Uhlamvu?"

"Like I said, they were in danger and needed help. Now they are safe here as inyasis and with our Gatekeeper, Ms. Mable being deceased, she can't take care of them. They need us. She is happy her babies are safe in the world her human ancestors' created."

"You had a relationship with the Gatekeeper and now human inyasis? That's outrageous. Can you trust this situation? Are we safe? Do you really want to be this involved with humans?"

"Yes and oh, Sunny, they're amazing. You would fall in love with Patience, Theo and Marcus if you knew them."

"Sis, this is just so scary having them integrate with us. What will become of our world if we let humans live here?"

I better focus on her love for me. Hopefully it will be strong enough to get her to help. I can't save them without her support. "Don't forget, their ancestors created our world. Haven't you heard of them or met Ms. Mable Jefferson-Johnson?"

"Father and the elders told me about her but I thought it was all just make believe, just some silly story – but you're saying they're for real? Wow! Why would you risk your life for them? Even if they were Jefferson-Johnson still, they violated our sacred tree. No one gets away with that Star. No one does!"

"Sunny they're young and didn't know what they were doing. In fact they were taken by force into Mbaba. Our Gatekeeper Ms. Mable made that happen and I believe it's their world we live in. Who are we to judge the Gatekeeper? I will admit I was terrified, scared too, but after spending time with them I fell in love with these remarkable children."

"Sis, this is very complicated but you make it sound so simple."

"It can be, but it depends on what or who rules your heart. God, love, hate, or fear," Star said.

"I fear nothing. Nyukis' are fearless but were not stupid."

"No we are not. As Nyuki I have learned more from these remarkable children, especially Patience about consciousness. How important it is

253

to always be aware of what's going on in your mind. To not let emotions like fear, jealously, anger and hate poison your mind. When the children came into my life I experienced so many different emotions that scared me too. These emotions challenged my mind to rise above the negative thoughts. I refused to let these thoughts compel stop me from doing the right thing. I never would have returned to the human world, befriend and loved Ms. Mable, or adopt and protect Patience, Theo and Marcus. Have the courage to return home to Taboo. Loving these children forced me to grow my mind into a more awakened and conscious Queen. Love in my mind and heart taught me to do what's right.

I became more conscious by my determination to help these broken children to heal with love. Maybe if you experience the miracle of another species love, it would be easier for you to understand. Imagine what would have happened to me if Queen Tulip, an uju-inyasi didn't adopt me but she did because she was a conscious Queen. If Ms. Mable had lived, I would have introduced you to her and I know how surprised you would be to know how much Uju-inyasis, Nyukis and humans have in common when it comes to hearts, minds and souls.

Regardless of your species some are conscious thinking doing the right thing to make their world a better place. Some are unconscious having hateful, destructive, and planet destroying thoughts. As Nyuki we ought to set a good example of being awakened conscious species if especially since we are the most powerful species here in Mbaba!" Star said.

"Maybe if their grandmother lived, she never would have brought them here – they're probably hoodlums in their world. I can't get over what they did to our precious tree!" Sunshine yelled.

"Sunny, I'm no different from you. We have a lot in common, although I was raised by another species. Love is more powerful than blood or species. It's truly what connects us all!"

"Sis, I can't let you raise humans. It's not the natural law. It goes against it!"

"There's no law against love for another species or God our creator wouldn't have put love in every, heart, mind or soul."

"True. I still think that you're crazy wanting to raise human inyasis'!" "What if there are consequences if we don't and risk destroying everything we love because we refused to help these kids? Our crazy cousin wants to destroy them or do worse and Adui has issues with them too. Obviously, I need more time to develop my level of consciousness. I can learn to be a wise queen from having thoughts like yours. Star our victory, the salvation of the Human's and the death of the madness that is Enchantress and Adui!" Sunshine yelled.

*   *   *

"We got to help him!" the twins said.

"Don't you guys notice that something strange is happening?" "What are else could be stranger than this?" Theo asked.

"Look at what is to happening Mbaba. Mbaba is changing! This world is changing; Look around you! Since this trouble began its colors have been fading more each hour and each day."

"Your right Patience it is fading, so much going on I wouldn't have noticed. I wonder what that means." Marcus asked.

They looked around them and noticed that the plants were no longer glowing as bright and the colors looked dull too. Their colors stood out more because everything around them was fading.

"I did see changes before but I thought I was imaging it because so much was going on. But it's true and I think we are not the only ones in danger."

"Patience, is it our fault are we the reason why Mbaba is in trouble?" Theo asked.

"Maybe, I don't know but we got to save Adui and when we do maybe we all can figure out what's happening."

Patience you must save us, help us we are dying!

"Did you guys hear that?" "Hear what?" they asked.

"It sounded liked hundreds of soft childlike voices – what's happening to me?" Suddenly she hugged herself tightly and looked around her then rubbed her forehead. Theo and Marcus watched her frowning. Marcus went over and hugged her.

"Patience, don't worry we'll be okay everything will work out after we save Adui."

Theo couldn't believe Marcus. "What, are you guys nuts? Those Formicas will eat us alive. We can't help him. That's why he told us to stay here!"

Oh Lord, why can't I catch a break? Always making things happen to test me more. How am I going to get us out of this mess? You better have another miracle for my brothers and me.

"He saved us from that crazy Queen. We'd better try to save him before that Queen gets to him." Marcus said.

"Yeah, he's our only hope, Guys. Everyone has helped us and Adui is family. When do we get to give some help right back?" Patience asked.

"Child the best way to be strong is to help the weak!" the familiar yet disembodied voice of Ms. Mable said loudly.

"Did you hear her?" "Yeah!"

"I just heard Grammy speak to me!" Patience yelled. "Me too!" Twins said.

"To risk our lives for an umuvi that probably still hates us are we crazy?" Theo asked.

"No. We all grew bigger hearts and conscious minds that make us more caring and less selfish. I'm not letting the negative thoughts mess with my mind anymore. Not even about Adui. That's what Grammy would want," Patience said.

"Yeah how do we help him when we can't even help ourselves, Patience?" Marcus asked.

"Hey, look over there at the tree next to us. There is a weird creature with a head like a bird but has a human face he looks a bird man because of the wings on his back. The colors of his feathers are beautiful too purple and blue. He is tall handsome especially the cool tweed outfit too," Patience said.

"It kinda looks like it might be a robin because of its head. He is so cool," Marcus said.

"Marcus, I think you learned the most from our Gram. I can't believe you're smarter than me sometimes," Theo said.

"He's the biggest creature I've ever seen in Mbaba. But he's very handsome too. Let me talk to him okay?" Patience said.

"Yeah!" the twins said. They moved over to the far end of the branch and started to wave while clicking their antennae. The humanoid bird moved closer then flew over and landed on the same branch.

"Hi, my name is Patience, and these are my brothers, Theo and Marcus. Thank you for coming over here. We need your help."

Finally they noticed me, those beautiful inyasis'. Today's my lucky day or is it. The world looks different today I have never seen our plants look so strange are these kids the reason for what's happening. I've been dying to meet them. "What are they doing out here by themselves?"

He extended his winged hand and shook theirs the children stepped back and looked up at him, smiling nervously.

"Greetings, my name's Thaddeus from the Inyoni tribe, at your service." He bowed gracefully towards Patience and she smiled and curtsied awkwardly in return. They stood there staring at him and Thaddeus smiled as he tilted his head to the side looking at them.

"You said you are in need of my help?"

"Oh yes, we are. Our uncle, he's old, injured and isn't capable of flying up the tree again to help us. My little brother Marcus can't fly that good and needs help to get down from this tree. Can you please help us?" "Well I have never done this before. Let me think about it. I think I can help you out. This little guy should be easy to manage."

"Oh, no, not Theo. My other little brother Marcus needs your help." Patience pointed at Marcus and Thaddeus's eyes widened in surprise. Thaddeus was taken aback by Marcus' size. Marcus smiled broadly trying to encourage the robin to help.

How or why would she refer to him as her little brother? "Well I have recently finished dining and physically attempting to carry him on my back would be a tremendous strain on my digestive system. Why don't I return in a few hours to help you out?"

Thaddeus turned to leave but Patience grabbed his wing. He stopped and now faced her, frowning when he saw Patience eyes brimming with tears.

"Thaddeus we really need your help right now. We've got a situation!" "What situation?"

"We are in hiding from that crazy formica Queen. Do you know who I'm talking about?"

"Yes. There is only one crazy, insane Queen in all of Mbaba. The Enchantress!"

"Enchantress is after us because of a tragic mistake. Queen Star has adopted us and found a way to protect us but we don't know where she is now. We are family. She was protecting us from her but had to go back to her birthplace to get help from her tribe of Nyuki. She needs to get a more powerful army to win a war."

"War what war? Star is returning to her Tribe after all these years? That's incredible. What will you do when you get down from the tree?" "Try to save our uncle who was protecting us. Adui fell out of the tree from exhaustion because he had to fly Marcus up here. Now we owe him our lives and we need to try and save his!"

"I don't believe it! That vain old dramatic, Adui, actually helped you children? Yes, I know him and personally, I can't stand that umuvi. He is my cousin but his ego makes it impossible to tolerate him!"

"Yeah, I know what you mean I used to hate him but he has changed. He's not selfish, cold or nasty. Lately he has been so helpful and nice we care about him. We want to help him now," Patience said.

"He was a coward and used to talk a lot of junk too, but I kinda respect him now. He has changed into a decent person, uncle and we think he's worth saving." Theo said.

"Adui is different. Now I know you would like him. He's totally cool dude," Marcus said.

"Thaddeus are you friends with Queen Star? If you are it would break her heart if anything bad happened to us and him. We are her family as she adopted us," Patience said.

"Please help us!" the twins said loudly.

He looked at them now all on their knees hands clasped together as if praying, their remarkable eyes blinking multiple colors like out of control stoplights. Thaddeus laughed while covering his eyes. They got up and stood before him, now laughing too.

"You children really know how get to me. All right, but only if you let me help you plan how to rescue that miserable old Adui. You must agree to let me be in charge. I trust that your word is golden true?"

"Better."

"As good as gold!" the twins said.

Patience, Theo, and Marcus, went over to Thaddeus and gave him a big hug. He enveloped them with his powerful arms. "Now Marcus, climb on my back. Good lord, child! You must consider going on a diet. Pray for me children. I have never done this before."

With Marcus on his back, he glided down gracefully with Patience and Theo following. Within minutes they were all on a large tree with dense foliage. Adui had unexpectedly been seized and trapped by Formica soldiers. "Oh, no, those Formicas have him trapped. How will we help him?" Patience whispered.

*   *   *

About fifteen massive Formicas' surrounded Adui. Their Queen was not in sight, but that did not stop them from being vicious. Adui laid there unconscious but suddenly moved when he was being jabbed at by sharp red poles that look like pitch forks.

"Dance for us and sing, you snobby umuvi!" Uno yelled. "Yeah, you don't look smart now," Dos said.

Adui slowly got up and started to dance and sing. Dancing was difficult because his leg was injured. The Formica' was laughing and taking turns poking him. He fell down and lay there on the grass. Uno and Dos walked over to him and spat in his face. He screamed because it burned like acid.

"Thought you could escape us, umuvi!" Uno yelled. "I am not surprised the umuvi is a traitor, Uno!"

"He could not be trusted. He betrayed his own Queen, Dos!"

"Ah, Uno if only we could have fun and torture him to death now!" "Our Queen will want to do it herself. We cannot deny her that pleasure, Dos!"

"A pleasure I shall happily reap!" Enchantress cackled emerging from beyond their view.

The children and even Thaddeus gasped, eyes widened – then their mouths dropped open when they all saw for the first time Queen Enchantress.

"She's enormous and what a fabulous gown and jewels. I wonder who her designer is. I thought Adui was vain, look at how she sits behind all those glass panels. No one can go near her. She's untouchable." Thaddeus whispered.

"Oh, no, she's here!" Adui screamed.

Adui passed out from fear and his wounds and laid there lifeless. With Adui passed out the others turned their attention to their Queen.

They cleared the way as she was carried to where Adui was. Her Drones encircled Enchantress and him. She watched Adui lying there while seated on the strong backs of her drones.

"Uno and Dos, where are my yummy Funky inyasis. I am positively famished. All this stress and time wasted. My royal belly has suffered enough!"

Uno and Dos, now on their knees crawled before her and bowed their heads until they touched the grass. Everyone saw their trembling bodies as Enchantress gazed down on them, her eyes cold and hard like two large shiny black marbles.

"Your royal most beautiful Queen, we have captured the Umuvi traitor and will soon capture the humans too!" Uno said.

"I want them now. How can you expect me to continue to tolerate your failures? All I want to eat are three humans that live in our world and yet still I must wait. Estupidos, I am starving. Your heads are like seedless grapes. I won't accept that you two have heads that are empty. Must I find two brains, cut off your heads and insert them to make you estupidos successful? Is that what I need to do?" She yelled.

This is it for us Dos. We'd better beg more powerfully than before.

I know we might not live another day, Uno, I will miss you.

But I will . . . No! We will not die so meaninglessly. Enchantress or not, though we serve her respectfully as our Queen she will learn her limits.

We just have to ensure we are alive to witness that day!

"You are right. We are estupidos, brainless, losers and beg you to forgive us for having empty skulls attached to our bodies. I wish I had a brain but sadly, I do not. I am a simpleton, foolish, mindless, and my brother is worse. We worship, adore, and would cut out each other's hearts for you to eat if you demand it. We love and live only for you our beloved and most desirable Queen!" Uno said.

I love it when they beg for their lives and tell me how much they adore me too.

"Enough, estupido idiot you bore me with your failures. Capture them by tonight or you will truly feel what suffering is!"

"The umuvi, shall we prepare him to be your tasty meal. My Queen I love you too much to have you lower your royal appetite by eating filth like him. Please, let us torture him and make him talk so that we can bring those children to you!" Uno asked.

"Torture him well, but make sure he doesn't die so that I can torture him some more. Now find my humans!" she screamed.

Her massive army left with her, leaving behind the twenty drones including Uno and Dos.

"I cannot believe she let us live, Dos!" "Yes, it's a miracle Uno!"

Uno let go of Dos and slapped his brother's hand away then suddenly he slapped him across the face. He walked over to an area of dry grass and wiped his feet, fury glowing from his eyes.

"I am so sorry, Uno, she scares the piss out of me!"

CHAPTER FIFTEEN

LOVE CONQUERS?

"Children, our advantage over them is that their Queen is as nutty as a Forzani nut. She lets her outrageous appetite control her.

Therefore, let her experience what it feels like to be on the menu for a change. I have a friend who will find her to impossible to resist and very tasty too. Now promise me Patience, Theo, and Marcus, that you won't try to do something crazy on your own, just stay here hidden until I return." Thaddeus whispered.

They promised and he departed. Patience, Theo, and Marcus, watched him quietly leave the bush from the back and then he was gone like a flash. They watched what was happening to Adui. The Umuvi was tied against a tree upright his head hung low and he appeared to be sleeping.

"Uno, I am tired. We should rest." Dos said. He yawned and stretched and Uno did the same. He gave orders to the Drones to watch Adui.

"Yes, Dos let us rest and continue our search in the morning. Guards, we have much work to do tomorrow so sleep till morning."

"Yes, General Uno!"

The children watched as Uno and Dos disappeared into a tent. The other drones slept lying down some on their feet, all snoring loudly.

"Wow, they fell asleep fast. Listening to them snore could wake the dead," Theo said.

"That is the loudest snoring I have ever heard. They sounded worse than Trevor," Patience said.

"How long have we been waiting? I don't know but it seems like ten hours." Theo asked.

"Nah, my Rolex watch says it's about three hours," Marcus said. "What if Thaddeus decided to take off? He seems more like someone who would watch a fashion show instead of a war movie." Theo said. "Just because a male is stylish doesn't mean he's not manly," Patience said.

"Ya right," Theo and Marcus said.

"Hey, with all those guards sleeping, now's the perfect time to free Adui. I'm going to sneak over and untie him," Patience said. "No don't, let's wait for Thaddeus," the twins said.

They were too slow to stop her and she flew out of the safety of their hiding place. Theo and Marcus went after her when they saw the large Formica suddenly come out of hiding and grab Patience. Two large ones threw a net over her and the other formicas did the same to her brothers. The siblings were each in a different net with a team of five drones each carrying them.

There was no way out of the trap. The Formicas landed on the ground dragging their prisoners on the grass. They struggled to free themselves but the nets were too strong. When freed from their trap, Patience, Theo, and Marcus were still surrounded by at least forty Formicas. Then two massive drones approached Uno and Dos, their size much larger and adorned with different uniforms from the other Drones. They looked menacing.

"Humans! My name is Uno, and you are my prisoners. If you want to live, you'd better do as I say!"

"Yes don't make us hurt you. Listen to my brother. My name is Dos. Uno is the only Drone with a brain. I listen to him all the time."

"Guys, we'd better listen. I'm sure that Star will save us." Patience said.

"You are fools to believe that Star can save you when she left you humans with your worst enemy. How do you think we found you, eh? Whom do you think left a trail for us to find you? That traitor Adui, he fooled your Queen and betrayed you humans too. He never told you about his meeting secretly with our Queen and they plotted your destruction," Uno said.

"Yes, he is like a jealous child who doesn't want to share his Queen. He loves her like Uno loves my Queen," Dos said.

"Dos quiet! How sad that you trusted him. You inyasis' are so beautiful yet sadly you will not get to grow up like other children. That loser, estupido umuvi is your enemy but we will get the chance to torture him on your behalf too. Maybe our Queen will let you watch," Uno said.

"I am sorry for my evil deeds. Please forgive me!" Adui yelled. "Never!" Theo said.

"I think he's changed. Am I right, Adui?" P a t i e n c e asked.

They could not see Adui because of the Formicas that surrounded them.

"I am sorry. I forgot about the trail. That happened long before I . . . we became a family."

"Yeah, whatever, like I'm going to believe you. The joke is on all of us you conned us into believing you cared. We played you into believing we cared about you too!" Theo said.

"Enough talking guards take them to their special prison and never let them out of your sight!" Uno yelled.

When the children entered the cave, they were surprised to find Adui there too. Adui watched them go to the far corner of the large camouflaged cavern covered with multi-colored Vines piled on top of a wooden structure. The opening had thick long vines that hung down over it like a blanket covering a football helmet. Adui sat there quietly with his back turned to Patience, Theo, and Marcus, and they sat close to each other.

There were two guards in the cave watching and about ten outside. The rest were busy preparing for their departure by building hideouts as part of their strategy. Places for their Queen's prisoners to remain hidden during the journey to their kingdom.

How can I get my family to trust me again, the uncle who betrayed them over and over again?

"I should a known he was incapable of changing his evil ways. He's just like Trevor, born without a soul." Patience said.

"Yeah, I almost believed him too," Theo said.

"No. We all believed in him because he could believe in us," Marcus said.

"Marcus, you're so naïve, always wanting to see the good especially when it's never there," Patience said.

"We all have changed for the better. I still believe that!" Marcus yelled.

"We've got to work together and find a way to escape," she said. "But how?" the twins asked.

*　　*　　*

Uno and Dos went to check on their prisoners and were pleased to see them sleeping. They kept their distance from Adui too.

"Ah, Dos, we finally have achieved the great challenge. I will finally win my Queen's heart when I present her with the prisoners. That Adui will no longer be agony-in-my-mind. I have won the brain war too. This victory is the sweetest of them all!"

"Yes, Uno, I never doubted who has the biggest brain. I don't think he has one. He is just very lucky, or use to be."

"Dos, our beloved Queen will treat me like royalty instead of formica dung for this muy grande successful mission."

"Yeah, no more worries about when we will be in her royal belly. I can finally relax. This feels good. I always worry about how much work your brain does. I wonder how long it will be able to help us with a Queen like Enchantress, Uno."

They re-entered the cave and saw the children sitting up and talking. Patience jumped to her feet and walked up to Uno. He was large and powerful, bigger than her yet she looked up at them hands on her hips. The brothers stood there watching their sister, too frightened to move. Uno had a scary expression while Dos smiled gently. Theo and Marcus suddenly came over to stand behind her but Adui stayed in the corner.

"It's not too late to save your lives if you let us go now, but you can keep that Adui. Pretty soon our new mother will return with a very powerful army. They will destroy your entire colony, including your crazy Queen. I don't think you realize who you're dealing with. I am a princess, inyasi royalty!"

"Well, now – a Princess, you say. Excellent, my Queen is really going to enjoy having you for dinner!" Uno said.

Patience raised her hand to slap him but Uno caught it just in time. He quickly shoved Patience towards her brothers, who broke her fall. Uno and Dos left the cave laughing and Adui suddenly flew towards his enemies, furious and desperate to escape but the large guards knocked him unconscious.

*   *   *

"Oh my, they're gone! I left the children here I must have taken too long and they were captured. Were too late, Dominic!" Thaddeus said.

"You summoned me from my deep sleep. I live alone preferring not to be around the surface dwellers. I was so cozy, comfortable in my underground home. I flew here from many miles. We flew all this way for nothing. That isn't easy for a someone like me!" Dominic said.

"Dominic, I had the most amazing surprise for you. This would have been the very best dining experience you ever had Imagine Argentian Formicas, the most exotic of all Formicas whose Queen would have been the most delectable of them all. I bet you would have been the first Formica eater to have devoured one. Now we just have to find them. They can't be too far away from here. Oh there's Devon the Impukane.

Maybe he knows where they are. I did ask him to monitor the children." Devon flew towards Thaddeus and Dominic, nervously looking around him as he fluttered around a few feet away. He was humanoid but had a serpent like body with arms and legs. His skin was light green and scaly.

His humanoid face, arms and legs were scaly too but he was cute because of his miniature size. He wore a light green cape and matching sack cloth pull over with short pants and green colored shoes. He was very tiny compared to inyasis.

"Devon, the children are gone. What happened?" Thaddeus asked. "Well those Formicas are fierce, and smart too. After overpowering and abusing poor Adui, I actually felt sorry for him. They tied him to a tree. Those kids must have been freaking out when they saw what they were doing to him. I couldn't approach them. It was too dangerous. I thought there were only about fifteen but the Queen secretly had some drones hidden. The Formicas pretended they went to sleep. One of those kids, the female tried to get closer but got caught, then her brothers too. They were all trapped in a net then taken to a cave. It was really scary. I took off before they caught me too!"

"Did you see which direction they went?"

"No, Thaddeus, I couldn't stick around. It was too risky. I was hiding close by waiting for your return to give you an update. It was the least I could do. Thaddeus we have much more to worry about just look around you."

"Thanks, Devon, we will find them. Yes our world is changing but am sure the Queen Star will make things right again in Mbaba!"

"Good luck, I gotta go!"

Thaddeus while on the powerful back of his friend watched Devon fly off while his old buddy Dominic did all the flying. He paced up and down, back and forth while on the back of the powerful Battalion.

Thaddeus stopped and flew suspended in front of his friend Dominic's face smiling.

"Dominic, we can still save them. You have amazing sense of smell to follow the Formicas scent. Let's go save those children before it's too late!"

They were an odd pair, the beautiful elegant blue and purple Inyoni eating dragon like creature with wings. Dominic's skin was a light golden color and scaly with tiny sprinkle of green dots wearing a green vest.

"That sound. Do you hear it, Dominic?"

"Yeah, it sounds like hundreds of thousands of Inyasis'!"

"Oh, how exciting I know it's Star, and she must have an army too!" "Dominic, you can leave now. It's not necessary for you to be here. I know that Star would prefer to handle this with her army. This is going to be a magnificent war."

"A war? I thought this was about me getting to eat some tasty new Formicas? I have been asleep for centuries now the crazy queen has declared war she has broken my sacred oath. To not consume her tribe as long as peace remained in Mbaba but I didn't sign up for a war. I don't like the changes the plants look so different they are no longer beautiful. You're right it may not be necessary for me to be here but I will eat some Formicas whether they be in the heat of battle or fallen. Good luck with your war buddy. I know what I am going to do but what will you do?"

"I must make sure that I can supervise the war make sure that everyone has what they need and looks good to win of course. Now I must be off. Thank you Dominic, I will be in touch. Take good care!"

*   *   *

Star spotted Thaddeus and his companion Dominic. She told her sister and Storm who he was. Storm directed his generals to order the army to hold their position in the air. Thousands of them hovered almost motionless in mid-air, their wings fluttering so fast you couldn't tell what was holding them up. Star, Sunshine and Storm, had stunned expressions as they looked downward from seeing the horrifying transformation of the plants, vegetation as one hundred guards flew towards Thaddeus to meet him. He stopped and remained in mid-air too.

"Sunshine, Star, and Storm, this is our cousin Thaddeus. I can't believe what I'm seeing our world is changing I wonder why it looks and feels so different here." Star said.

"I was afraid of what might happen to our world and now this is far worse than I imagined dear god help us." Sunshine whispered.

"Darling Star, dear cousin thank heavens you are here in time. I don't know what's happening our world looks sick, ill as if its beauty is fading. You have no idea as too what has been happening with those poor children. I was trying to keep them safe when the Formica captured Adui first. I tried to keep the children hidden and I left to get my friend Dominic the Formica Eater to help us."

Everyone turned to look over at Dominic the Battalion and he greeted them with a simple nod. Sunshine turned back to Thaddeus. Sunshine quizzed him in earnest.

"But?"

"But something went horribly wrong and now they are prisoners too.

Adui shockingly tried to protect them. I cannot believe he tried to help!"

"She's got my babies? Are they okay?" Star demanded.

"For now yes. If only they stayed, and waited for my grand attack plan. You will be thrilled to know that I . . . we have a very powerful weapon, my old buddy Dominic the Formica Eater, who will make sure no Formica escapes the field of battle. Our crazy Cousin has no chance against a powerful army like yours, very impressive indeed, and oh, look who's joining us too!"

Star, Sunshine, and Storm, turned around and saw a swirling mass of about one thousand orange and brown uju-inyasis approaching.

Leading the army was Violet, dressed in a stunning battle outfit. They were all amazed as she approached because of what she was wearing.

She embraced her then held her hand to escort her over to her sister and introduce them.

"Violet, I am so happy to see you and I love you as much as my own sister. Violet, meet my fraternal twin sister, Sunshine, and Storm, the Commander of her army."

"Violet, pleased to meet you and thank you for taking care of my sister. Now that she's back where she belongs, just know that you're welcomed to visit her at our home anytime."

Violet was taken aback. "She is your fraternal twin?! How incredible and exciting that must be! I wish it could have been under better circumstances. Star our kingdom is in a crisis. The life of Mbaba, our plant life everywhere is fading! It's so scary to think what their death can lead too! We tried everything but they continue to slowly fade. I fear they are all dying."

Sunshine looked at Violet with a cold and determined expression. Taking Star's hand she spoke out to the group.

"Our Family and World will never fade as long as we fight for it together."

She looked at Storm who nodded in agreement. He moved towards her side and beckoned the rest to join them on a field they formed a circle than began to pray, sing and they all sung in unison.

With the Prayer finished, the circle unbound itself and the question became who would lead the fight. A tussle of wills began between Violet and Sunshine but Storm and Star put an end to their discord.

"Look, you two, there's no time for this. We have got to save my babies and Adui too! If we win just maybe we can save our beloved Mbaba if it's not too late."

"Yes, ladies, we must ensure no harm comes to them and fight to save Mbaba." Storm said.

Both of them nodded their consent. Sunshine stepped forward and spoke to all who flew above them. "My Brothers and Sisters! We have a war to win, so let's get to it!" Having spoken taking Violet's hand together both Sunshine and Star vaulted in to the sky with Storm and sunshine following suit. Dominic the Formica Eater and Thaddeus flew lower underneath the swarm of inyasis, one thinking of the war ahead, the other of a feast. So dark was the shadow cast by the swarm cloud that flew overhead of them and flying in a hurry, nobody noticed the hidden, terrified formica drone that immediately went off to report to Enchantress what was headed their way.

*   *   *

Queen Enchantress was in seclusion at her royal camp waiting for her Human inyasis, Adui, and news of Star's capture too. She was standing in front of her magic glass trying to figure out what to wear for the occasion. As she stood before her glass, suddenly she held her hand to her mouth, eyes widened, staring at herself looking terrified.

"Servants, am I getting smaller?" she asked.

"No, your royal highness you are bigger and more beautiful!" they said. There were ten in her chambers including her royal crown holders. "My Queen, your drone number Forty-nine has returned with news!"

"Finally, let him in. Everyone get out so I can speak privately!"

Her royal crown holders never left her side. They couldn't hear while the others disappeared. The drone stood there by himself shaking and looking around nervously.

Oh, no, I'm alone with her!

He knew all too well what usual befell the bearers of bad news. He got down on his knees while Enchantress stood in the center of her magic panels and stared at him with sea blue eyes, smiling and looking larger than life.

"I have news, my most precious and beautiful Queen, I am sorry to tell you that you won't like it," he said.

"Talk!"

"The Queen Star has a very powerful army of Nyukis' from her own tribe. There are at least fifty thousand or more joined by an army of small uju-inyasis'. They add about ten percent more warriors for the Nyukis' number as well."

"What! Nyukis' in her army, how did that happen?" "I do not know but they are very powerful and..." "Get out!" She screamed.

He turned and ran fast, and he didn't stop running. Stunned, she returned to her throne and sat there staring into space. Then she stood up and looked deeply at herself in her magical glass watching her reflection smiling at her. Enchantress suddenly frowned, but her reflection the image of her in the glass laughed hysterically.

"The drone is lying and cowards like Star would never be able to muster or command any army of Nyukis. The Drone lies. She can only have an army of Uju-inyasis. She cannot win your war!" her Reflection said.

"Yes, she rules uju-inyasis only and they are harmless. My army is the most Powerful!" Enchantress said.

"Yes. You are invincible and you are the most beautiful Queen too. However, never forget who the better Queen is. Do not feel fear, Enchantress!" her reflection said.

"Guards! Summon the council! I will meet and eat all these Uju-Inyasis in war, saving Star for last as she watches me eat them all!"

CHAPTER SIXTEEN

HOME IS?

Uno, Dos, and the guards were on route with their prisoners about fifty miles from the camp where their Queen was hiding. As they were walking, suddenly a familiar drone was captured by one of their guards.

He was taken to Uno who recognized him. As they were walking Uno's eyes widened in surprise as he looked around him surprised by the appearance of the land.

"Forty-nine, is that you?" Uno asked.

"Yes General Uno. Please let me go. We are doomed!" "What madness are you talking about?"

"I saw them truly with my own eyes. There are thousands and thousands of the deadly Nyukis'!"

Now Uno and Dos looked at each other. Uno suddenly grabbed Forty-nine and slapped him across the face then shook him. Patience, Theo, Marcus, and Adui, where tied together too far to hear the commotion. Uno and Dos dragged Forty-nine and took him to a secluded area.

"Forty-nine, what are you saying?" Uno whispered.

"Uno, I am telling you the truth. Believe me when I say we are doomed. The Nyuki Queen has a deadly army on their way to destroy us!"

"Oh, no, Uno, what will we do?" Dos asked.

"Have you told any else of this, Forty-nine?" Uno whispered.

"Yes, our Queen. She is why I ran away too. She screamed at me to get out of her chambers and I have not stopped running since. Who would you fear more?"

"How much time before they reach us?"

"Less than twenty four hours if we are lucky!"

"Forty-nine you must stay with us and say nothing!" "Yes General Uno!"

"We must hurry everyone, our Queen is waiting!" Uno yelled. Within a few hours, they arrived at the royal hideout and the prisoners were taken to another secluded cage.

"We need to escape just in case Star doesn't make it here in time," Theo said.

"Yeah, but how?" Marcus asked.

"I know how. I just remembered something." Patience whispered. Patience reached into her secret pouch and pulled out the similar flowers Adui gave her to make them invisible. When she saw these particular plants she instinctively knew their powers. She put her finger to her mouth to stop her brothers from speaking, thankful that she had two of each flower – a total of eight.

"These flowers will make us invisible to the Formicas". We do nothing right now until they are sleeping, got it?" She whispered.

"Yeah, but what about him?" The twins asked quietly.

"Leave him here." Theo said.

Patience knew that the guards in their cage were the last ones to sleep. She told her brothers to pretend they were sleeping. She waited until Adui and the guards were sound asleep. When Patience heard the guards snoring, she opened her eyes and looked around her slowly then quickly opened the pouch took out the flower she popped two into her mouth. Her brothers were close enough to take theirs they followed her lead and now were invisible. Just as she was about to pass Adui suddenly he reached out and grabbed Patience leg then pulled her down. She was on top of him Adui quickly held his hand over her mouth.

The boys stood frozen on the spot, horrified and watched as Adui held onto Patience. When she stopped struggling he kept his hand there until she was silent.

"Umuvis' can still see you. I know what you are doing. Please take me with you. It's too dangerous for you to escape on your own. Please let me help. You are my family and I want to help," he whispered.

He removed his hand from her mouth and let her go. He sat there and watched her get up quickly. The three of them stood there looking down at him. The guards were still out cold sleeping. Patience and her brothers were about to go but suddenly turned to face Adui and threw him the flowers he reached up and caught them. Within moments, they were out of the prison and flying as fast as their wings could carry.

It was dawn when suddenly Uno fell out of his bed because of the frantic shaking on his shoulder from Dos.

"Uno, Uno! The prisoners have escaped!"

"Oh no, that can't be! Guards, guards find them at once!"

They quickly formed two teams and some flew over the castle grounds while others searched on the ground for their scent. Patience, Theo, Marcus, and Adui, were flying as fast as they could without knowing if they were getting closer to Star or Enchantress.

"How long do you think the flowers will keep us invisible?" "At least two more hours, if we're lucky," Adui said.

"I'm starting to get tired," Marcus said.

"Marcus, you either fly or we all die!" Patience yelled.

He suddenly caught up to them and they all flew hopefully towards safety.

*　　*　　*

"All this flying is wearing me out, Sis." Sunshine complained bitterly. "Sunny, hang in there. I really can't do this without you!"

"Oh, yes you can. Now you have Storm and your army, a powerful battalion. Let's not forget that sad excuse for an army of uju-inyasis. Hopefully no one will notice that inferior tribe mixed in with ours."

"Sunshine, you really need to change your attitude. You sound racist and demeaning for your role as a Queen. No conscious queen would be capable of those negative hate filled thoughts. You could learn a lot from your sister Star. It is why she is most suited to be a Queen!" Violet said loudly.

"Really! Well, I know she would have had a different attitude if she grew up with me. My poor sister Star doesn't know any better, since she was kidnapped by your tribe!"

"Kidnapped? We saved her life. She never would have survived without us. Your tribe abandoned a helpless child!"

"You all should have a returned Star to us, rather than forcing her to be raised as an inferior tribe!"

Star flew between Violet and her sister. Storm was behind them laughing along with the other generals who all found it very amusing.

Star frowned and tried to ignore their constant bickering.

"Violet and Sunny how many wars must I deal with today? First Enchantress, and now you two this is crazy, please get along. You are both my family!"

"Nyuki never mixed with uju-inyasis!"

"If we had your attitude, Sunshine, what would have happened to your sister?"

"Ms. Mable taught me a lot about being a caring, conscious being. As a Nyuki or human still it's important to have love towards all species. Yes, Sunny, would I be here today if I were left alone to fend for myself in the human world. There was no else around to rescue me if Violet hadn't gone to our Queen Tulip. Can you imagine if Queen Tulip allowed prejudice to prevent or stop her from rescuing me? Do you understand how destructive that disease of mind is; hate, or racism?" Star said.

Sunshine looked at her sister then at Violet who was staring at Star too. Sunshine looked back at Storm and his eyes avoided hers, but everyone stopped laughing.

"I never realized that I was coming across as, racist but I was raised to think that way or maybe I wouldn't be if Mama had lived. Oh Sis, thank God you have opened my eyes and I will change my attitude from now on towards uju-inyasis. Violet – I'm so sorry, girlfriend. I know better now."

"Apology accepted."

"Good. Now the two of you will realize how wonderful it is to be a family that is about love, not hate. Plants and flowers get that it's about time all of us do too. Thank God for the blessing to recognize the power of faith, love, and harmony. Now let's focus on stopping this war instead of fighting one. We also need to figure out why it looks like the plants in Mbaba are sick. Hopefully we can prevent them from dying."

"That might not be possible." Storm said.

"I believe in miracles. You should too!" Star said.

*   *   *

"What is that sound?" The children asked, in awe off all the humming.

Oh, my God, we are going to be saved. It's Star and a massive amount of Nyukis'!" Adui said.

"Star, she's come back with an army, thank God!" Patience said. "Hurry, we must go and meet them!" Adui yelled.

"I can't see them and I'm tired. I can't fly anymore!" Marcus yelled. "No we can't stop now, Marcus, man up, we got to keep going!" Theo yelled.

Now Adui was flying with renewed energy, excited about seeing Star again. Patience was flying faster than Theo, but he wasn't too far behind.

"They are sounding closer Marcus, we are almost there. Marcus?" She looked behind her and didn't see him Theo and Adui were flying ahead while Patience turned around to go and find her brother. She searched hi and low but he was nowhere until she spotted Marcus, he sat on a tree crying.

"Marcus, you scared me. Are you okay?"

"I'm sorry Patience. I keep messing things up for you!"

"No, no, we all mess up, but just rest a bit then we'll catch up okay," "No you go get Star and bring her back. I'll be okay Patience honest." "No, we stick together. I promise I will never leave you again!" "Patience, go. It's not safe."

"No. I'm tired too. We will rest a bit and then catch up to the others. Cool?"

"Thanks, Patience."

They sat together silently on the tree Patience closed her eyes then suddenly had a vision of Mbaba in darkness. The inhabitants of Mbaba like the Uju-inyasis', Nyuki, and all the creatures big and small crying out and suffering from trying to breath and starvation. Patience stood alone by the Inhlakanipha, the sacred tree of life chanting, praying and singing her beautiful Starlight song. Then a miracle was taken place in front of her the Inhlakanipha glowed as the unlamvu fruit started to grow rapidly and flourish.

The sacred tree spoke thanking her for restoring the consciousness of Mbaba and waking everyone up and making them care for more than themselves and power. Patience came face to face with the presence of five generations of Gatekeepers who stood before her thanking her for restoring the planet more importantly saving it.

Suddenly she was startled out of her trance like state when she felt nets tossed over Marcus and her. They were violently yanked down from the branch. Adui suddenly reached out and stopped Theo from being trapped too. He directed him to a large bush to hide.

"We've got to help them!" Theo whispered.

"We will, but we must be careful. There are a lot more Formicas around. They can't see us but can hunt from our scent. Be quiet. We must be closer to Enchantress's castle. I just need a minute to think!"

Back at the Enchantress' castle Uno and Dos stood before her wrath as she was in utter ire over the prisoners escape.

"How could you let them escape, Uno I should tear you apart for this. How dare you continue to make me starve?"

"My Queen, Forty-nine returned informing me that the Nyuki Queen has a powerful army of killer Nyukis'. How could you not be more concerned about that?"

"No. Star is trying to ruin my war but just because she has a powerful army does not mean that we will not fight. I refuse to let her win and command you to fight this war. Uno, but first you must capture my humans. I fear that I will start to shrink if I do not eat soon. It's not fair that you focus on a war instead of my royal appetite!"

Dos, she is more loco then I thought.

Yes, loco beyond nuts. Man what will we do? Be silent and listen, yes bro, I will.

"My beautiful powerful Queen we must surrender to save our kingdom we have more serious problems our world is looking scary. It is changing in a way that I have never seen before and that could be very dangerous for all of us. We have no chance against that army and there are more than sixty-thousand strong to our ten. How can we win?"

"Uno, you always find a way to make things right. Come to me after the war is won. Fear shouldn't affect a brainless idiot like you. How dare you try to tell me our world is changing when we both know that I am the only one suffering from your constant mistakes? I will be hiding in my private chambers under my castle. Bring me those humans before I decide to settle for you as my royal meal!"

"You are our Queen and you must stay. How can you leave us?" "Stop being an estupido drone! You expect me to risk my precious life, the only one worth saving. Now I command you to fight this war and bring my royal meal. If you lose I will make you pay, but first get me my humans!"

"As you wish!"

Uno and his brother left her chambers quickly. She gazed into her reflection, thrilled about the lovely new gown that her ladies in waiting were going to put on her. Now dressed, she clicked her antennas together and danced in front of her mirror while her reflection clapped her hands and watched, smiling.

"Enchantress, you never looked more beautiful!" Enchantress' reflection said.

"Yes I am surprisingly more stunning. How that is possible?" Enchantress asked.

"If only you were not starting to shrink. You better hope your dinner arrives soon!" Enchantress' reflection said.

"I am starting to shrink?" Enchantress whispered.

"Do not worry; your humans will get here soon!" Enchantress reflection said.

Her reflection blew her a kiss and Enchantress smiled and started to twirl with her arms raised above her head, awkward and clumsy.

* * *

"Adui, why are we just hiding here? Were invisible how will those Formicas' find us?"

"If we leave, they will capture us!"

"If we stay do you think they won't, Adui? Time to man up! We have got to make a move. It sounds like Star and her armies are almost gone!"

"I know but I don't want to take that risk!"

Theo looked at him and frowned when he saw how much he was trembling. He looked him up and down then shook his head disgusted.

My nephew thinks I am a coward but I have no power as an umuvi.

That punk Adui I gotta make a move. Only one of us is man enough to do the right thing.

Suddenly, Theo flew upward, flying as fast as he could then Adui went after him.

"Theo, Theo, come back!"

"Star help I'm here!" He yelled, shouting hoping to get their attention. Theo could see a few of the Nyukis' in the air and tried to get to them when suddenly he couldn't talk or fly. He was falling and passed Adui on the way down. He was frozen too and fell motionless both passed out before they fell into the large net.

"Uno, you have the best brain in the world! We are saved!"

"Not yet. Take the prisoners to the cage and search each one. We cannot let them escape again. Then we go on a secret mission."

"Where?"

"To the African Nyuki Queen Star!" "Why, brother?"

"I captured them to save ourselves. I believe Enchantress plans to punish us permanently whether we return with them or not. I do not believe the other side will do the same. Perhaps, it's time for Enchantress' end and time for us to rule in her place."

*   *   *

"My head hurts. What a wicked headache. I must tell Adui I know how to save Mbaba from destruction. There cannot be a war, the plants are upset, frightened by all the negative emotions of anger, hurt and fear from everyone. We must stop the war or none of us will make it." Patience said.

Patience sat up slowly and held her head looking around slowly feeling groggy. Her eyes widened and she put her hand to her mouth to suppress a scream. Their prison had changed. It was massive; a large beautiful room with bright red walls, carpet, and furniture, but it was sparse.

There were more guards and Adui was lying unconscious while her brothers were curled up on the ground and held their heads too.

"Guys, this doesn't look good. They have moved us and Adui isn't moving."

"What?" the twins said.

Theo and Marcus slowly sat up and looked around them, eyes wide from shock when they saw that the prison was different and Adui was lying there silent.

"Patience, what are we going to do?" Marcus asked. "Is he alive?" Theo asked.

Patience was about to crawl over and check on Adui when a guard stopped her. She quickly returned to her brother's side.

"I think so!" she whispered, with the guard still in their presence. Enchantress' voice boomed cutting their conversation short. "Adui better be because he must suffer for making me wait too long for you delicious humans. I can see why Star wanted to keep you humans, but now you are mine. It won't be long before you are in my royal belly!"

The children jumped to their feet and looked behind them. About five feet away, on a platform on the backs of ten powerful Ant drones sat Enchantress. There were glass panels encircling Enchantress who sat in the center on her throne smiling. She looked beautiful in a burgundy and black gown with gold piping down the center of it. Her eyes shone a beautiful sea blue and her full lips turned upward, smiling.

"Don't look into her eyes. She will hypnotize you!" Adui said.

Adui watched Patience, Theo, and Marcus, walking towards her but Adui quickly flew into his niece and nephews knocking them down. They sat up and looked at Adui, watching as the guards quickly dragged him away.

"Please do not look at her eyes. She will hypnotize you. Protect yourself from her eyes!"

"Listen to him. Don't look at her eyes!" Patience yelled.

Patience grabbed her brother's hands and led them to a far corner away from Enchantress. Now she was barely visible. "Oh my God, she is here!" Patience said. *I must tell that crazy Queen to stop the war or we all will die but how?*

"Star's got to get here soon or we'll all be Formicas' food!" the twins said.

"Children do not worry. I will protect you!" Adui yelled.

"Ha! That Umuvi always makes false promises. Shall I destroy him for you since he has been plotting with me all along to capture you humans?"

"No, he is on our side now so stop talking junk about him!" Patience yelled.

"Really, you are foolish enough to believe his lies still when he has turned against his beloved Star and her kingdom too. You, female human, he despises more than anyone in Mbaba. That power-hungry umuvi doesn't know the meaning of loyalty!"

"Oh, yes, I do. I am loyal to Star and the children, my family!" "Your family? Liar! You silly, brainless Umuvi fool humans can never be related to us!"

Adui got up and went towards Enchantress and the guards. They left him alone, frozen from fear when they saw her shiny black orbs. Adui stood before her fearlessly and they stared each other down.

"True, but I'm not an Umuvi. How could I be capable of everything I've done when we both know drones don't have brains with intelligence? I have knowledge and intelligence about this world because my ancestors created it. I am proud of being a Jefferson-Johnson and their uncle Trevor too!"

"What! Impossible." Patience yelled.

"You proclaim to be human?" Enchantress whispered.

"Yes. I am their uncle Trevor!" he yelled. This time his voice changed and Patience, Theo, and Marcus, looked at each other, shocked.

"Oh my God he really is our uncle Trevor!" Patience yelled.

Her brothers caught her because she suddenly fainted. Adui stood boldly before the Queen staring into her Black orbs. His eyes were like two green laser beams when he was angered. He knew that he was in for the fight for their lives.

"Human!" she screamed. "Yes, I am human too!"

CHAPTER SEVENTEEN

OUR JOURNEY TOO?

Uno and Dos looked up at the sky terrified. Dos suddenly turned to run but Uno grabbed him and dragged him back. They stood there shaking when they saw the sky change color from the swirling mass of Nyukis' army headed towards them.

"Oh my God, we must hide!" Dos said.

"No, we must stop the war. Dos get ready and do what I do but no talking!"

"Yes!"

Uno suddenly pulled out a massive white flag and so did Dos. Both waived frantically in the air until they saw the swirling mass stop motionless suspended in the air. Then half of the powerful Nyukis' broke away, flying towards them. The army situated themselves above the two trembling Formicas. Dos struggled to stay still.

"My Queen, I will go with my guards to ensure it is not a trap!" Storm said.

"It better not be because they can't be that stupid, seeing all of us here we out number them!" Sunshine said.

Storm left his Queen, Star, and Violet, while he and five thousand s' Nyukis' split up and searched the massive vacant field. They were about ten miles from Enchantress's castle. Storm and ten lieutenants landed in front of the two shaking Formica Uno and Dos that were equally sized in comparison, but out armed and outnumbered!

"We surrender, we surrender. I am Uno the number one General and I command our mad, loco Queen Enchantress army. I am here against her orders. I know we cannot win. Please, I beg of you do not destroy us!"

"If this is a pathetic trap, it is suicide for your entire kingdom!" Storm yelled.

"No, no, we are here alone trying to save our kingdom. Please, we are here to help you save those beautiful children, too."

Uno and Dos got down on their knees hands clasp together and then walked on their knees heads bowed as an act of submission. Storm looked at them and motioned to the other guards to bring his Queen, Star and Violet to him. They landed beside Storm and looked at the two Formicas with their heads bowed.

"Where are my children, and Adui? Don't lie to me because I guarantee that the only way to save your lives and kingdom is to help me to save them!" Star said loudly.

"We are here to help you. We submit to your will and now only serve you from now on royal Nyuki Queen. That we no longer serve that Queen who is so loco, crazy and out of control that no one is safe to have her as our Queen right Dos?"

"Yes. She should be fired. She is crazy!"

"My children, are they safe, and Adui too?"

"Yes. We will take you to them but you will want to destroy that Umuvi Adui!"

"Why?" They asked.

"He is the reason why the war started! He secretly met with our Queen and plotted to destroy your kingdom and the children too. His jealousy makes him a traitor!"

"Oh my God, how could he?!" Star, Sunshine and Violet said. "Please follow us!" Uno said.

They soared into the air leading Star and her army to Enchantress castle.

*　　*　　*

When Patience regained consciousness, her brothers and two guards surrounded her. Theo and Marcus helped her up and they stood beside each other. Marcus was between his sister and brother suddenly he reached out grabbed their hands. Now each of them held on tight and looked at the back of their uncle Trevor, who stood before Enchantress.

"How could you be human?" Enchantress whispered. *Why has my voice changed but I look the same?*

"My ancestors created Mbaba and I am the son of The Gatekeeper known as, Ms. Mable Jefferson-Johnson. The Gatekeeper serves Mbaba this world and protects and preserves the beauty of your world.

Only a human female can be the Gatekeeper. Before my sister's birth it was going to be me. I learned of my mother's, Ms. Mable's, unique gifts from childhood and she taught me many things enough to assume her role.

I would proudly have been the first male. The birth of my sister Thandee destroyed that dream when my mother informed me that she would be The Gatekeeper after her passing. The lessons began for Thandee. She was returning to live on the farm when sadly Thandee lost her life. I went to my mother, begging her to let me take her place.

She insisted that Patience and her brothers live with us and in time when her granddaughter was ready would replace Thandee. I was devastated, and furious too that Patience had no love for our land or animals.

I watched secretly as my mother tried in vain to teach Patience about our secret world too. She had no interest or passion for anything to do with nature or mother's stories. I hated her even more and hardened my heart towards my niece then manipulated her brothers to punish her too after my mother passed. I did everything I could and succeeded in making them treat each other badly I wanted to destroy the bond between them.

I tore my family apart and blamed them for my mother's death too. I was not only jealous but crazy from grief. I refused to honor my mother's wishes to teach Patience about how to fulfill her unique role in life. My jealousy, so much envy and hatred poisoned my mind. I wanted to get my niece to hate us so much that she would leave and run away. Poor Patience I made her life a nightmare when I physically abused her too." He turned around and watched his family cry as they stood there listened to him. Patience saw tears flowing from Trevor's eyes too. He turned to walk towards them but Patience, Theo, and Marcus, stepped back. This stopped him and they stood a few feet away Adui, who used his handkerchief to wipe his eyes then blew his nose.

"He is Trevor!" Patience, Theo and Marcus said.

"All those years, punishing me for something I didn't even know about? How could you?" Patience yelled.

"I was consumed with jealousy and it poisoned my mind and heart. I'm so sorry for everything, Patience, can you ever forgive me?"

Suddenly, Patience flew across the room and slapped him hard across the face. He held his hand to his cheek as he watched her return to her brothers. The siblings held hands again though Marcus was the only one crying. Patience and Theo's eyes were beaming pure hatred at their uncle. "This is much better than I expected. Now I have four humans to make me more beautiful and powerful. How splendid. So that's why I was convinced you had a brain. Now it makes sense," Enchantress said. No sooner had she spoken of her intent, a thundering vibration rose from the ground below them causing the walls and throne room to shake. The ground in front of Enchantress ruptured open and out from the burst Dominic the giant Formica eater on whose back Star, Sunshine, Storm, Violet and Thaddeus rode. The tremor had caused the supports below Enchantress to collapse and suddenly Enchantress grabbed onto the arms of her throne to save herself from falling as her platform crashed to the floor. She watched in horror as her crown smashed against a glass panel causing all of them to shatter in turn.

Enchantress sat there while putting her hands to her face to hide from the glaring eyes of her cousins Star, and Sunshine. Her platform was on the floor and everyone was staring down at her because she was only one quarter of the size her magic glass projected. Shaking with fury she rose from the Rubble. With the group surrounding Enchantress, Thaddeus smirked satisfied all was in order and hopping once more on

Dominic's back, the Duo disappeared back in to the hole they had come from to join the battle that raged below.

"You!" Enchantress screamed. "Guards!" She screamed for her soldiers but none came. Violet gestured to the window and from her vantage point, Enchantress saw her entire army engaged in a fierce battle for survival within and beyond her castle walls.

"Cousin, you have gone too far. Thank God I made it here on time!" Star said.

Patience, Theo, and Marcus, were free to run to Star because the Formica drones were so terrified they scattered, leaving Uno and Dos. Adui went towards Star too but then stopped and stood alone. Star, Sunshine, Violet, Storm, Thaddeus, and twenty guards from Sunshine's army were in the secret meeting room too that was now a prison for Enchantress.

"Thank God my sister found me in time to deal with a nut-case like you. Now you're going to pay for your actions," Sunshine said.

Sunshine and Storm went and stood before Enchantress, her green orbs were wide then she narrowed her eyes and sucked in her lips. She looked pathetic, small, and harmless sitting on her throne.

"Good Lord look at you now. You're so small and wearing tacky rags with no decent crown. You are a poor excuse for a Queen, having no sense of style and being crazy just shameful!" Sunshine said.

"Enchantress, your mental state makes you not fit run a kingdom. You should be dethroned!" Violet yelled.

"All of you have no right to hate me. It is not my fault that Adui poisoned my mind against you, Star. You should blame him. He said the humans were dangerous too. He is a traitor. Destroy him he should suffer for what's happened!"

"Me suffer? You crazy Formica, I have suffered enough and my family too. I did everything I could to save my family!" Adui yelled.

Enchantress surged forward at Adui and reacting to her threat, Sunshine and Star attempted to seize her. They however had underestimated her power and she flung them back before once more charging at Adui. She however was stopped by the wall that was Storm.

Storm struggled furiously to control her and aided by Violet and several members of his command, they succeeded in bringing her to her knees and subduing her.

With Enchantress subdued, Star and Sunshine were helped off the ground from where they lay in awe, by the children and Adui.

"Star, you won't believe who Adui is. He is my Uncle Trevor!" Patience said.

"Yeah, he conned us all!" The twins said.

Star was stunned suddenly went towards Adui. "Adui is your uncle? He's another human from your world?"

"Yes. I have been pretending to be from here because Mbaba is the world where I feel I belong. My Mama, Ms. Mable, wouldn't allow me to be here, but that didn't stop me. She never knew of my life here. I made sure that we never visited at the same time."

"All these years you played all of us, Adui? How could you!" Star asked.

"You don't understand. I love this world more than my own. It is why I thought I was protecting it by sabotaging Patience and destroying my family. My grief about losing my Mama and not being the next

Gatekeeper made me insane. I became Adui but instead of wanting to be loved. I choose to be feared so that no one would discover I was human too. I planned eventually to assume that role but then the children were kidnapped into this world and that changed everything. I had to plot to get rid of Patience, but in the end, she is the most worthy to fulfill that role of being the Gatekeeper. I am truly sorry for what I've done to everyone." He stood by himself weeping and dabbing at his eyes while everyone watched. Uno and Dos were shaking their heads as if he should be ashamed of himself.

"Star, now we know why he was always mysterious," Violet said.

"He tried to kill those children and wanted to steal our kingdoms too. He is so devious and should pay with his life!" Enchantress yelled.

"First the children and now Adui, a human who from the onset has affected Mbaba our world in negative ways. The health and wellbeing of this world has been impacted by all the destructive thoughts that have manifested because of these children. Now, as we speak, our Mbaba is suffering from all of the anguish, plotting, lies, and evil that has contaminated our minds. We were so focused on rescuing the children instead of focusing on our precious home." Violet said.

"Yes your right Violet we really need to do what is right for Mbaba our survival depends on what we do next and I don't believe my sister Star can be objective when it comes to doing what is necessary for us." Sunshine said.

"What are you saying Sunshine?" Star asked.

"Storm take the children and Adui into custody we have no choice but to remove them from Mbaba we cannot allow them to live amongst us." Sunshine said loudly.

Patience, Theo and Marcus ran towards Star but were stopped by the guards. Adui went towards the children and a semi-circle of powerful guards formed a barrier to prevent them from moving. Star went to her sister but was stopped by the powerful guards who prevented anyone from interfering with the meeting she was excluded from. Star stood there in the middle between the children and her family. Her outrage blazing from her eyes as she watched Sunshine, Violet and Storm in conference with each other it was clear what was happening and Star was shocked by their actions.

"You should give the humans to me! I know what to do with them." Enchantress yelled.

"Stop!" Patience yelled in a thunderous voice that shook the room. Everyone looked toward Patience who now was glowing all over a fiery orange as she slowly rose, ascended into the air. She was glorious, radiant, as if she was on fire all could see how her eyes appeared to be like burning flames when she spoke her voice was changed too.

"I am the voice, consciousness of this world. I am 'Vukisa' the awakened voice and thoughts of all that grow from the soil in Mbaba. Know that we are an advanced species of plant life that is capable of thoughts, feelings and emotions. We are not only food, or serve only one purpose to make your world beautiful but the vital life force energy that makes it possible for life here in Mbaba.

We deserve and expect an equal level of consciousness. A consciousness that is reflected in how you treat yourselves and each other so that we do not feel condemned to survive in an atmosphere that feels sick and destructive. We no longer want to exist in your world and therefore you cannot exist." Vukisa said.

There was a loud gasp then silence as everyone stared up at Patience who remained suspended above them. She neither expressed nor showed emotion as she stared down at them she looked as if she was in a trancelike state. The guards frightened backed away from Adui and the boys ran to Star who embraced them. Adui unconsciously moved closer eyes fixed on Patience and found he was standing by Star. Violet was trembling while Sunshine needed support from Storm who stared at Patience too. Enchantress looked around her smiling and when she saw Uno and Dos crying suddenly she stopped.

"Did she just say that we are going to die?" The twins whispered. "Yes." Star replied curtly.

"Patience, you can't let those plants kill us. Patience, make them stop". Marcus yelled. Patience eyes suddenly changed as quickly as a flash light shutting off as if her brother's words penetrated her mind she looked at him.

"I will! I have been trying with all my life to save all of you. Grammy, help me! Please help me!"

"Look!" Marcus said.

Everyone looked at where Marcus was pointing and saw a beautiful orb of light descend down towards them and remained suspended in front of Patience. They were separated by six feet above the frightened spectators. In the center of it was a stunning Humanoid Dragonfly. The rarest of specie from the 'Uzekamanzi' tribe. Only the gatekeeper could take this form. She was like a hologram with a halo above her crown.

Her wings were expanded and six-layer spiral pattern colored purple, gold, black, silver, and gold. She was clothed in a simple, but radiant gold trimmed black robe.

Her whole ensemble was uniquely beautiful in design right down to the purple satin gloved hands that matched her dress shoes. Everyone formed a circle and surrounded Patience and the orb with the exception of Enchantress who was now standing on the remnants of her throne. The stunning Uzekamanzi with Miss Mable's face stared at Patience she gasped when she saw her eyes the right one was lit as if it were a burning flame while the other was hazel vibrant a single tear dripped down her cheek. Patience was immobile unable to move but the close proximity revealed that there was some level of awareness.

"Ms. Mable, is that you?" Star asked. "Yes, the one and only!"

"Welcome Gatekeeper, we have been expecting you!" Vukisa said. "My granddaughter, your Gatekeeper has proven to be worthy and now I will help you to understand, Vukisa, how they all have learned to be worthy of life and value your continued existence. I beg of you to allow all of us to demonstrate our personal and spiritual grown and to allow your mind and heart to be transformed from a place of pain to one of healing."

"I will allow it." Vukisa said, releasing her hold on Patience. "Grammy, Grammy, is it really you?" Patience asked. "Gram, you're back!" The twins shouted overjoyed.

"She was the butterfly too." Patience whispered. "Yes, I was!"

Trevor could not believe his eyes. "Mama?!"

"Good lord, she's for real and is more beautiful than me too!" Sunshine said.

"Bow!" Storm said loudly.

Everyone including Trevor and the children bowed except for Enchantress, who stood there straining to see what was in the lighted ball.

"No need for formalities when we have got so much we need to deal with. Just give thanks to the good Lord for allowing me to return. You all came so close to destroying yourselves and this beautiful world too.

Thank God, you all woke up on time with the exception of Enchantress. Now we must share with Vukisa who is the voice for all plant life in Mbaba what we have learned and how transformed we have all become too.

I cannot force, control or change the outcome of what will happen here but I do have the power to remove my family from this world. I apologize to all plant life on Mbaba and am realizing learning is an endless journey and never stops regardless of passing on to the next life still I am learning more about consciousness. I have learned something from everyone especially my granddaughter. All of us are here to serve, honor and respect the lives of these remarkable plants that are the source of our wisdom and lives too. We have life because they make it possible for us to have oxygen to breath, we have food because they provide sustenance for our bodies, we have homes, plant life that make our world look and smell beautiful too. They provide the wisdom to respect and learn about harmony because they live amongst each other peacefully without conflict, war or violence. There is no hate, or racial issues they are the utopia of beauty because they have achieved what no other species have managed to do.

To exist in an unconscious mental state is the most destructive way of life because a sleeping mind is like a blind soul. A soul not seeing how ego, hate, fear, jealously, anger, greed, selfishness, lying, stealing, vanity, and being unforgiving can destroy your spirit. The letter 'I' represents our 'Spirit' and, the word 'Me'; represents your 'Mind'. Your 'Spirit' needs your mind to lead, go into love by having thoughts that are positive, enriching, and love based.

It's time to become aware of your mind and emotions how you let your mind affect others.

Teach your mind what to do, how to function, and not get messed up by thoughts. Negative thoughts don't have to exist if you make yourself aware and stop them from growing fight against your negative thoughts about, 'Self'. Thoughts like I hate, I can't stand, I don't like myself, I don't care about anything or one makes you have a sleeping mind. Your body is a unique beautiful house for your spirit and mind to live in so stop messing things up by focusing only on pleasing your physical being, think of your soul's happiness too.

Always try to stay conscious of your thoughts, words and actions we rarely pay attention, learn to listen to your human spirit. Every thought that begins with 'I' is your spirit talking first wanting thoughts and actions about, I love, I am going to be nice, fantastic, I was kind to, I feel good about, I can do this. We all must focus on positive 'I' thoughts about yourself, others and all things of the world.

When we are all about the 'Me' trapped in self-hate, doubt, hateful of others, no faith, emotions, then we are living dangerously in our heads. Saying, doing, thinking about what's hurtful to you and others, not trying to help others or trying to keep someone down, It's like training your mind to hate your 'Soul'.

I know you all are just starting to understand what I'm saying but, 'thoughts' and 'thinking' when it's negative is having an unconscious mind. All of you experienced sadness, pain, anger, fear, and jealously. Patience when you physically transformed and then said 'I' love 'Me' you transformed your human spirit into a conscious one. All of you remember, don't let your mind destroy your soul's focus on the positive and live a life that will help it to grow."

"Yes, Grammy, I remember whenever I said, I hate me, you would ask who is the, 'I'? You broke it down about my soul lives in my body with my mind and I am, 'two'. My soul is, 'I' and my mind is, 'Me, myself', right? I get it now about how important it is to, 'I love i'.

"I love i, i love i, i love i." Patience kept chanting the words while she slowly looked at everyone making eye contact. Her eyes looked enlarged to everyone that stared into them they were beautiful, but painful to gaze too deeply into because they were the windows of pain filled humanity. "Yes, Baby girl, I love, 'I'. That's very empowering and so on point child. Your Grammy is very proud of you and how your soul is so wise and grown. You'll remember to, 'I love I' is to love your soul. Remember to be conscious always." Star said.

"Yes, Mama, I'm so sorry that I let my mind become filled with dark thoughts, but from now on I will always focus on positive love, giving thoughts. I lost focus on how my actions, thoughts affect everyone and thing around us especially here in Mbaba. I am truly sorry Vukisa for not being conscious of the pain I caused. Please forgive me." Trevor said. "Patience, you are truly amazing I have learned so much and I thank you for teaching me to always, 'I love I' always focus on putting love into my soul. Become mindful of what makes my soul happy and put my soul's happiness above my minds selfish needs." Trevor said.

"I love I! That's so sick. It's crazy but I get it, Gram. It speaks to not having a jealous mind. It makes a jealous soul selfish all about the 'me'. I am sorry Gram and Vukisa and I promise to be conscious of my actions and Marcus too." Theo said.

"I love I, is totally cool. I get too. Don't have a haters mind because your soul can't get love with hate we, I am sorry too Gram and Vukisa living here has been the best school in showing me how to think about life." Marcus said.

"Vukisa, I never meant to harm our beloved plants and am deeply sorry for any thoughts that created such pain. Please forgive my actions and believe in my commitment to provide an environment that will promote loving energy. I love I, that's so empowering and beautiful Patience, I thank you for teaching my soul this lesson. I am so grateful and blessed Ms. Mable because we all have learned so much from you too." Star said.

"I have dishonored and been neglectful of the plants that make our world so special and I now realize I must always be conscious of their wellbeing. Please Vukisa accept my apology and know this will never happen again I promise. I love I is a concept that we all now embrace I believe that everyone agrees with me". Sunshine said. Everyone was nodding in agreement all voiced loudly their apologies to Vukisa with the exception of Enchantress who had a sour expression.

"This world was created for sleeping minds to grow into the wakefulness of, 'love.' I have watched how love affected all of your hearts and minds, turning everyone but Enchantress into a loving, conscious being. All of you have learned about the power of love for your spirit and others there is no better way to give the best of who you are. Patience, my beloved grandchild learned the most out of all of you. I am so proud of her. Trevor, I always knew who you were and believed you would always let love fill your spirit. No child of mine could stop love. I had to focus on my faith after I passed and believe everything would work out for the better. Thank God it did. Now do you see why our Patience is most worthy to become our future, Gatekeeper? She is still a child, but Patience mind became conscious and awakened before yours Trevor."

"Yes, Mama, I am so sorry!"

"Grammy, he almost got us killed and he was so awful to me since you been gone. He made me hate my brothers too. All because of a world I never knew about. How could he be so twisted?"

"I'm so sorry, Patience. Your uncle's jealousy was always a constant struggle. I have tried very hard to stay true to my faith. My belief in my son's upbringing had me believe it would transform his mind into a conscious one. It is why I never stopped him from coming to Mbaba – I knew the love he would discover in this world could wake up his mind.

Trevor, I can't believe it has taken you so long to become the man I raised you to be!"

"Mama, I can't believe what I've done and I don't know if I will ever be able to forgive myself. I don't blame any of you if you can't too!"

They formed a two-layer circle around the Orb with the inner circle having the children, Star, Sunshine, Violet, Adui, and Storm. The outer circle was made up of Thaddeus, Uno, Dos and the guards who remained kneeling with their heads bowed.

"Trevor you have hurt so many and did a lot of harm to your soul too. What have you learned?" Ms. Mable asked.

Everyone was looking at him but he focused his attention on Patience, Theo, and Marcus, the kids stood close to him holding hands watching. "Everything I have learned is because of Patience. Regardless of the nature of your being or species, if love isn't rooted in your heart, mind or soul you cannot provide the true nectar of life. Love is soul food that God put us on this earth to nurture the world, feed it and fill every soul, heart, mind, and all life with love. Love is what keeps our minds healthy and conscious. Love keeps our minds aware of what we should and shouldn't do to each other or ourselves. Harmony and peace is love too, helping each other to live and co-exist peacefully together, I believe that is our souls journey and purpose on this earth. That's all I have ever seen you do and Patience try so hard to do in spite of her youth, pain, and adversities' still she is so like you in having a beautiful soul. You tried Mama and have always been trying so hard to raise me in the likeness of you!"

"No. If we are love, we are the likeness of God, our creator. We are created in the likeness of him we should always be awake and conscious of everything we say and do. Always remember, I love I, love thy soul!"

"Amen!" Adui, Star, Sunshine, Violet, and Storm said. "Amen!" The children and guards said.

Patience suddenly found herself in front of Trevor. Her eyes soft but vibrant as she walked towards him then gave him a hug. He was so shocked that he needed a few moments to move his arms to embrace her. His rose and wrapped around her and he kissed her forehead. She stood back and held his hands looking up into his eyes. She smiled at the love she saw and felt too.

"Vukisa is still here listening and watching us I can feel her thoughts as she is trying to decide if she should believe in us we must continue to share our thoughts by speaking about our lessons learned. I forgive you Uncle Trevor. We both have changed and learned so much here and if it wasn't for our ancestors and this world, we never would have grown our souls or awakened our minds. I now get it about love and how much we need it to give and receive the best of who we are!" Patience said.

Her brothers went over and Trevor hugged them too, and he kissed their foreheads. The children were standing before him when he looked over their heads and saw Star standing behind them. Patience tapped her brothers, they stepped aside, and now Trevor was facing her. There were tears in Star's eyes but she was smiling at him too. He held out his arms to Star and she quickly went into them.

"My Adui is Trevor? The big tough black man I use to see singing and talking to his flowers in his Mama's garden? You spent more time with the flowers and plants than you did with the children. It's hard to believe that someone like you could be anything like Adui. It's outrageous. Your voice, style – everything is amazing. Being in Mbaba really changes a human. You came to this world and helped to change all of us for the better, although your methods were destructive and selfish. In the end, your actions helped to put us on all the path of Love, faith, and courage. Now we're all living with awakened minds, righteously as we are born to do. I see a very different Adui from the one I first met now that you are sharing a love-filled heart with everyone. I hope you can forgive me too for having my doubts about you."

"Me forgive you?" Adui whispered.

"I believe that we all forgive you. Forgiveness is the key to opening the door to love too!" Patience said.

He stood there smiled as everyone hugged or shook his hand even all the guards too. He was emotional and wiped at his eyes with his handkerchief while smiling with his watery eyes and when Uno approached him his tears stopped and he looked at him they stared at each other then suddenly they burst out laughing Dos joined in.

"I cannot believe that I, Uno learned something from a rival drone about love, loyalty and consciousness. I no longer despise you Adui and will honor the wishes of the Vukisa to the best of my mental abilities."

"That Adui shouldn't get to live. He is so evil and he ruined my mind and made me hate everyone with his hate. Destroy him!" Enchantress yelled.

Everyone turned to look at Enchantress. She stood on her throne jumping up and down. Suddenly she jumped off her throne landing on the floor on her back. Her arms and legs flailed wildly in the air while she cried buckets of tears.

"I hate him. I hate all of you for ruining my life!" She screamed in an eardrum shattering tone.

"Silence!" Ms. Mable yelled.

The room shook from the powerful vibration of Ms. Mable's voice. Everyone held on to someone to steady themselves. Enchantress suddenly stopped and lay there, too frightened to move.

"Get up, or I may make it so that you never get up again!" Enchantress suddenly got up. She backed away when she saw the Orb over her head, but low enough to crush her. Suddenly the Queen walked closer and peered into it so that she could look at Ms. Mable. Enchantress' eyes were now a tranquil sea blue smiling as she stared up at her.

"You are beautiful!" Enchantress said. "So are you!"

"No, not anymore how can I be without my magic glass?" "It was the magic glass that made you ugly, not beautiful!"

"No. It was the only thing that made me look beautiful. I know you are not blind!"

"Is beauty only external? Isn't true beauty represented by having a loving mind and soul?" Ms. Mable asked.

"Beauty is what you can see. No one can see my mind or soul. Who cares about tiny small Formica?"

"No cousin it isn't. Beauty is what you feel within. If I were cruel, selfish or had dark ugly thoughts about myself then I truly couldn't feel beautiful. Why do you think I believe I am beautiful?" Star asked.

"I'm no fool because of your looks!"

"No. How I look has nothing to do with it. If I hated myself, others hated or feared me, and if I hurt myself or caused pain then I would not feel beautiful. I would be ugly. The only reason why I believe I'm beautiful is because of loving who I am, being loved and loving others. I love myself because of my loving soul. Love is un-conditional we should want to give and receive love." Star said.

"I am beautiful now because of my thoughts that are good and love based. There's no hate, self-hatred, anger, jealousy or selfishness and best of all I can forgive. That's like a miracle in my soul, not holding on to anger. It makes my heart feel so light and free. Even though my mind is smaller because it's the size of an inyasi, I'm surprised that it now feels ten times larger than when I was Human. I am and feel beautiful because I just want to feel and give love. I love that I am love, my human family loves me, and so does my new family here in Mbaba. I can feel their love too. You got to love yourself first no matter how you look to know what real love is. I learned that by turning into a bee like creature and I use to hate them and think they were ugly too. I had to become what I thought was ugly to learn how to be beautiful," Patience said.

"Yes. If I looked like you I would still love myself because I'm special, one of a kind. There is nothing better than loving yourself!" Sunshine said.

"Without love in your mind or soul for yourself cannot give or receive the gift of love. We all need to love ourselves first," Violet said.

"Enchantress, love of oneself, the mind and soul is unconditional. Love and respect how our creator made you. In his eyes, you are perfect, so why should you believe otherwise? He didn't put you here to hate yourself because only pain, suffering, sadness and destruction would manifest. You filled your mind with hate, ugly, and evil thoughts, and that's what makes you, 'ugly'. Your journey on this earth is to know self-love, then grow in soul-love, become conscious and make sure that your mind is about loving thoughts. Share the inner beauty of yourself with others to empower this world!" Ms. Mable said.

"I am so small. No one will care about me!"

"It is not the size of your physical self but the size of your love that makes you big, large, muy grande!" Uno said.

"Really?" Enchantress asked.

"No one can see God, but we all believe and love him too!" Marcus said.

"Everyone loves God and we can't even see or touch him, but he is powerful and amazing to all of us!" Theo said.

"Yes. You are just small, but God's invisible and he is loved more than anyone on this earth!" Patience said.

Enchantress came out from behind her chair and then stood on it. Smiling suddenly, she raised her arms and started to dance. She

stopped and pointed, squinting at Ms. Mable as if she was trying to see her more clearly.

"So all I have to do is be beautiful on the inside to be beautiful on the outside. I have to learn how to love myself and others?" She asked.

"Yes!" Everyone said.

"I have always loved you even without the magic glass!" Uno said loudly.

Uno then stepped from behind the others went on the platform and stood before Enchantress smiling. He held out his hand to her.

Surprisingly, she held it, coming down from her throne standing by his side. Uno stood there proudly, his chest puffed out while Dos wiped at his eyes, blowing his nose and shaking his head.

"Everyone is here and will help Enchantress, but you got to commit to change. Are you ready?" Ms. Mable said.

"Yes!"

Suddenly Patience went towards Enchantress and stood before her staring eyes made Enchantress start to back away she clearly feared her when Patience spoke it was not her voice. Uno ran back to his brother leaving Enchantress alone looking around bewildered.

"No, you are not ready! I cannot be fooled by your lies Enchantress." Vukisa roared, returning to the forefront. Everyone gasped as they saw Patience raise her hand slowly than point a finger at her. Patience eyes shot out a beam of light that completely encircled the Formica Queen.

All watched as Enchantress struggled to break free from it in vain. She vanished with the light. Uno and Dos ran to the spot where their Queen last stood than dropped to their knees heads bowed as if waiting.

Patience walked towards them and tapped them on the shoulder indicating they should rise they stood in front of her heads bowed. She turned to face the audience who watched some with mouths still open from witnessing Enchantress's fate.

"Stand and I will always be watching over all of you who are permitted to remain here. We will allow Mbaba to return to its former glory as we are now feeling an energy that is healing and conducive to our wellbeing. We now believe we can trust that the level of consciousness has risen here. Enchantress can no longer harm anyone she is now in a place where she can no longer contaminate our world with her thoughts."

Patience shook her head as if she just became conscious of her surroundings she looked around her eyes no longer had that eerie look and returned to their natural state. She ran to Star who embraced her as she trembled from the shock of her actions. Trevor and her brothers approached her and then she went into each of their arms for comfort. Patience then returned to Star's outstretched arms. Ms. Mable lovingly watched her granddaughter, son, and grandsons, quickly dabbing her eyes to stop the flow of tears of joy from feeling and seeing the love within her family. Everyone looked upward when they heard her clearing her throat.

"All of us have experienced the miracle of forgiveness even Enchantress but sadly Vukisa decided she could not be trusted. I believe she is in a place where she will receive a level of learning that will one day enable her to return. Now it's time to send my family back home where they belong." Ms. Mable said.

"What!" Everyone said loudly.

"Mama, are we not we better off here staying in this world? All of us are happy here."

"No. Humans' aren't allowed to live here. Our purpose is to nurture and enrich all life to preserve the beauty of both worlds with the wisdom of conscious love. Your journey in Mbaba has taught you much but the journey must continue. The time has come for my family to take what they have learned and empowers others by awakening their minds. For my family there is still much to learn, lessons that are waiting for them at home in Mystic Krewe Jefferson!"

Suddenly Patience grabbed onto Trevor and her brothers they held on to each other too.

"Grammy I'm so tired. I don't want to go back. I love it here!"

"Yes, I know and one day when you're ready you will return, Patience!" "Mama, please let us stay. We all belong here!"

"Gram, we want to stay too!" the twins said.

She was smiling down at them when suddenly Trevor, Patience, Theo, and Marcus lay down a few feet away from each other. Star was beside Patience on her knees. She smiled while the tears fell down their cheeks. Star held her hand then leaned over and kissed Patience forehead. Patience smiled up at her while her tears flowed too.

Patience felt so tired and too weak to move but her remarkable eyes were like golden light as she looked at Star.

Star kissed the hand that was stung by her mother then held it to her cheek then placed Patience hand over her heart. She leaned over and gently kissed her forehead again. She then placed Patience scared hand over her own heart and watched her lovingly. Sunshine and Violet helped her to her feet. They all stood close, Storm, Thaddeus, Uno and Dos all looking down at her and they smiled while they wiped at their eyes too.

"I will always love you, Star. I don't know how I'm going to live without you. I wish I didn't have to, you saved my life. Thank you. You will always be my Starlight too. Thank you for giving me love and teaching me how to trust and value it and for showing what real beauty is about too. I know we'll see each other again soon," Patience whispered. "Patience, child, you're in my heart and I will be seeing you, my love, I promise." Star quickly went over to the twins and Trevor and quickly kissed them good-bye. Star went into Storms arms and he held her as she cried.

"We love you Star. Thank you!" the twins said. "I hope I see you again dear Star!" Adui said.

"I will see you all again. Be blessed always!" Star whispered. Suddenly a loud piercing noise arose that rumbled through the air, accompanied by a bright shining light that blinded them all. "What is that noise? Make it stop!" Patience said.

Suddenly, Patience, Trevor, Theo, Marcus and Ms. Mable vanished from everyone's view.

* * *

She yawned and rubbed her eyes then sat up and looked around her. Patience eyes widened then she quickly backed away when she saw who was snoring so loudly.

"Oh no. No, no, no, no. Oh my God, Trevor's here!" She yells. Suddenly, Trevor, Theo, and Marcus jackknifed into a sitting position they looked at Trevor all wide eyed and frightened. Theo and Marcus quickly crawled over to their sister. They sat there frowning before looking at each other and staring at their Uncle Trevor, who watched sitting up looking at them, stunned.

"Trevor, stay away from us!" Patience yelled. "We are really back!" Twins whispered.

"I'm not a beautiful inyasi. I'm not a princess anymore. No more Star, Mbaba – what are we going to do now? Was it all some crazy dream?"

Trevor stood up and he held his head then shook it and looked at them frowning. Patience, Theo, and Marcus backed further away. He suddenly started walking towards them but stopped just a few feet away he stood still facing them.

"Patience, Mbaba is real! We were all there. Now we were sent home because we are a family that experienced the healing power and miracle of love. All of us were transformed not just physically but mentally and spiritually too. Patience, you were taken into a world that you will eventually take care of. You are so incredibly special because you came to Mbaba and empowered everyone. You taught me Patience the true meaning of a Gatekeeper. A Gatekeeper's role your actions and thoughts that provide the wisdom to make other's conscious of how they love themselves and everyone. To be conscious of their world and all species and care enough to make it a better place to live. I remember everything and now that were back, I hope that you will let me love and treat you as the princess you are born to be. I want and promise from now on to be the uncle you all deserve. I will make your Grammy and your parents' proud of me by raising my family with love. Now I know I can do it because I love i!"

Patience looked up at Trevor her eyes widened mouth opened she couldn't speak. She could only smile through her tears at him. They sat there and looked at each other then Marcus nodded his head, smiling broadly at his brother and sister. He got up and ran into his uncle's open arms. Trevor held him then kissed the top of his head. Theo got up and ran but then suddenly stopped as he looked back at his sister who sat alone, still crying. Theo ran back to Patience got behind her straining to pick her up but he couldn't move her. He then went in front of her grabbed her hands tried to pull her onto her feet and she slowly got up.

Excited he quickly grabbed her hand and tried to run with her but she didn't move. Suddenly he tried to pick her up she laughed everyone laughed because he fell down.

Patience and Theo looked at each other laughing. He reached up his hand to her and she grabbed it pulling him up. She hugged him tightly they held each other and he awkwardly patted her back till she calmed down as she laughed and cried. She wiped away her tears and stepped back smiling then quickly kissed him on the forehead and grabbed his hand tightly. Together they walked hand in hand towards their Uncle Trevor and Marcus.

THE END

To find out more about the author and her projects, please visit:
http://www.joypetersonnovels.com/

www.ingramcontent.com/pod-product-compliance
Lightning Source LLC
Chambersburg PA
CBHW050552260626
47157CB00002B/530